THE WHISPER OF STARS

Nick Jones

Acknowledgements

This book would not have happened without considerable help from others. So, in no particular order – deep breath – here goes.

Charlie and Ella: I have spent a lot of time sat in a chair staring at my screen and appreciate your love, support and patience.

Ian Hughes: Thank you for your constant enthusiasm, hard work and dedication to the cause. You are a storyteller, like me.

Stuart and Jo Key: Awesome cover shot and a really good day. You helped make all this real.

Chanelle Jones: The second I saw you I just immediately thought 'Jen'. Thanks for being so cool.

Murray Bruton: You could argue this is all your fault, you made me believe I could make the world spin for me.

Kay Renfrew: You told me I was a writer before I believed it myself and for that, I will be forever grateful.

Nikki Wiggins: Coffee, friendship, walkies and talkies.

John Woodford: For keeping the wheels of *real life* moving while I created another world to play in.

Steve Parolini: Thank you for your insight, mentoring and hilarious comments on the first draft.

Sarah Kolb-Williams: Your bubbly infectious manner and eagle-eyed proofing deserves much praise.

Dan Hall: Weapons, security and frozen eyelids. Cheers Dan.

Mark Ravenscroft: Your advice on how the UK Police force and Government agencies fit together was invaluable. I hope I didn't get it too wrong.

Louis and Alfie: For their company during those long nights tapping in the studio.

Dedicated to Sarah.
You kept telling me to write it. Well now I have.
I hope you are proud. I miss you.

PROLOGUE

GCHQ, Cheltenham, England.
July 2058

Jacob Logan's hand trembled as he lifted the device from its secure chamber. He admired its smooth, dark surface and felt the familiar pulse of energy passing through him. He had done this many times, but today was different; today he was stealing it. He glanced around nervously before sliding the pebble-like object into his briefcase. It was Sunday afternoon and his laboratory, normally buzzing with activity, was deserted.

Today, David Jameson, Secretary General of the reformed United Nations, would announce his vision for the future, and while the world was distracted, Jacob would slip away. He checked the time: 2.14pm. Jameson would be talking of tipping points and accelerating climate change and asking if mankind could adapt, mobilise and join together. Jacob paused, absorbing the room's calm ambience one last time, knowing that on Monday morning the men in suits would be shouting and the lab would be in lockdown.

I've spent the best years of my life down here.

He lingered, drifting through the past, wishing it could have been different. The intercom flashed once, interrupting his thoughts.

'Professor Logan. I'm seeing an alert,' a voice said. 'Looks like chamber two has been accessed without clearance.'

Jacob brought his hands to his brow, closed his eyes and concentrated. The voice belonged to a guard stationed on level three. Jacob sent him a thought, pushing it into his mind, deep enough – he hoped – for it to feel like the guard's own.

< *It's okay. It's an error. You can disable the alert.* >

Jacob watched his screen, the seconds feeling like hours until the warning light disappeared. He exhaled heavily, his pale features accentuated in the glow of the computer console. His lab was sublevel six.

Come on, Jacob. You can do this. You have to.

He grabbed his briefcase, strode to the door and placed his right hand onto a glass panel. His presence on a Sunday was unusual, but not unheard of. He closed his eyes and waited. Lights pulsed and distant machines agreed he was authorised to exit. As he approached the lift, he recognised the guard on duty: Stephen Lowe, a stickler for detail and procedure who seemed happier at work than anywhere else. Jacob suspected he'd volunteered for this shift.

'You didn't stay long,' Lowe noted.

Jacob strained a smile and cleared his throat. 'Just had to set something running.' He handed over his briefcase.

Lowe snatched it, returning a brief smile before feeding it into a scanner and comparing its contents against arrival.

'That's weird,' Lowe said, his eyes flicking between two monitors.

Jacob spoke words suitable for such an exchange while simultaneously transferring thoughts into Lowe's mind, assuring him that the discrepancy he was seeing was nothing to worry about.

Lowe looked up, curled his lip and tutted. 'Bloody machines. And they reckon they can replace us.' He gestured towards the lift. 'Enjoy the rest of your day, Professor Logan.'

Jacob entered the lift, pressed zero and ran a shaking hand through his hair. After a rapid ascent he stepped out into a busy entrance hall. Cameras were everywhere. As he passed through the final stages of security – persuading another three people to ignore various alerts and protocols – he imagined how they would scrutinise every piece of footage in the aftermath.

He felt the cool air, the tantalizing promise of freedom, and paused for a moment, the sun warming his face. He finally allowed himself to think of his wife and daughter and days spent on the farm together. Sunday would usually be family time. He fought back tears that had been threatening an assault all morning.

Please forgive me.

His legs buckled, and he struggled to keep his feet. Collapsing would be a relief, but it might alert security and raise the alarm. He forced himself to walk to his car, climbed in and then pulled away from GCHQ for the last time. He drove through empty streets eerily quiet for this time of day, his hand hovering over the dash.

Does that man deserve to be heard? After all he's done?

He jabbed the radio dial and the car filled with Jameson's familiar, authoritative tone.

'...was time to accept the truth. Accelerating climate change was real. I urged every thinker, every dreamer, every man, woman and child to imagine our future anew. Incremental innovation would not save us. We required genuine breakthroughs in science, engineering and renewable energy. We needed to rethink innovation itself if we were to survive.'

He's slick, Jacob thought, shaking his head, his bloodless lips set in a hard line.

Jameson continued, 'Now, we have our best scientists, our

best ecologists, our greatest minds working together. And today I would like to share a vision with you. A long-term vision that will take many years of hard work, of faith and unity, but I know we can achieve greatness. I know –'

Jacob punched the control and the car fell silent.

Fuck Jameson, and fuck his plans.

There were tears of frustration, of broken promises and deception. Jacob was trying to remember how he'd become so involved in all of this. It had been easy to justify in the early days; back then it had been exciting, a challenge, and he believed they could do good. He should have known it wouldn't last. Power corrupts – it always does – and now the well-oiled political cogs would grind the truth into dust. He glanced at the briefcase and reassured himself he was doing the right thing. The truth would be heard, even if it killed him.

Jacob was right about lots of things.

The men in suits began their shouting early on Monday morning, and by midday on Tuesday he was dead.

The device glowed faintly in the darkness, a gentle pulse like a heartbeat.

Uncaring.

Hidden.

Waiting.

CHAPTER 1

December 2091
(33 years later)

Jennifer Logan stood on the corner of South Street and waited. It was a typical Monday morning, and the City of London was bustling and alive.

< *Logan in position,* > she said without speaking, her mind augmentation translating her thoughts into text.

From inside London's MI5 headquarters, surveillance officer Jonathan Cole guided a small, insect-like camera towards a penthouse apartment five storeys above her position. The microcamera attached itself noiselessly to a south-facing window. Cole now had visual on the target: Mrs Victoria Harvey, a successful businesswoman picked up by UK Border Control on a biometrics discrepancy – a suspected body swap.

Cole's hands flashed over his holographic console, bringing up details of the operation and names of the assigned agents.

```
- Operation Penthouse: Strike Team -
Logan: South Street, Mayfair, opposite target's building.
Collins: Entrance to Green Park tube station.
Smith: Henrietta Street, Covent Garden.
```

Cole attached another camera to the entrance of the building and zoomed in, framing Logan. Her details appeared on-screen. Jennifer Logan, eight years in the Met, three in Duality – a division with a unique remit: Enforce Hibernation and control illegal cloning and mind replication. Her list of arrests made for good reading.

Cole glanced around and then zoomed in even more. She was dressed in civilian clothes, dark jacket, grey jeans and trainers. He moved the camera up her body, mentally listing her attributes. Good legs. He checked if she was enhanced with bionics. *Interesting. All natural.* Her leather jacket was zipped up over her vest. Cole continued moving the camera, feeling a pulse of excitement upon seeing a sliver of flesh between her jacket and belt. He settled on her face: cocoa skin, emerald-green eyes and a shock of red hair. It was the eyes, though, that intrigued him most, a green so intense people often assumed they were enhanced. He checked the time again – 7.04am – and decided he could spare a few more minutes. He imagined running his hands through her hair and –

'She has her mother's eyes,' a voice behind him said softly.

Cole spun around. 'Jesus, Mac, you scared the shit out of me.' He turned back to his console, face flushing red. 'I didn't hear you come in.'

'You're not her type,' Jim McArthur said, strolling into the room smiling. 'And also? She's out of your league.' He passed Cole a plain white cup and sat down. 'Are we all set?'

Cole suspected Mac was right. The old man knew Logan better than anyone. He thanked him for the coffee and turned his attention back to the camera feeds. 'Just waiting for the target to leave. She's taking her time.'

The internal video feed showed Victoria Harvey standing in front of a large mirror. As if on cue, she let her gown drop to the floor, revealing a slender body adorned in white underwear.

Expensive underwear. She turned, faced away from the mirror and bent over, placing her hands delicately on her buttocks, craning her neck for a better look. She admired herself for a while.

Cole glanced sideways, trying to stop the smirk breaking across his face.

McArthur sent him a sharp look. 'You recording this?'

'Shit.' Cole switched the recording function on and took a large gulp of coffee. *All these bloody women*, he thought. *I can't concentrate.*

The split-level penthouse was the epitome of London splendour. Five paned windows stretched its full height, flooding the apartment in natural light. On the walls was an assortment of traditional paintings and modern artwork; in the centre, a contemporary steel staircase that floated up to a spacious mezzanine. Plants and seating had all been carefully placed, everything designed and considered.

Mrs Harvey sat at her ornate vanity table applying light makeup. She squeezed her lips together, pouting at her reflection, tilting her head, exposing her neck. The Harveys had always known money, even during the troubles. Her husband, Phillip, had made a killing on the financing and distribution of renewable energy. She had invested his money in a chain of successful fashion boutiques, selling to people who only trusted one of their own. That was all before the announcement, before Hibernation.

Hibernation. On that, the Government was inflexible. It didn't matter who you were or how much you had – in the end, everyone would be drafted. The Harveys had known they couldn't buy their way out, not this time.

'We should have left when they made cloning illegal,' her husband had protested, and in a rare moment of solidarity she had agreed. That's when she'd decided on the illegal operation. If she was going to hibernate with the masses, then she would at least be young again. In moments of raw honesty, she had to admit the real reason she had wanted to be young: so Phillip would find her desirable like he used to.

She sighed. All of that was a long time ago, before separate bedrooms and distant lives. Divorce had been discussed, but it was such a degrading business, and anyway she didn't have to like her husband. Most of her friends didn't like theirs. Separation suited her just fine.

Her thoughts drifted happily and settled onto the other man in her life, the one who mattered now, the one she couldn't stop thinking about: Marcus. When had it started? She couldn't remember exactly, but when she thought of him she felt a rush of heat to her groin and lightness fill her being. Her libido was definitely stronger this time round. She felt alive in a way she hadn't since she was a teenager, drifting inside her thoughts, sometimes losing hours. Was it love or lust? It didn't matter. She was young, but this time with the benefits of age, wisdom and confidence, and it was even better than she remembered.

She allowed herself a final look in the mirror, admiring her firm, young flesh. Thirty years younger. It really did make all the difference. She sprayed a little scent onto both wrists, imagining Marcus's strong arms around her waist, pulling her in, and felt another rush of warmth. She stroked her neck, her red lips parting, chest flushing to match. Only he could do this to her. Her hand drifted down her right breast. She wanted to masturbate but decided to save herself for him.

Love or lust?

As she slipped into a smart oyster-coloured dress and picked jewellery to complement the outfit, she decided: both.

CHAPTER 2

Jen mounted her bike, a Yamaha EZR electric hybrid and one of the only possessions she cared about. Gloss black, liquid pearl and fast as hell. Standard issue just didn't bite hard enough. Twisting the throttle brought the reassuring purr of raw electric power beneath her.

Cole broadcast, 'Target is about to leave the building. Strike team stand by.'

Jen knew that Cole, even with all his technology, could still lose a target, especially during rush hour. One mistake and they might miss the chance to make an arrest. She took a deep breath and rolled her shoulders, aware of the distant hum of automated cars. Police and emergency services had exclusive rights to manually control their vehicles, but weaving through the chaotic solar streets of London required precision, agility and fierce concentration.

Stay relaxed.

Victoria Harvey appeared, and by the time she reached the edge of the pavement a luxury car was waiting, door open. With an easy elegance she slipped inside the vehicle. Logan waited for the car to pull away and began to follow, her active contact lens displaying the vehicle's speed and location. It was unlikely Mrs Harvey would notice her, but Jen decided to maintain a safe distance between them.

< *Logan following. I have good visual.* >

'Target is traveling southbound on Hay's Mews,' Cole reported to the team. 'The vehicle has been programmed to her office address. Logan has visual.'

On two previous occasions, Victoria Harvey had made long, unscheduled stops near Green Park before continuing to her office. MI6 suspected she might be meeting the handler responsible for her mind relocation. Jen had seen the results of mind rejection and it wasn't pretty. Mrs Harvey was probably buying antirejection drugs. If that proved true, the strike team was to move in and make the arrest.

The target vehicle, heading east, reached Piccadilly, paused for a few seconds and then joined the frenzied blur of traffic. Jen timed her entrance carefully and slipped in amongst the jostling transportation. Vehicles ebbed and flowed in balletic unison, occasionally darting like fish across lanes. Jen reminded herself to breathe. They stopped briefly at Piccadilly Circus to watch a sea of people cross the street.

< *Mac, you there?* > Jen asked. It was a transitory moment of calm.

'Yeah, I'm here, Jen. Nice day for a ride, eh?'

The traffic lurched forward as if starting a race, each vehicle reaching and then settling into its natural place in the pack.

< *I'm almost enjoying it,* > Jen thought, accelerating hard into a small gap in front of a bus full of schoolchildren. Their eyes were on her, but she had no time to acknowledge them. The chase continued across Haymarket before joining the Strand. They were now heading northeast toward Mrs Harvey's office. Jen felt a twinge of disappointment. Perhaps it wasn't going to happen today.

Cole spoke. 'Logan, traffic is heavy up ahead. Try and get closer if you can.'

Easy for you to say, Jen thought to herself, leaning, accelerating and pushing into the impossibly tight spaces between vehicles.

Cole's voice again. 'She's just made a stop at Adam Street. It's close to the office, but…' There was a brief pause. 'Hang on, vehicle's on the move again.'

As Jen approached the turn for Adam Street, she saw the target vehicle. It was empty.

< *Target has exited the vehicle,* > she informed Cole, eyes narrowing.

She pulled in, dismounted and started a facial recognition scan, adrenalin through the roof, eyes darting everywhere. This was one of those times when she wished the Government had been successful passing mandatory tracking chip legislation. The Central Transport System moved millions of people; the fact that they had to rely on old-fashioned methods to find one of them was ridiculous. They needed to actually *see* this woman?

'Still nothing,' Cole said.

Jen imagined him scanning local camera feeds on his array of monitors. *Needle in a haystack,* she said to herself.

'Nearest tube station?' Jen shouted, frustrated with her lack of movement.

'Presuming she isn't going to Covent Garden, then it's Arches or Embankment,' Cole replied.

Jen processed the options. Embankment also included a sublevel tube. The fastest route appeared, a luminous overlay in her vision. It was a seven-minute drive, four on her bike. She thought about Mrs Harvey, scanned the map, looked up and made her decision.

She likes to walk.

'Logan proceeding on foot to Embankment,' she said, pushing her way through the crowds towards Victoria Embankment Gardens.

'Is Logan always like this?' she heard Cole ask. He had forgotten to mute his microphone.

'Not always,' McArthur answered. 'But generally. Yes.'

Jen smiled, then launched herself up onto the bonnet of a parked car and vaulted over the tall iron railings that surrounded Embankment Gardens. She landed, rolled and was up and running towards the tube station. She darted through trees, dappled by golden sunlight, until she came to a clearing. To her left she could see Waterloo Bridge and the River Thames, the sun sparkling on its silvery surface like a thousand excited bulbs. She turned right and continued running along Victoria Embankment, passing the pier towards the station. Her breath was controlled, her fitness paying off.

'Just picked the target up at Embankment,' said Cole. 'Logan, she's just ahead of you.'

Victoria Harvey appeared in her retinal display, fifty metres from where she stood. Jen smiled again. Her intuition had been right.

CHAPTER 3

Jen arrived at the station entrance and considered the various options highlighted in her retinal display. She couldn't see the target.

< *Old tube or Sublevel?* > she asked, flicking her attention left and right.

Cole had a possible match, but he explained it was taking multiple cameras and way too long. A transaction linked to the account of V.HARVEY appeared on his screen.

- London DTL: Embankment: c8.60

'Sublevel,' he replied quickly. 'She's just bought a ticket.'

Jen pivoted and raced towards the SUBLEVEL signs, pushing her way through queues until she reached a giant lift already crammed with at least a hundred people. She squeezed in as a large semicircular door span closed and the lift dropped in a rapid descent. Jen worked her way through the faces she could see, but it was difficult to move without arousing suspicion, so she reluctantly stopped and waited.

'Target is already on the platform,' Cole informed her. 'The next train is approaching.'

< *Understood.* >

Jen composed herself, sending the thought as calmly as she could. There were other thoughts, laced with failure, but she kept those to herself. She exited the lift and broke through the mass of people to see a train waiting at the platform.

'She's on that train, Logan. Don't miss it,' Cole advised.

Jen cleared the platform in three strides and jumped, the doors closing behind her. The train levitated, departed and quickly accelerated. She only managed to advance three of the eight carriages by the time it reached Canary Wharf Station. On Cole's instruction, she stepped onto the platform and discovered she had, completely by luck, gained an advantage. She was next to the only exit stairwell, so the target would have to pass her. A crowd of sombre faces trudged past.

< *Logan holding, awaiting visual on target.* >

Nothing. More faces.

Finally, as the wave of people thinned out she locked onto a confirmed identification. Victoria Harvey stood alone at the far end of the platform.

< *Confirmed visual on target. Canary Wharf substation, Platform 1.* >

Jen watched the target move out of sight into a nearby walkway tunnel and tried to anticipate her next move. Catch another train? Why? She might as well have stayed on the last one. She glanced up at the station clock. 8.27am. Would the target really meet her contact down here?

The lift opened and a fresh group of busy commuters spilled out, blocking Jen's line of sight. Cole offered her a video feed from the platform camera and she accepted, reducing the transparency until it floated, ghostlike, at the top right of her vision. She waited and watched as Victoria Harvey glanced nervously around the platform. She appeared to be waiting for somebody.

< *Cole, do we have ears yet?* > Jen asked silently.

'I've been trying, but there isn't anything down there I can use. You might need to use a drone.'

Jen took a small bug-like device from her pocket and placed it on the palm of her hand. It flickered to life before floating silently and attaching itself to the tiled ceiling about fifteen feet from the target. The tiny drone inched closer, seen by no one. Jen turned her attention back to the target and was surprised to see that Mrs Harvey had started a conversation with an unknown male.

'Logan?' Cole said, tentatively.

< *I see him, but why can't we hear him?* > she asked.

'I'm working on it. Give me a few seconds.'

Jen scanned him. The man was Marcus Aldridge, an investment banker. Middle-aged, smartly dressed with a serious countenance – pretty much the same as half the people on the platform. In the distance she heard the rumble of another approaching train. If they decided to take this one, Jen wanted to be close. She walked slowly towards them.

McArthur this time: 'Jen, it's okay, this train doesn't stop. Keep your distance. Let's hear what they have to say.'

Jen's relief was short-lived. Something wasn't right. Even at this distance, it was obvious the conversation was turning into an altercation. Victoria Harvey was standing awkwardly and shouting.

'How could you do this to me?' Her words became a scream as the drone opened its audio channel. 'You told me you loved me!'

Marcus Aldridge looked stunned, all colour sucked from his normally healthy-looking face. He was blinking and mumbling, shaking his head.

'Listen, I'm sorry, but I... can I get someone to help you?' he offered in desperation.

'Sorry!' She crumpled to the floor in apparent defeat, a discarded shoe next to her. 'It's been agony without you. Why are you acting as if you don't know me?'

The crowd of people near them started to move away, leaving a circle of tension around the pair.

'I... I... don't...' he mumbled, then asked, 'How do you know my name?'

Jen was running now, praying she was wrong.

Not again. Not another one.

She could feel the ions crackling around her as the train approached the station, pushing a large pocket of warm air ahead of it. Victoria Harvey looked to be in pain, her eyes darting like a lost and confused animal. Her face stretched into a grimace, and then for a brief moment, as if a shocking revelation had overwhelmed her, was calm.

'Of course,' she sneered. 'It's that bitch. That twisted, selfish bitch. She's taken you away from me. She's poisoned you against me.'

Jen was running at full pace. 'She's splintering!' she yelled, but her voice was swamped by the growling power of the approaching train.

'She's what?' It was Cole's voice. There was no response from McArthur.

Victoria Harvey began shaking uncontrollably, her perfectly symmetrical face now smeared with mascara, creased into a sickening grin. Marcus Aldridge began shouting for help, backing away from the woman.

Jen was still thirty feet away as the train flew past at impossible speed. She screamed through a pocket of nervous bystanders, bashing into a man and knocking him sideways, and just made it through to see Aldridge on the edge of the platform attempting to sidestep his assailant. Jen drew her weapon. Mrs Harvey was yelling, lips drawn over her teeth like a snarling wolf.

'This is what happens when you promise someone the earth!' she cried. 'You promised me, Marcus! You told me you loved me.'

'Don't move. Stay where you are!' Jen shouted.

The woman didn't react.

'Victoria!' Jen shouted again.

She watched Mrs Harvey leap up and push Marcus Aldridge hard in the chest. He flew back and away from the platform, seeming to hover in the air for a second before disappearing in a sudden, sickening rush of steel. The terrible image of the train smashing his body was followed by a hiss of brakes and the screams of unfortunate witnesses. Mrs Harvey was on her knees, a look of simple confusion. Jen kept her gun trained on her, knowing that Marcus Aldridge's terrified expression would stay with her forever – a horrifying mix of shock, disbelief and fear – and that Operation Penthouse had just become a lot more complicated.

CHAPTER 4

Nathan O'Brien glanced around the empty lounge, fresh magnolia paint covering memories of a life long gone. Notes were spread randomly around him, pieces of an elusive puzzle that remained just out of reach. He studied them, mumbling, looking for a connection he'd missed. His wife Katherine had been onto something, a story she believed would be the biggest of her career. It had become her obsession, and it had gotten her killed. Nathan corrected himself. *Murdered.*

He played her final message again, her voice cramping his stomach and tightening his throat. Kat was meeting a man she thought might have some answers. She told Nathan she loved him, that he shouldn't worry. The message ended.

At first, Nathan thought he might be able to accept the official story. 'Katherine O'Brien, investigative journalist for the *Montreal News*, tragically killed in mugging gone wrong.' It was believable. That sort of thing happened. Just not to people like Kat. She was streetwise, capable and smart.

Nathan gathered his notes, each name, word and place memorised. He would burn them in the garden and then leave this place for good. A place where grief had owned him and days had threatened to stretch on forever. He couldn't say how, but he'd eventually crawled his way out of that all-consuming grief, a simple word nourishing him back from the edge.

Revenge.

He would find those responsible and kill them. Gradually, the singular clarity of revenge became something more, something richer and deeper. He knew that retribution would only offer a brief respite from his pain. He needed to honour her somehow, finish her work, write the story – even it meant bringing down the whole house of cards. Then, and only then, would he would allow himself his sweet reward.

If revenge meant his own death, then so be it; he would have nothing left to live for. A few years ago, all of this would have been impossible to imagine. He had been a lecturer in computer science and programming, a loving husband with a future stretching out in soft focus ahead of him. It had been a quiet life, and it had suited him just fine.

All that was blown away in a second.

The death threats had started a few months back. They scared him at first, but then he understood; it meant he must be close. They had helped him realise what he needed to do. If he was going to track them down, he needed to become a ghost.

He took one last look around the house, their once-happy home, wincing at the Sold sign on the front lawn. The money from the sale combined with their savings should be enough. It would have to be.

He played her final message again. How many times had he listened to it? A hundred? More? Her upbeat tone and excitement crushed his heart anew but also strengthened his resolve. He almost played it again, his mind hovering for an age, but managed, in the end, to delete it. He needed to move forward.

He burned his notes as planned, the words turning to ash and drifting on the wind, and then left their house and all those years behind him. It was time to say good-bye to his body, his identity and to Canada. It was time to be reborn.

CHAPTER 5

It was Friday 6 December. Jennifer Logan sat in the window of the Shipwright's Arms pub and stared blankly outside.

'Tell me again it's not my fault,' she asked Jim McArthur as he arrived with their drinks.

'It's not your fault,' he replied, nudging a glass towards her. 'You should drink up and move on.'

Operation Penthouse had consumed their week. Debriefs, press conferences and plenty of finger-pointing. Yet somehow, within the department, it wasn't considered a complete disaster. Chief Superintendent Paul Richards had seemed unusually calm about the whole thing. The operation hadn't delivered the source of the body swap, but Duality Division still had a chance to secure a prosecution. Negative press for backstreet replication was always good, and the Harvey case would be in the news for weeks: an innocent man murdered – smeared across half a mile of train track – and a 'swapper' in custody. It was a good opportunity to highlight the dangers and feed the fear of splintering. Bronze Team had done a sterling job; Richards had said so in front of the whole department. Praise from him was rare, but Jen didn't feel even the slightest shred of satisfaction.

McArthur pulled at his tie and sighed. He was solid, some would say stocky, befitting a man of his age. He kept in shape, dressed well and had allowed his hair to vacate residence, a decision that Jen thought suited him. They sat for a while, processing the week in shared silence. The traditional pub, a short walk from the Duality offices in London Place, was filling with after-work revelers and the smell of ale and history was comforting.

'Are we still making a difference, Mac? I mean, really?' she asked, her eyes searching his for answers.

'It doesn't always feel like it.' After a long pause, he asked, 'Jen, do you know how old this place is?'

She glanced around. 'Older than you?'

He smiled, picked up a beer mat and rotated it in his stubby fingers. 'Established 1884.'

Jen smirked, her trance broken. 'No wonder you like it here; you fit right in.'

McArthur ignored her and continued to spin the beermat. 'This place is over two hundred years old and still going strong.' He leant forward. 'People all want the same thing, Jen. They want to keep going, they want to cheat death.'

Jen made no effort to hide her sarcasm. 'So it's our job to make sure they die. According to the rules, of course.'

Mac didn't take his eyes off her, his stare remaining fixed below a solid frown. It forced her to look down at the table again, huffing.

'Making cloning and replication illegal was the right move.' The humour was gone from his voice. 'If people carried on sidestepping the system and living too long...' He paused. 'Well, we'd still be in that mess.'

The *mess* he referred to was an understatement. The 2066 Superflu had killed nearly a billion people. Then came the riots, the blackouts and of course accelerated warming, millions of refugees seeking asylum in the safe zones. The suffering had been horrendous. It was a mess alright, the biggest of them all. It meant the elusive dream of immortality had been just that.

Jen rubbed the back of her neck and sighed. The last legal replication – an older mind transferred into a younger clone – was over twenty years ago. Hard to imagine now, she mused.

McArthur continued. 'If people want this life – the security that the UN safe zones bring – then they have to hibernate. That's the deal and it's a good one.' He paused a beat, his tone softening, eyes meeting hers. 'You know it.'

She did, deep down.

The Hibernation programme offered longevity, security, and prosperity. It wasn't quite the immortality of science fiction novels, but it was more than fair, especially when you considered the options. If mankind *didn't* hibernate, there wouldn't be a habitable planet in which to spend eternity. Accelerated warming had reached tipping point and drastic measures had been needed.

Jim McArthur was always right, Jen thought, but she'd noticed his eyes had lost some of their sparkle recently. Decades of MI6 crap taking its toll, maybe. She could understand that. The world had changed a lot during his lifetime, and Jim McArthur had seen more than his share of suffering.

'We do make a difference, Jen,' he said, staring into his pint as if the answers lay there. 'You just can't always see it.'

Small cogs in a big machine, Jen thought.

It triggered the unwelcome image of Marcus Aldridge, his terrified expression as he disappeared under that speeding train. He was the small cog, smashed under a big machine. She winced at the clarity of the memory and thought of Victoria Harvey, probably rocking back and forth in a padded cell somewhere. She wasn't the first and wouldn't be the last.

Splintering was becoming too common for Jen's liking. It was one of the risks of an unregulated procedure, the mind transfer equivalent of a dirty needle. Fragmented memories of the previous owner's life – as embedded and real as their own – made the new host unbalanced and dangerous, or in this case murderous.

'I spoke to Callaghan on Wednesday,' she said, thinking how quickly Operation Penthouse had spiraled out of control. 'We had *fifteen* splinters last month.'

McArthur shook his head but didn't seem worried. Bigger problems, she guessed, more important things to worry about. They both took a drink and McArthur changed the subject.

'Did you hear the news this morning?' he asked. 'They're ahead of schedule.'

The controversial draft system had been tested and deemed successful, and that morning the rumours that had been circulating homes, bars and workplaces for weeks were confirmed. With 9 billion people living in the safe zones and a global population approaching 12 billion, the UN had released their new, more aggressive Hibernation targets. During the next two years, 80 percent of people within the zones would be in the Hibernation programme.

The message was clear: Plan your alignment with friends and family. Choose your cycle – alpha or beta year – and claim a slot before the system chose one for you.

Jen hiked her eyebrows and lowered her voice. 'Like it or not, people need to get used to the idea. Hibernation is happening, and if they want to choose their year, they should do it – and soon.'

A group of men laughed loudly in unison. Logan checked the time and looked around the bar. She didn't want to socialise with anyone else from work.

'You going to be okay?' McArthur asked.

'I'll be fine,' Jen replied, finishing her drink. 'Say hi to Cole and the other guys.'

She stood, pulling on her coat. 'See you Monday. Oh, and give my love to Sally and the kids. Remember to do that.'

As they hugged, Jen whispered in his ear, 'Only a week to go, old man.'

His expression suggested he'd almost forgotten – retirement – something Jen never thought would happen. Although he didn't like to admit it, Mac was tired. They both knew the nanobots cleansing his blood and repairing his ageing cells could only do so much.

'I'm not *actually* retiring for another two months,' he reminded her, and then said without any hint of importance, 'Top brass are coming, apparently. Some posh meal or something.'

Jen smiled warmly and left. That *something* was a surprise party. A big one.

From his window seat, Jim McArthur watched her cross the street and disappear into a mass of people. He was going to miss the job, but most of all he would miss her. He had made a promise to watch over her.

He'd been on this earth for one hundred and nineteen years.

I guess for some people it's never enough.

He drained his glass and ordered another pint.

CHAPTER 6

The Friday evening sky dressed London in soaked purple linen. Jen looked up, shrugged and decided to walk home. It would take her thirty minutes and the fresh night air, rain or no rain, would help her forget what had been an awful week.

As she crossed London Bridge, she paused to watch a large airship cruise above St Paul's Cathedral, its blinking red lights cutting through the gloom. She looked up at the moon and found herself thanking it, as many did these days. It had pulled the tides forever, and now it might just turn the tide on the energy crisis, too. There were mining colonies up there now working triple shifts, pulling water and energy out of the ancient rock.

In the distance, the nearly complete Thames solar receiver stood majestic, rising up out of the water. Once operational, it would supply nearly half of central London's power needs. It was incredible to think that a combination of technologies could end up giving the planet free energy, a fact that seemed all the more impressive as she watched the city glow into life, preparing itself for another power-hungry weekend. Jen continued on, deciding she would have a quiet night, a glass of wine and some mind-numbing entertainment.

Simon, her roommate, had other ideas.

Their apartment was on the third floor of a newly constructed smart building on Ropemaker Street. Her rent was heavily subsidised by the Government, a perk of her position at Duality. Simon had been an obvious choice for a roommate. He was clean, tidy and worked long hours as a healthcare assistant. That suited her. Only once had he made a move on her. He'd been drunk and suggested it would be 'Fun!' and might do them both some good. Logan had been careful not to hurt his feelings but made sure he wouldn't suggest it again.

She made her way through the main entrance and up the stairs, and as she approached the door, she heard music. She opened it to see Simon and three friends in the kitchen, downing shots, dance music blasting from multiple speakers. The smell of warm food hit her immediately: pastry and spices, fresh herbs and cumin. She couldn't remember the last time she'd eaten.

'Officer Logan!' Simon raised both hands in surrender, then grabbed a tall bottle and poured a generous measure into a shot glass.

Jen knew the friends. They were good people. They'd had some crazy nights out together, but she wasn't in the mood this time. She walked over to them, planning to exchange pleasantries and make her excuses. Simon pushed a drink into her hand.

'Your face?' he said with mock concern, his infectious smile catching her.

'Yeah, tough day.'

'Rules are rules, Jen.'

They had made a pact. If either of them had a Friday that was beyond crap, then they had to go out. No questions. Drink, hit the town and blast the hell out of work. It was stupid and immature, but Simon had a contagious kind of optimism. She needed that sometimes.

His smile had become impossibly wide. 'We are going to

party!' he screamed and resumed dancing.

'Can I at least eat something?' Jen pleaded.

'You've got half an hour.'

She swore, knocked back a vodka shot and decided that actually, this might be just what she needed.

★ ★ ★

A few hours later, Jen was lost in herself, dancing alone, music pounding through her. From an open-air veranda she looked down onto a cobbled street packed with people. The Dome Nightclub, so named because of its huge clear glass ceiling, was crammed full. Projected colours and imagery flashed over its neon-blue floor as a sea of bodies swayed like tribal warriors, laser projection changing their appearances like flames licking a sea of ice.

In that brief, exquisite moment, Jen's day ceased to exist, the stress gone. Most of the club members were augmented, linking and planning the rest of their evenings, the power of speech dwarfed by the ability to think together and share thoughts and feelings. Jen preferred to dance alone. It was a form of release for her, a kind of meditation. Later, the clubbers' mind chatter would become flirtatious invites revealing desires and dreams, but for now the mood was exuberant anticipation.

Jen had turned off her social linking – she didn't want to meet someone random tonight – but accepted the club's audiovisual feed. She wanted to experience it alone. To her, that was the point. Which was why she was so frustrated by the man blatantly staring at her. Jen knew her dancing wasn't overly sexual or erotic, and she wasn't advertising or broadcasting herself as available. She ignored him and allowed her thoughts to wander. *Thomas.* She hadn't seen him in a while. She sent him a message and waited, the music traveling through her. Minutes later she received a reply.

It read: < *So good to hear from you. How about my place at 1?* >

She felt the unexpected, welcome rush of sexual anticipation. She continued to dance, trying to ignore the man still staring at her. She moved away as he approached, but he followed, smiling, eyes all over her. He closed in, seemingly unaware of the invisible boundary, the line between them. Jen stopped dancing, folded her arms and stared at him, the hypnotic trance broken.

'I'm leaving,' she shouted.

'I'll come with you.'

The man was drunk. As he placed his hand on her shoulder, he soon found himself on the floor facing the opposite direction, his arm twisted. He cried out, almost loud enough to be heard over the music. Jen released the wrist lock and walked away. The man sat there for a while, staring into space, rubbing his arm, shaking his head.

A large bouncer approached as she neared the door. 'You okay, miss?' he asked, his voice almost as deep as the sub-bass shaking the floor. 'That man bother you?'

'Thank you, I'm fine,' she replied with a wry smile. 'Nothing I can't handle.'

The exit, a large circular tunnel, was reminiscent of a steel igloo. She stepped out into the cool evening air, called a taxi and disappeared into the night.

Fifteen minutes later Jen was in Thomas's apartment. They shared a few drinks and kissed, warm, lingering kisses that lit her up inside. Thomas had shown her how sex should feel. It wasn't an exaggeration to say he had unlocked its elusive mystery for her. Now they were naked, making love, entwined as one.

This dance, like the music earlier, was another way of losing herself, of giving herself away. Luckily Thomas was in no hurry. He had undressed her slowly, ensuring he paid attention to every curve, every delicate inch of her skin. Time ceased to exist as his movements led her towards orgasm.

Control. Jen spent her life in control, calculated and considered. But not here. Here she was free. She cried out as she climaxed, an intense wave of emotion and pleasure. It wasn't something she decided to do; it just happened, natural and involuntary, and that made it beautiful. And yet, with each passing second, those feelings of purity left her, along with all thoughts of love and companionship. Those were the dreams of ordinary people. For Jennifer Logan, they were always fleeting, elusive and so quickly distant. She could never hold on to them. She lay silent for a while, nearly content, the warmth of his body permeating hers. Thomas fell asleep and Jen slipped away quietly, leaving money on the table next to his bed. It was a good arrangement. She would see him again when she needed him, when the time was right.

The rain was coming down in a thin mist, the street buzzing with traffic, people and energy. Simon was right. Tonight had been just what she needed, the day forgotten for a while. Her thoughts turned to Mac. She was going to miss having him around. The old man would be flat out by now. She thought of him snoring and smiled. Retirement was coming at the right time for him. Jen, on the other hand, had work to do. Duality never stopped. She would need to take it easy the rest of the weekend and make sure she was recharged before it all started again.

CHAPTER 7

Jen awoke late on Saturday morning and spent most of the day at home, enjoying the calm lethargy a mild hangover can bring. By the time Sunday arrived she was feeling better prepared for the week ahead. She ran before dinner – the cold shift to December subtle, yet enough to invigorate – and then settled in for the evening.

That night, a recurring dream returned, one that hadn't surfaced for a month but had featured heavily over the years. It always started, and finished, in the same way.

Jen found herself in a large cornfield, above her a ghostly moon behind drifting clouds. A sound like breaking surf shook the crop, clacking its tall blades in unison. She sensed him first – her father – and then saw him in the distance, moving through thick, green stalks.

'Daddy!' she cried, running. 'Wait!' Her voice was young, the voice of the child she once was.

She ran hard, but somehow the distance between them remained, the earth pulling at her, slowing her down. They were both in danger. She could feel something closing in, dark figures with claws and sharp teeth. Did her father know they were here?

'Daddy, they're coming. Don't leave me.' She was in tears now. Up ahead, in the inky darkness, a warm glow. She headed towards it, crashing through the sharp corn until she reached a circular clearing. In the centre stood a framed doorway, and in front of that her father, silhouetted in warm light. He spoke, his voice clear and caring.

'Daddy has to go away.' He sounded calm as he opened the door and stepped through. 'I want you to forget me.'

The sickly sweet comfort of his voice warmed her heart, but those words twisted in her gut. Sounds crashed around them. Closer they came. Jen ran, but the door was closing. She grabbed at the handle, her hand slipping repeatedly on its smooth surface. The door continued to close, eventually slamming shut: just a door and its frame, upright and solid. Jen fell to her knees, pushing tears out of closed eyes as the creatures approached. From every angle she could hear them, thrashing through the cornfield, snarling.

'Don't leave me!' she screamed, pounding the door. The dark shapes broke through into the clearing. 'Daddy, how could you leave me?'

They descended, sharp claws sinking into her back. Her pain rose above adrenalin and she screamed, but no sound came, no one would save her, he was gone, her father was gone.

The dream ended there, as it always did, in a vacuum of silent pain. She awoke covered in sweat, heart racing, a ringing in her ears accentuated by the deathlike quiet of her apartment.

She cried for a while, waiting for the power of the dream to fade, knowing that sleep wouldn't come again. The dream – horrible as it was – also left her with a nagging feeling of absence, of something missing, like a ripped section of a map or a name you couldn't quite remember. The day's first light cut the darkness above her. She decided to get up, shower and focus on the day ahead.

The order had come through last night. She was to extract Phillip Harvey – husband of Victoria the train killer – from

Hibernation and interview him. His wife had splintered, the result of a back-street body swap, and Jen was determined to get to the source. At least *that* was in her control; at least *that* was real. By the time she left home, the nightmare had lessened its grip. But her father's words lingered:

Daddy has to go away. I want you to forget me.

CHAPTER 8

The silver Mercedes sped west, finally free of central Brasília's dense traffic, the temperature pushing its tired air conditioning to breaking point.

'Put these on,' the driver ordered, passing sunglasses over his shoulder.

Nathan leant forward, grabbed the glasses and did as he was told. Relief from the fierce glare was instant and he was able to gaze out the window without squinting. The colourful vibrancy of the capital had been gradually replaced by sprawling urban towns framed in scrubland and separated by rows of tired telegraph poles stretching far into the distance.

'How long will it take us?' Nathan shouted over the engine noise.

The craggy-faced driver glanced up at the mirror but didn't answer. Nathan struggled to see him and realised it seemed to be getting darker. He panicked briefly, thinking he may have been drugged, but then relaxed. It was the sunglasses; they were actively blocking his vision. As the world gradually turned black, he understood: he wasn't supposed to see where they were going. He scanned as far as he could in all directions. Nothing. The glasses masked even his peripheral vision. His only input was a dark void, and the monotonous drone of the engine.

Better than an old-fashioned blindfold.

He'd left Canada a week ago, traveling carefully and slowly, arriving in Brazil as planned. The previous evening had been spent at the Imperial Hotel. His contact, Raul Ferreira, had arranged it all. Apart from the impossibly thin waiter who delivered room service, Nathan hadn't seen or spoken to anyone. His sleep had been restless, waiting for the telephone to ring. Could the people who murdered his wife know he was in Brazil? He wasn't sure, but it was better to be safe and suspect everything and everyone. In just a few hours he would be in a new body, he reassured himself, he would become somebody else.

The car banged over another pothole. Nathan cursed his delicate stomach as tiny beads of sweat appeared across his brow and his mouth filled with saliva. The lack of vision combined with the driver's sour body odour sent ripples of nausea through him.

'I'm going to puke. Stop the car,' he pleaded, knowing there was nothing he could do. 'Stop the car!'

The driver slammed on the brakes. 'Be quick,' he shouted, turning the radio up. 'And mind the seats.'

Nathan stumbled out, pulled the glasses from his face and heaved, ejecting most of his breakfast. He paused for a while, hands on his knees, eyes adjusting. The area was desolate, mainly scrubland. It smelt like a tinderbox waiting to go up. *Jesus, this heat,* he thought and puked again, the air burning his lungs.

'Let's go,' the driver barked a few minutes later.

Nathan spat a large globule of bile onto the ground and watched it curl and disappear in a thick ball of dust. He wiped his mouth, got back into the car and pulled the door shut.

'It's not far now, just hold it in,' the driver ordered without any sense of compassion.

Nathan studied him, noting the cheap jewellery, fake watch

and lack of hygiene. The driver amused him, acting the big man. Nathan wasn't trying to be anyone. He was simply living day to day, moment to moment. He wasn't acting anything, he just was.

The driver scowled at him in the mirror – 'Glasses!' – before pulling away, kicking up clouds of orange dust. They didn't speak for the remainder of the journey, which felt longer than two hours. They stopped only once. Nathan heard a short conversation, something about roadblocks ahead, then nothing. Just his darkness and thoughts, images of his murdered wife, a different world, long gone. After what felt like days he felt the car lurch, turn a full circle and stop. The engine died. There was a pause.

'We're here,' the driver said, tugging the handbrake. 'Leave the glasses.'

Nathan did as he was told and stepped out of the car, blinking against the sudden assault of sunlight. His stomach was complaining again.

He was in a car park bordered by a tall wire fence. In the centre was a large four-storey building, flat-roofed, primarily concrete, with regular square glass windows. Numerous cars were parked neatly in spaces, suggesting it might be an office. Nathan looked out beyond the fence to connecting roads, dry desert and the odd cluster of residential buildings. In the distance he could hear a lone dog barking and the tidal hum of highway traffic. Again, it was the heat that struck him. Oppressive and unforgiving, it surrounded him, robbing his body of moisture. His face and ears prickled.

'When do I see Mr Ferreira?' Nathan asked, licking his dry lips.

The driver walked around the car, dumped his bag onto the ground and tossed a small bottle of water at him. 'Drink this and wait here.'

Nathan caught the bottle, twisted the cap and took a long gulp, the water harsh against his burning stomach. The driver was back in the car and seconds later Nathan was alone, baking in the midday sun.

I will miss our conversations, you ignorant prick.

He could hear machinery grinding inside the building and guessed it was a workshop of some kind. He waited. Nearly five minutes passed. He scanned the area again for shade. Nothing. He considered walking around the building but decided to wait as instructed.

The sun pounded his head, the heat making each breath a determined effort. A chorus of crickets, quiet on his arrival, were now building to a deafening crescendo. He had noticed them on the hotel menu and wasn't surprised; there must be billions of them out here. He gulped down the remaining water and placed the empty bottle on the ground, noticing the heat haze shimmering like wet glass across the tarmac. He could feel paranoia welling up inside him. An unwelcome thought bobbed to the surface of his mind, making him frown.

What if I've just been left here? Dumped? Three hundred thousand credits lighter, and nothing to show for it.

He didn't know where he was, and he had no way of getting back to the airport. He could steal a car, but what then? He wondered if he was being watched. *'Check it out! The idiot from Canada – the so-called "smart" one.'* He shook the thoughts away, gritting his teeth. This wasn't a time for weakness.

Stay focused.

As he regained his composure, a small metal door at the base of the building opened and a woman stepped out. She was petite and smartly dressed, in her thirties, he guessed. She gestured towards him and Nathan walked rapidly, joining her at the door.

'Your name?' she asked politely.

'Nathan O'Brien.'

'Thank you. Please confirm you aren't using any recording devices, augmentation or implants.' Her voice was clear and precise.

Nathan shook his head. 'No, nothing, I don't have anything.'

'This way,' she said, and walked back inside the building.

CHAPTER 9

Nathan's eyes adjusted to the dimly lit corridor. It was narrow, paint flaking away from the edges of its dirty green walls. He followed the woman into a large open workshop. Blue sparks flickered through the air, lighting up the floor like an electrified sea. The smell of oil and hot metal filled his nostrils. Cars, old but still usable, were being converted to run on biofuel. Busy mechanics crawled over them like sweaty ants. The woman, young and attractive, with hair pinned neatly to her head, crossed the floor ahead of him. Not a single one of the hard-working grease monkeys looked up.

They're used to seeing her. Jesus, how many of these do they do?

He joined her and they entered a small metal lift. She pulled a safety cage in front of them and pressed a large yellow button. The lift whined into action and descended slowly, the sound of the workshop giving way to the steady metallic drone of its machinery. This wasn't what he'd expected at all, but Nathan was learning to embrace the unexpected. That was the cost – and the wonder – of living in the moment.

They faced forward for a while, not speaking. He could smell her, feminine like floral soap, and looked over to see her wiping grease from her fingers with a dainty handkerchief. With polite will he forced her to return his smile, which felt like a minor triumph after the taxi driver's inability to connect on any level. She seemed harmless, but he watched her carefully. The car conversion business seemed to be viable in its own right, but he hadn't forgotten why he was here. He wasn't going to be taken out by some honey trap in a tight skirt.

The lift slowed to a halt. Its doors slid open, and stretching out in front of them was a modern medical facility. Nathan felt an invisible wall of chilled air wash over him and took a deep breath, his lungs thanking him. Groups of people were milling around in the long white corridor. It reminded him of a private hospital wing, clean, bright and pleasantly cold. The contrast to the heat and industry of the workshop above couldn't have been stronger. They exited the lift. The woman turned and Nathan noticed that her cheekbones were unusually pronounced, her dark skin somehow richer under the fluorescent light. It had been a long time since he'd had a woman. Probably wouldn't again, he thought without sadness.

'I'm sorry if your trip was… difficult,' she said, gesturing to her left. 'Please wait in here. Mr Ferreira will be with you shortly.'

Nathan nodded. He entered the room and looked around. It was simple, unadorned: a steel table with two matching chairs and what looked like an airlock in the left corner. It reminded him of something, but he couldn't place it. He brought his shoulder blades together, aware of the sweat now cooling his back. Moments later Raul Ferreira entered the room, smartly dressed in a pale blue shirt, grey trousers and polished black shoes.

'Mr O'Brien. Good to meet you.' He shook Nathan's hand. 'My colleague has already apologised for the journey, I believe. I'm afraid it's necessary.'

Ferreira had a warm, friendly demeanour and, although born and raised in Brazil, spoke impeccable English.

'It's fine,' Nathan lied.

'Please sit.' Raul pulled out the chairs and they sat facing each other. 'First, some formalities. As we discussed previously, your candidate is European, very fit, healthy, no distinguishing marks. He is exactly as ordered. Prepped and ready.' Raul paused, frowned and tipped his head, 'But there has been a slight change.'

Nathan shifted in his seat. 'Change?'

'Yes, the donor's travel visa is now four weeks, not six. Since you and I first spoke, the UN have changed the rules. *Again.* Unavoidable, I'm afraid.'

He spoke as if they were discussing a simple tax return.

'Why didn't you mention this before?' Nathan asked. Two weeks less would make things more difficult.

'UN law is outside of our control,' Raul said confidently, 'and therefore outside of our agreement.'

Nathan couldn't argue. He remained focused on Raul. 'Is there anything else I should know?'

'Everything else is as agreed, but I will take this opportunity to remind you of something.' Ferreira leant forward, his eyes tightening. He spoke slowly and clearly. 'I don't ask your intentions, but I do make it my business to correctly ensure the safety of my clients. Your security deposit is repayable on *return*. Your donor understands the risks involved, hence the higher premium, but you are only *hiring* his body. It is on loan. He wants it back. I just wanted to be clear on that.'

Nathan would have preferred a permanent body jump, but it just wasn't possible. They cost millions. He had to rent instead, knowing that he might not make it back, might never see his old body again. If that happened, they would eventually restore the donor into a clone of his original body – an expensive, complicated procedure. That's what the excessive deposit was for. Nathan supposed it went some way to appeasing his guilt.

'I'll be back for my deposit,' Nathan lied again. 'It's a lot of money, Mr Ferreira.'

'Yes, it is. So are you happy to proceed?' Raul asked.

Nathan pulled a clear data card from his trouser pocket. 'It's all there,' he said, handing it over.

Raul took the slide and placed it onto a flat glass console in the centre of the table. Nathan watched the two connect. Digits formed for a few seconds and then disappeared. The secure bank transfer was complete. Raul smiled, and his behaviour changed almost immediately. He seemed keen to conclude the meeting. Nathan presumed he had other clients.

'I will leave you now,' Raul said. 'Please undress, step into the sterile chamber and follow the instructions. The procedure takes around one hour. Once complete, a driver will take you back to the airport. Your ID and luggage are all prepared.'

He stood, smiled and shook Nathan's hand firmly. 'I will see you on your return.'

Nathan followed the instructions and undressed, finally realising what the facility reminded him of. The thought made him smile. It was a moon base he'd seen on the news, a Helium 3 processing plant. This was simpler, though, like the old science fiction films.

He entered the booth and felt vulnerable as a laser rotated and scanned every inch of his naked body, removing all traces of bacteria. A burst of chemicals washed him clean and suction cleared the air with a hiss. He grabbed a thin gown, wrapped it around himself and stepped out into a small room that resembled an operating theatre. In the centre were two beds surrounded by high-tech machinery. A gowned nurse wearing a mouth guard and hairnet was being advised by a virtual doctor. Nathan was reassured; artificial intelligence meant less chance of error. His donor body lay on the right-hand bed. The left-hand bed was empty.

'Please lie down and try to relax,' the AI instructed him, its voice calm and authoritative. The nurse barely looked up.

Nathan approached the empty bed, stealing a look to his right. The donor was as described, tall and physically strong. Even lying there apparently lifeless, the man appeared trustworthy. He was perfect. Nathan took a breath, sat on the bed and lay down. He had already said his good-byes to his current body. It could be traced and was therefore useless to him now, but he wondered about his donor. What would drive a man to hire his own body out? Even for such a large sum of money?

The nurse shone a green light into his eyes and attached two warm rubber nodes to his temples. The mind transfer itself was actually pretty straightforward, as long as it was executed correctly. The donor's mind would be backed up, stored and then restored to its original body on Nathan's return. For the donor, the weeks wouldn't exist; the operation would seem almost instantaneous. At least, that was how it was supposed to play out.

What would drive a man…?

Nathan felt another pang of guilt for his donor but pushed it aside. He knew all about sacrifice, about doing whatever it takes.

'Sleep now,' the AI said softly.

He felt himself slide away, the small tablet he'd taken helping him relax, making him more obedient. With his guard lowered, primal instincts took over. He thought of the girl who had accompanied him in the lift, the sound of her heels and the sway of her body squeezed into that tight skirt. No guilt.

Women… Women are good. She could tell me what to do, he thought, smiling, glassy-eyed. *I would be a very good boy. Do as I'm told.*

As his thoughts became echoes, Nathan drifted from consciousness, suspecting this might be the best sleep he would have for some time.

CHAPTER 10

Doctor Leon Povis paused, staring at a gowned patient in the theatre below. The subject was no one special, but today was an achievement, something to be proud of.

He returned to his terminal and initiated the operation, reminding himself that forty thousand was just the beginning. It wasn't yet time to crack open the champagne. A large robotic arm jerked to life obediently, rearing up like a praying mantis before creeping slowly towards the patient's head. As Povis checked the man's vitals, a nurse to his side confirmed all was ready.

'Synchronising Hibernation chip with biorhythms,' the nurse said.

The doctor watched as a unique link was made between the host's brain patterns and the Hibernation chip's magical circuitry. It still impressed him. That thin slither of nanoengineered genius, so advanced not even he understood it. That didn't matter in the grand scheme of things. What mattered was that it worked. A dark wisp of smoke licked the sterile air as a laser burnt a thin slit into the patient's neck. The robotic arm, which tapered down to a thin point, inserted the tiny chip before retracting quickly to its original position. Povis and the nurse waited a few seconds. Data streamed into view.

'Chip is active. Bonding complete,' the nurse said, her voice dry and mechanical.

Understandable, the Doctor thought. *We've got millions of these to do.*

In the right-hand corner of his vision, an alert bobbed annoyingly. Having already ignored it twice, he glanced at the icon and answered the call. It was reception.

'Doctor Povis?' the woman asked, her squeaky voice grating down his spine.

'*You* called *me*,' he said flatly, wondering what the point of direct-thought comms was if you still had to check who you were talking to. There was a long pause, presumably while the squeaky-voiced one caught up with him.

'Doctor Povis?' she repeated in exactly the same tone.

'Yes,' he snapped. 'Christ! This is Doctor Povis.'

'Officer Logan from Duality is waiting to see you,' she said, and then added deliberately, 'Three o'clock, as arranged.'

The Doctor glanced at the clock. It was nearly half past.

Great. This is all I need.

★ ★ ★

Jen looked around the atrium of the Hibernation centre and sighed. She'd listened to the informative voiceover twice and didn't want to go for a third. Opposite her a family of four waited, fidgety and nervous. The centre may have been purpose-built, designed to calm and ease concerns, but no amount of peaceful music and water fountains could make you forgot what it was. The couple were in their fifties, she guessed, although it was becoming harder to tell; the average life expectancy was almost a hundred and forty now. Their kids, a boy and girl, aged around ten, were becoming agitated. The couple quietly mumbled to each other, probably discussing the draft, a common subject for those chosen. There were another thirty or so people dotted around the space, all of them looking equally apprehensive.

The woman opposite caught Jen's eye and smiled. 'Are you here to join Hibernation?' she asked.

'Already in,' Jen replied. 'Two years ago. I've completed one cycle.'

The boy inched along the sofa, prodded repeatedly by his sister. 'Does it hurt?'

His mother tugged his jumper and explained it wasn't a polite question.

Jen reassured her that it was okay, that the procedure was painless. 'You go to sleep, then you wake up. A whole year has passed, but it's like a dream. Like a really good night's sleep.'

'Are you a police person?' the girl asked, eyeing Jen's clothing.

Jen nodded. 'Kind of.'

The couple resumed their conversation and the boy saw his chance to make up for his sister's constant poking: a single thump to her arm. The girl nestled against her mother, crying. The boy smirked at Jen, but couldn't take his eyes off her gun. Jen tightened her stare but was smiling inside. Kids are nice, she thought, as long as you can give them back.

'Ms Logan?' A man in a white coat, presumably Doctor Povis, stood next to her. 'Apologies for keeping you. One of those days.'

There was no sincerity in his voice. Jen said her good-byes to the family and followed the Doctor, who seemed rushed and annoyed by her presence. She took an instant dislike to him.

'You were expecting me?' she asked.

'Yes.' He walked quickly, as if trying to lose her.

'You seem aggravated. Is there a problem?' Jen asked.

The Doctor stopped and looked her up and down slowly.

'I take my work very seriously, Ms Logan.' A sharp sigh. 'People seem to think Hibernation is simple. That we just flick a switch off, and then flick it back on again.' He mimicked the gesture of a switch. 'Click. They're back.'

Jen eyeballed him. 'No one takes extraction lightly, Doctor Povis. I can assure you of that.'

Approval to extract Phillip Harvey, husband of the train killer, hadn't been easy, but it was a high-profile case, one that Richards seemed determined to capitalise on.

'It's not standard procedure, Officer Logan,' Povis continued. 'When we hibernate, we aren't designed to be pulled out of –'

'Doctor,' Jen interrupted. 'There's been a murder, and under the Hibernation Act we are permitted *by law* to extract anyone, at any time.'

The Doctor scowled, raising an eyebrow that remained set in place. Jen crossed her arms and waited. Povis shook his head and muttered something under his breath before striding towards a lift, tutting. It was important to Jen that he was the one to break the stalemate. This man might be smart, educated and important, but she was in charge. She joined him by the lift doors.

'Ready to see behind the scenes?' He punched the lowest button on the console, seemingly pleased with himself. The phrase echoed in her mind during the rapid descent.

Stepping out of the lift, they walked a narrow corridor before entering a box-like room that appeared to be some kind of viewing platform. The entire far wall was glass. Jen walked to it and swallowed, her mouth hanging open slightly, eyes blinking rapidly. Her experience of Hibernation centres so far had been exclusively front-end. She had attended opening ceremonies, managed security, done her bit. And then, when her name was drawn, she had been through the pre-checks and finally the procedure itself. Never here, though, behind the curtain. She stared through the glass at a sight most people would never see, and knew then it was right they didn't. It was as awe-inspiring as it was terrifying.

As far and high as she could see were circular glass windows built into smooth walls. Behind each sealed door, a human, hibernating. The sight reminded her of a steel beehive, organised like a military unit, sterile and efficient.

'How many?' She turned to the doctor, her voice wavering slightly.

'At the moment, forty thousand. Next cycle will be triple that.'

He accessed the control panel and spoke a command. 'Chamber 26578. Mr Phillip James Harvey.'

The AI confirmed the subject in question and awaited his instruction.

'Extract and prep for acclimatisation.' He smiled at Jen, pointing out through the glass. 'You'll enjoy this bit.'

She turned back and watched as a huge robotic machine went to work. In the distance, she heard a hiss as Phillip Harvey was removed from his chamber on a tray and lifted high into the air. She could see his body – grey-blue and lifeless – wrapped in protective film. She frowned at the precision of it all, could feel her breath quickening, a chill setting into her core.

'How long will it take?' she managed eventually, doing her best to hold his stare.

'Two days at least,' the Doctor replied, his thin smile suggesting he was enjoying her discomfort. 'And to reiterate, this is not normal protocol.'

Jen tilted her head and stared at him. 'Noted. *Again.*'

She shook his hand – cold and limp, as expected – and returned to the ground floor alone, the lift rolling her stomach, the sight of the Hibernation chamber burnt into her mind. A tomb, people not alive, more like death.

Ready to see behind the scenes?

She felt her skin crawl and realised she was rubbing the tough nub of flesh on the back of her neck: her Hibernation scar. The doors opened, snapping her thoughts away. The family from earlier were sitting next to a man in a suit. The boy noticed Jen and waved.

You'll enjoy this bit.

She managed a weak smile but felt her face flush red. Hibernation was necessary, Jen knew that, but now, perhaps for the first time, she understood why they didn't want people to see the reality.

The false front of the waiting room was peaceful and calming. She walked past the group, her gaze set on the exit, not wanting them to see the irrational, creeping fear that had taken hold of her.

CHAPTER 11

Phillip Harvey's interrogation happened three days later. After a bout of Hibernation sickness – something he dragged out – he'd finally been cleared and brought in just after noon. Detention room 4, Duality Headquarters.

'It's too late, isn't it?' Phillip Harvey sat slumped in a small steel chair, head down, resignation in his voice. 'For her, I mean.'

'Yes, I'm afraid it is,' Jen replied coldly.

The file said it all. Phillip had screwed around. He wasn't a good husband. His wife, desperate to entice him back into their marriage, had undergone an illegal body swap. So far, so familiar. Then, as they often did, she splintered, and the next thing you know, Operation Penthouse is a murder enquiry.

Mr Harvey sniffed. 'She had the operation because she wanted me to notice her again.'

'But it didn't work, did it,' Jen said, colder still.

'It's ironic I suppose,' he continued, ignoring her, his mind seeming to drift.

'Ironic?'

'For years she craved attention, and suddenly, well, she had more than she could cope with. After the operation people noticed her again, she ended up leaving me. *She* was the one who ended up fucking around.' He shook his head at the irony, letting out a long, heavy sigh and looked at Jen for the first time, his eyes glazed with obvious regret. 'Not that I blame her.'

'Why didn't you just divorce?'

He frowned. 'Ugly business. No. We separated. And when I got drafted for Hibernation…' He stopped his face going through a gamut of expressions before seeming to accept something difficult. 'I was actually glad.'

'But you broke the rules,' Jen said sharply. 'Your wife wanted to live longer than everyone else. To cheat the system.'

Jen walked the sterile room towards a mirror spanning the length of the wall. Behind it three men stood observing the interview. Jim McArthur (Intelligence officer, MI6), David Ravenscroft (Senior strategist, organised crime, MI5) and Jen's immediate superior, Paul Richards (Chief Superintendent, Duality). They should be pleased. It could take hours to get information, to break a man down and weaken his spirit. Phillip Harvey had spilled his guts in just under thirty minutes.

'We didn't mean it,' Harvey said, sucking a strand of snot creeping from his nostril. 'I just wanted her to be happy. I'm sorry.'

'Sorry isn't going to save you,' Jen shouted. 'You financed the operation, Phillip.' She walked to him, her body language softening for just a moment, her voice calmer. 'Tell me the name of the person who organised the operation and you might get out of this alive.'

He stared at the floor, visibly shaking, and replied slowly. 'He never told me his name.'

'Then where did you first hear of him? Where do you meet?

'Victoria organised it all.' He blurted the words, looking up but not meeting her eyes. 'I just pay the bills. That's all I ever did. I pay the bloody bills.'

Jen slid a picture of Marcus Aldridge – the victim – onto the table. The train had done its work; his contorted body was bloodied and mangled.

'Jesus Christ,' Mr Harvey sighed, his voice a whisper.

'I'm afraid he can't save you either.' Jen pushed another gruesome reminder onto the table. This was a process she found tiresome. Always the same, so predictable. Why didn't people realise the damage they'd done? Why did they need to see it? Part of her wanted to just kick the chair from underneath him, push him to the floor and get her knee into his jaw. Screw all this psychological shit.

Of course, she wouldn't do that.

She would remain calm, in control. Part of the reason she'd run to work that morning was to shake some of the physical aggression out of her system – well, that and to forget that awful dream. Her routine was one of opposites, a kind of dual life. After Operation Penthouse went sideways, and *that* Friday night, she had spent the remainder of her weekend recharging, eating decent food, exercising and sleeping. Go to the edge, fall over, pick yourself back up. It kept her sane, made sure she didn't burn out under the pressure. Plenty had, and it wasn't just the police work. A world on the brink, accelerating climate change – it was a constant shadow hanging over everyone, like a global sword of Damocles. No. She needed to be smart, she needed to maintain balance, remain in control. So when she banged her fist on the table – the shock physically lifting Phillip Harvey from his seat – it wasn't real anger. It was all for show.

She shouted, baring her teeth. 'You traveled to Pretoria and you met a man!'

Harvey hungrily scanned the pictures on the table, rocking back and forth, eyes bulging, mumbling to himself.

Jen waited. Slowly, he placed a trembling finger onto one of the faces Jen had shown him earlier.

'That's him,' he whispered, his heavy frame collapsing with relief.

'That's the man you met, the handler who organised the operation in South Africa? You're sure?'

'It's him. I'm sure.' He began to cry again, big gulps of air followed by long, shaking sobs.

The interrogation had been scheduled for two hours. Jen had gotten a positive identification in less than one. She pressed a small device on the table. It flashed red once.

'Interview terminated by Sergeant Jennifer Logan. Wednesday 12 December 2091 at 12.53pm.'

'What will happen to me?' Harvey asked, his voice almost childlike.

Jen stood. 'You'll probably get ten years in the block.'

'The block?'

'Hibernation with ageing.'

He pursed his lips and nodded, a sorrowful gesture, an acceptance of his fate.

Jen left the room without looking back. The trick now was to forget him, to disconnect. Chief Superintendent Paul Richards joined her in the corridor, a tall wiry man whose appearance was made paler by cropped jet-black hair. It sat atop his long face like a nail-brush. He was always immaculate, uniform pressed, the lines on his trousers like blades. Jen couldn't remember a time she'd seen him in civvies. They walked together, his mood buoyant. After the grilling he'd given the team that morning, Jen wasn't really in the mood for the *nice* version now.

'Good work, Logan.' He smiled thinly. 'We got him.'

Jen fought the urge to question his use of the word *we*. In her opinion, he had been over-promoted, a yes-man given too much power. Her view didn't count for much though. Richards was a political animal, something she would never be.

'They're going to make an example of the wife,' he continued happily.

Any high-profile case that could scare the shit out of people was good for the cause, which in turn was good for Richards. He seemed to be glowing with pride. Jen presumed his insight into the potential sentencing made him feel somehow closer to the power.

'I wanted to be sure you understood.' Richards eyeballed her. 'She might get the death penalty.'

Logan hid her surprise, forcing a calm nod. She hadn't expected the sentencing to be so aggressive.

He continued in his best condescending tone. 'I know how that *conscience* of yours can let you down sometimes.'

'It's her own fault.' Jen said, managing to suppress the anger boiling up at his last comment. She took a breath and continued, 'The law is clear. Sir.'

'Yes it is. Swap job and now murder. I wouldn't want to be in her shoes.'

Jen observed him coldly. He seemed entertained, as if this were a sideshow. They faced each other in awkward silence. Richards was clearly trying to think of something he could give her to do, a job to keep her busy.

'That report,' he said finally, 'the Lady of Mercy bombings?'

Jen nodded. It had been an interesting case initially, a group of religious extremists planning to blow up a Hibernation centre. They were common targets, and well protected. Unfortunately for the group – and the twenty-two innocent civilians in the adjacent building – they managed to blow both themselves and their secret hideout to bits. It became a case no one wanted, the main players in the terrorist group dead, every lead as cold as the bodies in the morgue. Jen was left picking up the pieces, so to speak.

'I'll have it on your desk Wednesday morning,' she replied.

'Oh, and Logan – speak to Peter Callaghan, would you? I talked to him this morning but he didn't seem himself.' His eyes darted around in thought. 'We're going to need him to be pin-sharp when Penthouse goes to trial.'

Richards walked away, muttering something under his breath. He was, at his core, a good policeman. She respected him, but he could be an arse.

No mistake.

CHAPTER 12

Jen was back in her running gear, through security and out onto the street by early evening. Clock watching wasn't her style, but the interrogation had left her feeling mentally exhausted. She couldn't wait to be free of the place.

She glanced up at the tall glass building, home of Duality and various other agencies and departments. The Government had known the move towards Hibernation, or transition as it had become known, wouldn't be easy. This building had been imagined as a kind of hub. The idea – an emphasis on communication and sharing – was sound enough, but departments sharing information? For the greater good? That never worked as well as it should, same building or not.

She ran, the evening chill ensuring a good pace, her feet beating out a reassuring rhythm. In the distance, Christmas lights and decorations reminded her the holiday season was looming. Not her favourite time of year. Above her, silver and red flashes of light cut across the sky, the latest transport for those who could afford it. She passed other runners and cyclists, many of them tuned into something, listening to music or the news. Jen preferred to be disconnected, to stay in the moment, to focus inward. Running was a form of meditation for her, of solitude, of being.

She cut across Fenchurch Street and paused. There was a Hibernation block ahead, but it wasn't purpose-built like the one in Shepherd's Bush. In the UK, population had reached one hundred million and Hibernation targets were aggressive. In the next three years, eighty million would join the Hibernation programme and Fenchurch was part of a new initiative to repurpose existing dwellings and speed up the process.

Jen considered her route and decided the possibility of streets free from traffic was too good to pass up. Even if it was a little eerie.

Perk of the job Jen, and by God, there aren't many.

She passed through a checkpoint and ran the empty streets, glancing up at the shadowy outlines of sentry droids patrolling the layered corridors, their glowing red pulse on every floor. It was strange knowing that inside thousands of people were hibernating. Weird to think that in just over two months they would return, Beta year would become Alpha, life would resume and Fenchurch Street would be a bustling community once more. As she passed the centre's main entrance, an armed droid approached. It was humanoid in form but featureless, its body moving in a smooth, yet menacing fashion. Jen saw her reflection in its black outer shell as it scanned her.

'Clearance approved. Move along, Sergeant Logan.' It retreated back into the shadows, guarding the sleepers. It was the same in other cities, towns and villages across the world. Hibernators were kept safe, casualties nonexistent.

She was about to resume her run when she was interrupted by a call.

The name 'Peter Callaghan' flashed up on her retinal display. She berated herself for forgetting to call him, took a breath, smiled and answered.

'Peter. I meant to call you today.' Her attempt to appear upbeat combined with breathlessness made her sound slightly manic. 'How is Mrs Harvey?'

'She's stable now,' he said. 'I did my best to contain the splintering, but she doesn't remember much about the incident.'

Hearing the train murder called an *incident* sent a shiver through her. His emphasis of the word made it sound like an unfortunate thing, an embarrassment even. Whilst it was typical of Peter to be clinical, there followed a long silence, and that was unlike him. Richards was right, Callaghan was not his usual self; normally she wouldn't get a word in.

'The boss thinks you might be asked to testify,' she offered, hoping the chance of a court appearance might improve his mood. He did love an audience.

Another pause, this time with rustling in the background.

'Are you okay, Peter?'

A new alert appeared. < *Secure line request.* >

She accepted and switched to the encrypted channel.

Callaghan spoke quickly. 'Where are you? You sound out of breath.'

'Sorry, I was running home,' she replied. 'Peter, what's wrong? Why the secure channel?'

'Are you recording this?' he said shakily.

'No, Why?'

'Jen, you need to trust me.' His voice was trembling. 'You could be in danger. We could both be in danger.'

His obvious panic forced her to make a couple of quick calculations. *Home. Fifteen minutes run, about five in a taxi.*

'Can you come to the house, tonight?' he asked.

'You need to tell me what's going on first.'

'Come to the house. I will tell you everything. Just trust me.'

He disconnected.

Jen didn't like that call one bit, it was clear this day wasn't getting better any time soon. She looked around and instantly wanted out of the Hibernation block. She started running, her pace faster than before, her mind racing.

★ ★ ★

An hour later, Jen arrived at Callaghan's house, the low rumble of her bike cutting through the silence of the leafy suburban street. She dismounted and looked up to see him standing just inside the front door. The wait had obviously been agonising for him.

'Thank you for coming,' he whispered nervously, peering up and down the street. 'Your augmentation and comms – they're turned off, right?' He tapped his head.

'Yes, I'm off-duty and offline.' She did her best to hide a shiver of nervousness bursting over her back. He looked gaunt, almost skeletal, and his fear seemed to be catching. Callaghan stole one more look outside before shuffling inside, gesturing for her to follow. Jen hadn't visited the house since his divorce, over two years ago. Back then it had seemed warm and homey; now it smelt stale, a bittersweet smell she associated with a lack of attention. In the hallway a cluster of family photographs still clung to the walls. Jen paused and studied them. Peter looked impossibly young and confident, taller even, and she realised how much he had changed over the last few years.

'I do miss her.' He was smiling, trying to conceal his obvious sadness.

Jen smelled the faint odour of whiskey on his breath and noted his growth of pepper-white stubble. She remembered the split: Callaghan always working, his wife leaving him for a man who showed her some attention. After the Harveys' depressing tales of doomed marriage and infidelity, it appeared to be this month's theme. All very predictable and sadly poignant, with Christmas just around the corner. During the silence that hung between them, Jen noticed the layers of dust covering most surfaces. She probably could have done more, checked in on him maybe.

'At times I hate her for leaving.' He stared blankly at the wall representing his past, eyes glassy, tone defeated. 'But I don't blame her.'

'Peter.' Jen asked gently, 'Why don't you tell me what's going on?'

'Yes… yes, of course.' He seemed to physically shake the memories from his mind as he looked her dead in the eyes for the first time that evening. 'Follow me.'

He continued down the hallway, stopping at an undersized door and gripping the handle. After an audible beep, the lock opened. On hearing the familiar sound, a large ginger cat appeared and proceeded to swirl and weave between Callaghan's legs, purring loudly. He shushed it away, raising his eyebrows and smiling awkwardly before opening the cellar door and stepping through. Jen followed, instinctively placing a hand on her sidearm.

They descended dusty stone steps, lit poorly from above, the smell of oil and boot polish mixed with earth. At the base of the steps was another door, this one much larger and made of steel. Callaghan turned to face her, his eyes shining like black marbles in the half-light.

'I need your help.' He paused. 'But what I am about to tell you could put you in further danger.' He waited to be sure she understood the importance of those words.

'I understand, Peter. You can trust me.'

The damp smell, wet ash and freshly dug earth, was more intense now and conjured memories. Jen recalled her childhood, the wine cellar at Brook Mill Farm, and felt a strangely familiar sensation, as though they had skipped a few seconds of time. She was struck with a sudden, undeniable certainty. She couldn't explain how, but she knew whatever secrets were hidden behind this door would have deep significance for her.

'I *know* I can trust you.' He leant in close, eyes tightening. 'But it's not *you* I'm worried about.'

CHAPTER 13

The basement was a functioning laboratory, filled with expensive equipment and odd items of antique furniture, scattered without any sense of taste or consideration. This was a man's den, a refuge, and Jen wondered if she might be the first women to set foot down here. She also suspected it might have played a part in his divorce. Too easy to come down here and hide.

There were various machines, cooling fans whirring, data running down displays like rain. Callaghan closed the door, pulled two small leather chairs together and offered her a seat. Jen sat. He walked to an ornate wooden bureau, poured himself a whiskey and held another empty glass, raising his eyebrows at her. She declined his silent offer.

'This room is completely secure,' he said, sitting opposite her, his mood a little brighter.

She figured by *secure* he meant from surveillance, that they could talk freely. She observed him, his eyes a little bloodshot. He wasn't drunk, though, he was using the whiskey to calm his nerves.

'Okay, Peter,' Jen said. 'Tell me what's going on.'

Callaghan licked his lips and swallowed, a click in his throat followed by a deep breath. He looked at her twice, seemingly unable to start talking. He smiled limply.

'It's alright,' she tried to reassure him. 'Start at the beginning.'

He rubbed his hands down his face and nodded, finally managing to get words to leave his mouth by staring at the floor and blinking.

'I found things during my research into splintering, anomalies in brain patterns. Things that aren't…' He took a sip of his whiskey, wincing as it burned his throat.

'Aren't what?'

He replied reluctantly without looking up. 'Aren't. Right.'

'Go on.' Jen leant forward, placing her hand gently on his arm. 'Tell me everything.'

He looked up briefly and smiled. 'I ran some tests on our recent cases, using a new algorithm, something deeper. That's when I found them.' His right leg was jangling like a trapped eel. 'The discrepancies.'

'In English, Peter.'

'I'm still trying to figure it out,' he snapped, clearly frustrated, but then frowned, sighing. 'I'm sorry.'

'It's okay,' she said, reaching for his hand. 'You found discrepancies in brain patterns?'

'Yes, they exist, like scars on top of memories.' He held her gaze with a sudden intensity, his confidence returning. 'But they don't have an origination signature – they look like search echoes.'

Jen felt the knot in her stomach loosen slightly.

Search echoes.

She didn't need to say a word. Her expression must have done enough, as though she was telling him off and pitying him all at once.

'I know how it sounds,' he snapped again, his voice childlike and defensive.

'Do you though?' Jen replied, remembering the years of heated debate.

In the beginning, people had been scared. Mind interfaces,

augmentation, thought comms. They had been understandably concerned about thought privacy, but that was all in the past. All she had to do was reassure him, talk him down, make him see sense.

Callaghan stared into his glass.

'You're talking about mind searching,' she said softly. 'You know that, right?'

'I thought it was a part of the splintering at first,' Callaghan explained, undeterred. 'But then Aldridge came along, you know, our guy under the train. I ran the test on him, and others, to –'

'Others?' she interrupted, working to process the information. 'How many?'

'It seems that if you're a hibernator, you have them.'

That got Logan's attention. 'What do you mean?'

'Of the people tested so far, only hibernators appear to have the echoes.' He was more animated now, unable to help his enthusiasm even though the subject was clearly scaring him.

'Don't you think it's unlikely that you, and only you, could have discovered this?'

'Yes, okay, but once you know where to look…' He trailed off.

'Have you told anyone else about this?' she asked.

'No, why?' The question seemed to increase his nervousness.

'Because you shouldn't. The Symbiosis Act, Peter. It prevents all of this. Everything is bound by it. What you're suggesting is impossible.'

Callaghan finished his whiskey and shrugged his shoulders. The Act ensured data was encrypted within the biological host, that it couldn't be tampered with or interpreted in isolation.

'I think someone has broken the rules,' he said with resignation.

'So what, then? They're searching us right now, are they?

They're all in on it? Jim McArthur, Richards, the Prime Minister?'

Callaghan recoiled, and Logan instantly regretted the outburst.

He stood and began pacing the room. 'I'd rehearsed this a few times. I know it sounds crazy, but I can't deny what I've found.'

There was a long silence.

'I'm sorry,' Jen said in a feeble attempt at a truce. 'You need to understand how this sounds. Just, please don't start screaming conspiracy. Let me do some digging. You can run some more tests. Just don't do anything drastic.'

He nodded.

'So, do you think they're searching us now?' she asked, as carefully as she could manage.

'I don't know. But I doubt it. I think it takes time. I think they do it during the Hibernation cycle.'

His tone, so matter-of-fact, is what scared her. This man she had known for years, Duality's consultant of choice, trusted expert witness on a number of high-profile cases, seemed convinced of mind searching. She couldn't stand by and watch him throw his career away on a half-baked theory. That's when an idea came to her, so obvious she couldn't believe it had taken until now to suggest it.

Jen said, 'Test me.'

Peter stared at her.

'I'm serious. I've hibernated for a year; I would have the search echoes. Can you do it? Here?'

'I could try,' he replied. 'Yes. Probably.'

'Then do it.'

He grabbed a small square device from the table next to him and tapped it, launching a holographic interface. She watched him work, his face complete concentration. Thirty minutes later, he was set up and ready.

'Just relax, close your eyes, you won't know a thing about it.'

Jen sat back in the chair and said dryly, 'And tomorrow, you will wake up and realise how insane this all sounds.'

The scan took less than three minutes. Jen blinked and looked at him, unable to decide if his expression was confusion or fear.

He was rubbing one eye and repeating himself.

'That can't be right,' he mumbled.

'What is it?' she asked. 'What's wrong?'

Callaghan's eyes tightened, and he shook his head.

'For God's sake, Peter, tell me,' Jen shouted. 'Did you find echoes?'

He nodded. 'Yes, you've got them, you've got echoes, but there's something else.'

'What do you mean, something else?' Her stomach was doing flips, the moment charged with a dark destiny.

He grabbed the screen, turning it towards her. 'You can see it. There. It looks like a file, a memory, but it's been buried really deep.'

In the centre of the scan was a highlighted section, words she couldn't make out.

'Is it like the echoes?'

'No, those are searches; they're quite weak. This is a full and complete memory. It looks like it's been encrypted – and it's been there a *long* time.'

Jen had heard of thought encryption, sometimes used by the military to avoid details falling into enemy hands. Was this similar? If so, surely Callaghan would know how to do decode it.

'Can you unlock it?' she asked.

'I wouldn't even know where to start.'

'Is it Military?'

He paused and sighed. 'I don't think so. The encryption... I've never seen anything like it.'

Jen stood, peering over his shoulder at the offending, blinking dot. 'Well, if it's not one of ours, then who put it there?'

Callaghan didn't answer. Instead, he gasped, hands pressed against his head. 'I don't believe it.'

'What now?'

'It just disappeared.' He turned to her, his expression confusion, face drained of colour. 'I think it just unlocked *itself*.'

CHAPTER 14

Jen was on her rooftop looking out over a dark denim sky that bled into the orange glow of London. It was early on Sunday morning, and she couldn't sleep. It had been three days since Callaghan's *discovery* and she'd thought of nothing but that tiny flashing dot, the hidden memory and his claims that it had magically unlocked itself.

Three days and nothing.

She hadn't *felt* anything – although, to be fair, she wasn't sure what she was expecting. What would a new memory feel like?

She shrugged. So many questions. *Who put it there? And why?* She was concerned about Peter, too. He had supported her on some very difficult high-profile cases, been a confidant, a friend, but in all their years she'd never seen him in such a state. In his profession, such outlandish theories could kill a career. He could be struck off within days, metaphorically hanged. If he persisted, Jen doubted she would be able to save him.

She felt a chill ripple up her back, sending gooseflesh over her arms. The night was sharp, and despite three layers, the cold was settling in. She decided to try T'ai Chi. It always helped her think, and she had plenty of that to do, plus it would keep her warm. She glided through the movements, her hands pushing as if through water, fluid motions followed by passages of tension igniting heat in her core. As her heart rate steadied and her breathing became smooth, a thought arrived.

What if Callaghan was right?

Mind privacy had been such a hot topic during reformation, and with the Hibernation programme well underway, it was back on the agenda again. She looked out over London, millions of people already chipped and hibernating with more joining soon. Next year she would be back in Hibernation, part of the January switch. Surely they couldn't do it? They wouldn't be able to get away with it. She shook the thoughts away, convincing herself that Callaghan would call tomorrow. He would tell her, *"It's this old house making me imagine things. Don't tell anyone. Can we just forget it?"*

She completed the Tai Chi form, flicked the remnants of green tea from her mug and went back downstairs, where she lay awhile, staring at the ceiling. Although convinced sleep wouldn't come, she eventually slipped under its veil and into a deep slumber. Her recurring dream came again, except this time it was different, this time it didn't stop in the usual place. It continued, allowing fears long forgotten to rise up, scratching, hungry and restless.

★ ★ ★

It was a scene she knew all too well, the cornfield, clouds moving by, except she had an awareness of being asleep, along for the ride, an odd sense of voyeurism. To her right was a young girl she recognised instantly as herself, aged nine. As the familiar gust of wind whistled through the jagged corn, it brought with it a realisation. Jen would be watching the familiar dream as a spectator. The young girl turned, looked straight through her and darted away.

The dream was playing out as it always did, exactly to the note. A horrifying thought arrived, one that made her figurative legs go weak.

Am I going to see myself ripped apart, eaten alive? Is this how the dream ends?

In the distance she saw her father and the young girl chasing after him and heard the thrashing corn behind her, the creatures closing in. Jen followed and arrived at the clearing in time to see her father pass through the doorway. She watched her younger self, tears streaming down her cheeks, frantically twisting the door handle, eyes darting and bright with fear. Jen went to her, hands trembling, and watched, helpless, as her adult hand passed through the solid object.

I'm a ghost, she thought. *I'm already dead.*

The sound was building. She knew how this gruesome scene ended. In a moment the creatures would fall on this helpless girl and pull her apart, and Jen would be made to watch.

And listen, Jen, you get to hear the ripping and gnawing. The screams of youth. The sound of breaking bones and tearing flesh.

Jen stood defiantly over the girl, breath bursting in and out, tears welling up inside her. If she was a ghost, then defiance was pointless, but she had to do something.

You left us both, Daddy.

The first of the dark figures broke through the corn and Jen, struggling to process the information, finally faced her demon. Huge, midnight-black and encased in a thick shell, its small head twisted towards her, mandibles flashing in the moonlight. It was a giant beetle. She recoiled, fighting an overwhelming impulse to flee. The girl was crying and pounding the door as more beetles flooded through the corn into the clearing. There were at least seven now, closing in around them, their hungry mouths like razor combs, clacking and vibrating.

Jen felt a wave of nausea as her legs folded beneath her. She couldn't hold the tears back any longer. They burst out, weak, guttural sobs mixed with a terrible sound of insect feet scratching at the ground. There were too many beetles to count now, like a sea of black ink surrounding them. Jen turned to see her younger self standing, poised, ready to run straight into the solid door, and in a sudden rush of clarity she finally understood. What if this was the memory, buried for all these years, and the doorway is a metaphor? If the memory had been unlocked, surely all she had to do was open the door…

With that single, basic thought the door flew open, bathing the clearing in a thick column of blinding light. The swarm of beetles writhed and curled, their terrible, high-pitched screams like tortured whale song. The delay was long enough for the girl to dive into the light and Jen to follow. The door slammed shut behind her, silencing the nightmarish howls instantly and forever.

Jen lay on the ground, panting and crying. Time passed, tears flowed and she found herself praying that when she opened her eyes, what she saw wasn't somewhere worse. What could be worse? She smelt grass and felt a cool wind whipping up and over her. She rolled onto her back and opened her eyes.

A full moon hung majestically over a dark Cotswold scene, one she recognised instantly. She was home. The recurring dream, the nightmare that had been with her for so long, had finally been resolved. She had unlocked a memory and opened the door. Now, she needed to find out what happened next.

She looked around, praying she wouldn't wake. It was a strange feeling, being so alert and yet certain this wasn't real. She spotted the girl from the cornfield creeping along a hedgerow to the side of a churchyard. Jen absorbed the scene and remembered. This actually happened; this *was* real.

Jen stood but had to fight to stop her legs from shaking, still reeling from the horror of the beetles. Her younger self, wearing nightclothes now – *yes that's right, I remember* – slipped through the church gate. Jen followed, tracing along a low stone wall, recalling this night more with each step. In the churchyard, she found her father on his hands and knees burying something. Jen heard her younger self speak and instantly the conversation came back to her. It was as if she was learning, seeing and remembering simultaneously.

She studied her father. Seeing him again was so hard. She desperately wanted to throw her arms around him and never let go. She knew of people who had used dimensional films to relive past experiences, to see lost relatives again. She had tried a demo once but found the experience void of true feeling. This was completely different; she was *living* this moment, every sense, smell and feeling. The pain of love lost combined with the ecstasy of a rediscovered past.

Her father stood suddenly, horror in his face.

'Jenny, what are you doing here?'

Her younger self ran and hugged him. Jacob, rigid at first, wrapped his arms around her, squeezing her in return. Jen walked towards the pair, somehow knowing she would remain invisible for the duration of this performance. Her father's eyes were welling, his skin covered in perspiration. She remembered hearing him leave the house that night. She had been awake and followed, worried about him. How could she have forgotten all of this? Why had it been hidden from her?

'Jenny,' her father said.

The young girl looked up and waited patiently, her green eyes glinting in lamplight, melting his heart. Nobody called her Jenny except him.

'I need you to help me,' he said softly. 'Will you do that? Will you help me?'

'Of course.' The girl's voice was kind, innocent.

'Good girl. I need you to keep tonight a secret.' He leant

in, playfully. 'Really secret. We need to hide it away so no one can find it.'

'Like treasure,' she replied excitedly, craning her neck, trying to see the mound of earth behind him.

'Exactly.' He smiled, but the pain in his heart was obvious to her older self.

'I need you to forget this, Jenny. The church, tonight. Forget all of it. Can you do that?'

The girl nodded obediently.

Jen felt a weight lifted from her as his words echoed back through time. All these years she thought her father had wanted her to forget *him*. That wasn't what he'd said at all; he had only wanted her to forget *this* night, this moment.

'Daddy has to do this, sweetheart,' he explained. 'Trust me, okay?'

He placed one hand on the freshly dug earth and in the other took his daughter's tiny hands. Jen remembered how that had felt, a vibration pulsing through her, his hands unusually cold to touch, like they were made of chilled metal.

Without warning or fear, the churchyard scene, her father and the girl drifted away into darkness. Jen, still inside the dream, was back in her old room, warm and safe. Her father was perched on the edge of her old, ornate iron bed, looking down on his daughter, now tucked in and sleepy. Again, Jen remembered this.

'Daddy?' Jenny asked.

'I'm here, honey.' He stroked the hair from her face.

'I'm scared. I don't want you to go.'

'Baby, I have to go. It's important. Mummy is here.'

The nightlight cast a comforting amber glow across her father's face. The girl reached up and touched his dark skin, felt the roughness of his stubble. He leant forward and hugged her. Jen could smell him again, conjuring feelings of security long since gone. She lived the moment again, wishing it would last forever.

'Why do you have to go?' the girl whispered.

He paused and sighed heavily. 'There is something I need to do, sweetheart.'

'When will you be home?'

'A week, two at the most.' He smiled, hiding his pain. 'As soon as I can.'

The girl snuggled down into her blanket.

Her younger self seemed satisfied, but Jen knew better. Her father never came home. He died a few days later. Jen was crying now, shouting, pleading with him not to go. Her warnings fell silent, trapped inside a vacuum of time.

Daddy, you die! Don't go! Mummy never forgives you.

There was nothing she could do. She was on a tortuous rollercoaster, trapped and mute until the end of the ride.

'Good-bye, sweetheart,' he said softly. 'I love you. I'll be home soon.'

The girl was asleep by the time her father left the room, the memory of the churchyard locked away in her mind, where it would remain hidden for years.

Jen awoke in tears, her tattered voice breaking thinly in the darkness. She was struck by an immediate and cloying sense of loss. It had been such a gift to spend time with her father again, but the experience had bought fresh grief and new pain. The memory of that night, the one Callaghan had dislodged, was clear and thankfully remained with her. She remembered every detail and vowed she would never lose it again.

So it was her father who had hidden the memory, trying to protect her. But why? And perhaps more importantly, from whom?

A worrying thought came again, one she had dismissed

earlier on the roof. If Callaghan was right, and the Government were searching, she needed to be very careful. Whatever her father had buried in the churchyard and hidden away in her mind wasn't a secret anymore. It was out in the open. Callaghan had believed the searches were most likely performed during the Hibernation cycle. Well, soon *she* would be back in Hibernation. What then? She had accused Callaghan of being a mad conspiracy theorist. Now it was she who appeared to be spinning out of control.

This is fucking crazy, Jen. You know that, right?

She got up and showered, hoping to make sense of the questions banging around in her head. It didn't help. No matter how much she tried, she couldn't shake a growing certainty.

Whatever else she might discover, whatever the dream meant, Callaghan was right about one thing. They were in danger.

CHAPTER 15

`-Code Blue-` *What the hell is a code blue?*

Analyst 13 wandered down the hall, grabbed a coffee and arrived back at his terminal. It was still there, flashing. He rubbed his temples, glancing around nervously. There were around twenty other operators on shift that night, all of them young like him, worker bees, each assigned five hundred cycles per hour. Their job was to flag files of interest and then pass them on for processing. That was it, that was the job and he was good at it.

Mole. That had been his nickname in college and for a few years after. Until he came here. In this underground deniable bunker, everyone was numbered and faces would come and go. Mole had decided it best not to make friends. If he kept his head down for one more year, he would move up a pay grade and perhaps run his own team. He was a hard worker, he was sure that had been noticed.

Alerts, though? They were rare. That's why he double-checked the code blue – triple-checked, in fact. He didn't want to get this wrong. Protocol required him to make a phone call. Level three clearance. He wasn't required to interface with people very often and realised he was sweating heavily. Again, he squinted around the room at the ghostly faces tapping away in silence. *Come on, Mole, this could be the making of you.*

He dialed the number, fingers trembling.

CHAPTER 16

In the members' bar of the Royal Shakespeare Theatre, New York, Zido Zitagi entertained her guests with well-researched conversation. Wrapped in a silver kimono dress – a nod to her Japanese heritage – and standing tall on razor-sharp heels, Zitagi was a woman who demanded attention.

Her guests, two gentlemen from a prestigious manufacturing company, were discussing their excitement leading up to this evening's performance.

Immersive theatre, as it had become known, combined live performance with holographic projection and required precise choreography to ensure a seamless performance. When done well, the effect was mesmerising. Zitagi's dark eyes, displaying a wisdom beyond her years, scanned the two men politely.

'Gentlemen,' she said, her voice precise and warm. 'If you are ready, we can make our way to the private gallery.'

They nodded and she led each of them by an arm, making more polite conversation. The men surely felt special – this was her gift, perfected and used many times. The outcome of such an evening would always be as Zitagi planned.

Her party took their seats, a gallery situated centrally above the ground floor, and admired the impressive building. The orchestra ceased warming up and the audience hushed, the anticipation tangible.

Zitagi had seen it once before, and although her focus was

on her guests, she allowed herself a moment of wonder.

Two blue lights shone down, revealing the stark simplicity of the central stage. Then, piece by piece, an intricate scene appeared. First, a campfire with rocks and horses and tents, then to the left of the stage a tree-covered hillside, and to the right a steep cliff face. Finally, when a starlit night with moving clouds completed the panorama, actors walked out onto the stage and began to interact with the projected scenery. The tableau was complete, a rich, deep landscape that spanned the full height and width of the stage. The audience fell silent, transported by the stunning spectacle. Later, a horse would travel across the entire scene in an intoxicating display of live theatre, film and immersive entertainment. Zitagi noted her guests. One had a tear running down his cheek. The first time could have that effect on people.

Augmentation was automatically switched off during the performance. But Zitagi's equipment was beyond their control, set to receive calls of security level two or above. She was surprised when the call came in.

It was level three.

She slipped silently into the adjoining bar, clicking her fingers at the smartly dressed bar staff and pointing to the door. They shuffled out quickly looking worried.

She answered. A moment of decryption followed by a voice.

'Hello?' a male voice said, weak and hopeful.

Zitagi sighed, pursing her plump red lips. She preferred artificial assistants, but if they had to be human, at least make them sharp. This one sounded twelve years old.

'Go ahead,' she said in a harsh tone.

'This is Analyst 13.' There was a long pause. 'The protocol requires that I call the person named on the –'

'Analyst 13,' she interrupted. 'Have you ever made a level three call before?'

'No, I haven't,' he replied.

'Some advice,' she said. 'Take a breath and get to the point.'

'I've just received a code blue.'

'Subject?'

'Jennifer Logan.'

A pause.

Zitagi said, 'You're absolutely sure?'

'Yes, completely. I ran it three times.'

'Interesting. When?'

'This morning around 3am. The subject's brain pattern changed, we picked it up as she accessed the network on her –'

'Tell me,' she asked. 'Do you recognise the encryption?'

'Well, that's the thing,' he said excitedly. 'I've never seen this kind of encryption before. The date tag, it's old. Initially I thought it was based on something –'

'Listen carefully,' Zitagi cut in again. 'Tell no one about this, not even your supervisor. Copy the search data onto a secure server and delete any trace from your systems there. I have just granted you clearance to do that.'

She waited. Nothing.

'Is that clear?' she barked, already making plans.

'Yes. Absolutely.'

Zitagi disconnected, closed her eyes and smiled, savouring the moment. A code blue, at last. Presuming it was genuine – and she no reason to doubt it – she might finally get the chance to achieve her primary directive.

She made another call, this time to Victor Reyland. There weren't many people that could make her nerves swim, but he was important. She respected him more than anyone. He answered and she immediately felt the last twenty years fall away. She was a recruit again, standing before him. His commitment to the cause had been absolute and she had worked tirelessly ever since to gain his respect. That made this moment all the more special; his faith in her was finally being rewarded. She explained the situation and received her orders. His voice was calm and controlled. He briefed her fully and before disconnecting told her that she had done well.

Zitagi glowed with pride.

She returned to the performance, her two guests acknowledging her and nodding their appreciation. She tipped her head and smiled back, calculating that she could kill them, complete her mission and be in London by the following evening.

CHAPTER 17

It was the evening of Jim McArthur's surprise party. Three days since the dream had played out. Jen's father had buried something in the churchyard, and she needed to find out what. She began making plans deep in her mind but tonight needed to put them, and her building sense of dread, on pause. If only for tonight, for Mac's sake, she needed to pretend life was the same, that it was safe and good. He would be pretending, too, playing down the attention but secretly enjoying it.

Jen looked out of her apartment window at the waiting car. Richards had insisted they travel together. She checked herself again in the mirror, deciding he could wait a little longer. She wore her hair up for a change, leaving her shoulders exposed, and wondered how many times she would hear the phrase *You scrub up well*.

She hated that.

Entering the lounge, she saw Simon sitting in comfy clothes, his attention on the box. He glanced around and then again, nodding with absolute sincerity.

'Yes, yes!' he cried, approving the outfit. 'Black dress and heels. All men will be helpless.'

'No idea when I'll be home,' Jen said dryly, curling her lip.

'Come on, it can't be that bad.'

'You're probably right.' She thought through the guest list. Peter Callaghan would be there. Since dislodging the memory they had spoken daily, but she hadn't told him about the dream yet. She was hoping for a chance to talk to him tonight.

'See you later.' Simon smiled, 'Don't do anything I wouldn't.'

Jen navigated the stairs, folding her ankle twice and cursing her choice of footwear. She stepped out onto the street. The auto-car was an expensive model, silver and sleek with a large, spacious interior. The wing door was up and Richards was peering out. She climbed inside and sat opposite him. The cabin was clearly designed to be a statement — studded red leather, framed with chrome detailing — the ceiling an animated night sky. His eyes worked over her quickly.

'You look very *nice* Logan,' he said, his delivery reluctant, as if his mother had nudged him.

'Thank you, Sir.' Jen smiled graciously. 'So do you.'

It was a lie. Only Richards could make a dinner jacket look that bad. The car pulled away smoothly. They stared out the window for a while, the city streaming by. Eventually he spoke.

'Logan, I wanted to take this opportunity to speak to you before the party.'

She nodded, waiting for him to continue.

'There are some important people attending, and I would urge you to consider tonight an opportunity.'

'An opportunity?' Jen replied. 'I'm not sure I follow you.'

'You're a good police officer, Logan. Maybe I've never told you that, but you are.'

Praise from him was rare, and he seemed to deflate, the words clearly painful for him to say. Jen decided to enjoy the moment even if it did lack sincerity.

Richards continued, 'There is someone I want to introduce you to.' He leant forward, the smell of his cheap scent threatening an instant headache. 'I'm trying to help you.'

There was bitterness in his voice and his delivery felt forced, as if he were reading from cue cards. She'd worked Duality for nearly three years and in that time had never received a single word of encouragement. It was obvious he'd been put up to this. The question was, why? Was this linked to Callaghan and his theories on searching? Her dream? Or, perhaps less worryingly, was Mac putting in a good word before such blessings lost their power? Whatever the reason, she decided to play along.

'Thank you, Sir,' she managed finally. 'I appreciate it.'

Richards sat back, stretched and gazed out of the window. He seemed happy the conversation was over.

'I'm sticking my neck out here,' he said, in a more familiar tone. 'Just don't fuck it up for me.'

★ ★ ★

Across town, Peter Callaghan returned home, his car lights tracing across the garden and settling on the driveway before blinking out. Just enough time to change and still make the party, he decided. His cat slinked onto the porch.

He spoke in a higher voice reserved exclusively for his feline companion.

'Millie, I thought I left you inside.'

He was tired and tempted to stay home, knowing that a nightcap followed by approximately four minutes of reading would be enough to bring sleep. He wanted to see Jen, though. They needed to talk. He entered the house, closed the front door behind him and noticed a shaft of light spilling from his study.

'Is there someone there?' he called, his words reverberating through the old house. He waited, feeling ridiculous, half-expecting someone to answer. No reply came. He considered just leaving the light on and going to bed but couldn't. He crossed the lounge, lights turning on automatically as he approached, and looked around. Everything seemed to be in order. The door to his study was ajar, but there were no signs of forced entry, and anyway, the security would have notified him.

So it's a polite, considerate intruder. Intent on what, exactly? Reading my collection of worthless novels? I'm an old fool. Spend my days surrounded by senility and now it's my turn.

He entered his study. It was untouched. He walked over to an old standard lamp and reached under the shade.

'I'm not going to hurt you.' It was a man's voice, and calm.

Callaghan turned to face the intruder, a cold surge of adrenaline flushing through him. The man, tall and well dressed, was blocking the doorway.

'What do you want?' Callaghan managed, his heart racing, eyes searching the room for an escape.

'Doctor Callaghan,' the man said. 'I need you to come with me.'

CHAPTER 18

Dark clouds hung over London as the car pulled up outside the restaurant. Richards jumped out and insisted he open the door for her. Jen nodded, stepped out of the car and they entered the restaurant like an awkward married couple. The restaurant was one of Mac's favourites. It had a club lounge feel with lamps, glass tables and large leather sofas hugging the edges. Large dining tables filled the center of the room, each with a personal chef preparing food in front of the diners. It was expensive, popular and heavily decorated for Christmas.

Jen spotted Jonathon Cole and a new female constable standing at an ornate bar that stretched almost the full length of the room. She hadn't seen Cole since the Operation Penthouse debrief. He was a good option for pre-dinner chatting, and she'd met the constable once before and liked her. Maybe tonight would be okay.

The maître d' took her coat. Jen checked the time. Mac would be arriving shortly with his family, unaware of the gathering. She began the process of small talk, working her way around the gathering.

Thirty minutes later, Mac arrived. She was glad she recorded his arrival – now, whenever she needed an emotional lift, she could replay the video and watch the genuine surprise on his face. Sally, his wife, glowing with excitement, had organised the evening. So far it was all going to plan. His twin daughters, aged seven, captivated most of the guests, the rarity of children making them a novelty. Population was strictly controlled and had been for years. Mac had been lucky. After many attempts, Sally had finally conceived, and when twins were confirmed it had been a battle to keep them.

Jen wondered if her maternal instincts would ever be rekindled. Pangs of motherhood were a rare thing now. She didn't feel it was her destiny to have children, but she would certainly enjoy Mac's kids this evening. In fact, the first hour was already gone and she was actually enjoying herself. Eventually Mac made his way to her.

'Thanks for the heads up,' he said, referring to the surprise and her lack of warning.

She smiled, leant in and kissed him on the cheek.

Mac took a step towards her in mock secrecy. 'I need to ask you a favour.'

'Anything, Mac,' she replied. 'You know that.'

'I'm going to miss this.' A sad expression moved over him quickly. 'Too much, I suspect.'

Jen touched his arm and smiled. 'I know.'

'Keep me in the loop, okay?' he asked. 'I need to keep my mind busy. Sally has ideas for me. Gardening and cooking and other things.' It was a mixture of sadness and humorous concern. Jen suspected he was secretly looking forward to a quieter life but could understand the need to stay mentally active. She smiled again, attempting to reassure him.

'Mac. Listen. You're only what, early hundreds?' She knew he was a little older. 'You've got years left in you.'

Raising her hand flat to her cheek, she whispered, 'I will let you in on a secret. I can't imagine doing this without you.'

He laughed and seemed happy, but Jen felt a pain pinching her heart. It was true. They hadn't worked many cases together, but they'd often met, shared information and talked. Her intention was for that to continue, but people always said that, didn't they? She thought of Callaghan again. She wanted to make sure he wasn't derailing again, spouting more crazy talk. They needed to figure this out together.

'Wasn't Callaghan supposed to be here tonight?' she asked, sending Mac's eyes searching across the bar.

'Yeah, I thought so. But you know him.' He lifted his eyebrows playfully. 'Probably knee-deep in some experiment or case file.'

She decided that if Callaghan didn't show, she would call him again later.

An Italian-looking waiter with a dark blanket of stubble and long hair rang a bell, ushering the party into a private dining area. Jen was seated in the middle of the table. Mac, his family and four others were guided to the head. She recognised Ravenscroft. The other three she presumed were MI5, MI6 or high up in the Met. They had an air of importance about them. It seemed Richards had been right; it was a serious gathering. She thought of their earlier conversation in the car and wondered whose arse she would be required to kiss.

Once seated, Mac tapped his glass and stood. His speech had people laughing out loud. She really was going to miss him. As she looked around the table at people smiling and enjoying each other's company, her concerns of the past week began to fade. Tonight she simply couldn't imagine some terrible conspiracy. Whatever Callaghan had discovered, they would figure it out together – and that hidden memory? That was a long time ago. History. She would understand it all eventually, but tonight she was just happy to be genuinely enjoying herself.

The evening passed easily. The McArthurs were a nice family, decent people who attracted like-minded folk. After more speeches Jen decided the alcohol, which had worked its magic earlier, was starting to make her feel a little slow. Knowing she still had to meet her mystery guest, she eased off, joining Mac's wife at the bar. They chatted but within minutes Richards caught her eye and nodded to the far side of the bar, his expression like granite. Jen could see Ravenscroft and two other men talking to a Japanese woman she didn't recognise.

Jen was quite sure this woman hadn't been at the table during dinner; she would have remembered her. She was smartly dressed and classically beautiful. Jen wasn't surprised to see men clucking around her. Richards approached, apologised for butting in and escorted Jen towards the group.

'Where have you been,' he said quietly, not hiding his anger at having to find her. 'She wants to meet you.'

'Who is she?' Jen asked.

'Government, high up, asked for you specifically.'

Jen felt a pulse push up through her temples. *Government? Was this something to do with Callaghan?* She was suddenly nervous and wished she could grab her coat and leave, forget the whole thing.

'What's her name?' she asked, but it was too late. The woman turned her head and smiled and the men stopped talking.

'Ms Logan, a pleasure,' the woman said, stretching out her hand. 'My name is Zido Zitagi. I have heard so much about you.'

Jen was sure she had never seen such perfectly straight hair. It was pulled back and pressed against the woman's head and sculpted into a beautiful bob. Her outstretched hand looked doll-like, and when Jen took it she found it to cool to the touch, like porcelain. Ravenscroft towered over all of them. Before becoming a strategist with MI5 he'd been a copper and had conducted Jen's initial interview. She always remembered him for ducking under doors. Since then, she had only seen him at regional briefings and the odd function. He was red-cheeked and looked drunk, or close to it. She didn't know the other two men but suspected they were senior ranking officers from another region. They all seemed nervous. Jen guessed they didn't know the woman either, but their attentive nature suggested they knew she was important.

Richards stepped in. 'Ms Zitagi. As you know, Sergeant Logan has been with Duality – my department – for two years.'

Over three, you dick.

'In that time, she's been –'

'Thank you, Chief Superintendent,' Zitagi cut him dead. 'I am going to steal Ms Logan away from you.' Her eyes remained fixed on him, her expression cool and controlled. Richards' mouth was open but no words came. He wasn't used to being talked over. Ravenscroft was smirking.

Zitagi said, 'Only for a short while.' She turned to Jen and gestured towards a large spiral staircase leading to what appeared to be a cocktail bar above the main restaurant. 'May I steal you away?'

Jen's heart was racing, but she managed a confident nod and caught Richards scowling as they climbed the stairs, his face grey, jaw twitching. At the top of the stairs was an empty cocktail bar, no staff, and low lighting.

Zitagi turned, smiled and said, 'I apologise for dragging you away from your friends and colleagues, but this is important.'

'You asked to meet me specifically,' Jen said. 'Why?'

Zitagi nodded carefully. 'You and I work for the same people, the same Government, but I…' She paused and took a breath. 'Well, let's just say I work for a department with a *unique* remit.'

Zido Zitagi clearly didn't believe in warming up her engines. They weren't even going to sit.

She continued. 'Your record. Four years National Service, relief work in India, Thailand. Five years US Military. Tactical

Operations.' She stopped deliberately, for emphasis. 'Then back to England, the Met and then Duality.'

Jen nodded.

Zitagi's gaze burned into her. 'Initially that struck me as a little odd.'

'That I should choose Duality?'

'Yes. It's a little… pedestrian, for a woman of your talents. But then it made sense to me. You are a woman of morals and principles. Duality is honourable work. I admire that.'

Jen nodded again. 'Tell me more about what you do?' she asked, trying to stay calm, pleased that so far Callaghan's name hadn't come up.

Zitagi smiled gracefully. 'We have peace, but peace doesn't last. History proves that, Ms Logan.'

'Perhaps this time it will,' Jen replied, sounding more argumentative than she had intended.

'My job is to *keep* the peace we have fought so hard to attain,' Zitagi shot back.

'So why are you here tonight? Why do you want to talk to me?'

'A good question.' Zitagi leant forward and passed her a data card, eyes sparkling, mischievous and alive. 'The right question.'

'What's on this?'

'My details. Not many people get those.'

'Why would I need to contact you?' Jen asked defensively.

'These are interesting times, Sergeant Logan… Transitional. Loyalties will be tested. I need people I can trust. People who are willing to stand.'

'Loyalties?'

'Duality has a leak, and it isn't you.'

Jen processed the information, considering her response carefully. 'With all due respect, Ms. Zitagi, how do you know you can trust *me*?'

'Jennifer,' Zitagi said formally. 'Trust is earned. I am simply advising you. If there is anything you feel you think I should know, then please, call me.'

Her superiors words came to mind. Richards had a similar, slippery tone. *I would urge you to consider tonight an opportunity.*

There was no time to think; the conversation was over. Zitagi shook her hand and left, walking away with an elegance Jen knew she would never have. This woman was intriguing but also worrying, pretty much in equal measure. Jen rejoined the group, wondering what their exchange had *actually* meant, unsure if Zitagi was the snake or the snake charmer. Richards' head kept popping up over the crowd, searching for her. He would be desperate to cross-question her. The night went slowly after that. Zitagi appeared to have left shortly after their conversation. As people were leaving, Mac asked Jen about their meeting.

'You know me, Mac,' she said, brushing it aside. 'I hate the political side of things.'

Jen waited until it was polite to leave and stepped out into the cold air, the weight of the data card heavy in her pocket. Zitagi's arrival was no coincidence. It was obviously linked to Callaghan and her dream somehow, she just didn't know how yet. Duality, a leak? Jen doubted it. That all felt like an excuse, a way to intimidate her into sharing any hidden secrets. For the first time in months, Jen felt lonely. She considered calling Thomas but knew she would just be covering up the problem. She dialed Callaghan instead, on a secure line. Nothing.

She hung up and her thoughts returned to her dream. She hailed an auto-car, knowing what she needed to do. She needed to go back to the place she grew up, back to Brook Mill Farm and that churchyard. She just hoped that whatever her father had buried was still there.

CHAPTER 19

Just before eight on Saturday morning, Jen left her apartment and set off towards Oxford. The option of a flight into Brize Norton had crossed her mind, but that would mean easy tracking of her position. She wanted to at least try and do this without everyone knowing her whereabouts. She had packed an overnight rucksack and, despite the cold, decided to travel by motorcycle. Snow was forecast for Monday – Christmas Eve – but she planned to be back in London before then.

Home. It had been a long time.

Her journey would take in the rural zones, large areas of Great Britain exclusively designated to agriculture. People had abandoned the once-desirable countryside for the safety and security of the major towns and cities, UN Hibernation subsidies being the biggest incentive of them all.

In the cities, living was good. Jen could see it all around her. Affluence. It would be in stark contrast to where she was heading. The solar embedded roads of greater London gave way to regular tarmac as she reached the outer checkpoints. Here, most of the vehicles were either carrying supplies or workers. She entered the priority lane and pulled up in front of a booth.

A droid asked her to flip her visor, its green light flashing across her retina.

'Reason for travel?' the droid asked.

'Leisure,' she replied.

Once past this checkpoint, if they wanted to know her whereabouts, they would have to track her. She still couldn't believe she had to think like this. Her frequent use of the word *they* was worrying. Were *they* really now the enemy?

The droid opened the barrier and Jen pulled away, the road ahead strangely quiet. To her left, huge buildings flashed gold, bathed in the reflective glow of the morning sun. She decided to make the most of the decent road surface and pushed her bike up a notch. Twenty minutes later and the buildings of the past were all but gone, replaced by fields of crop and huge processing plants. Every few miles small, town-like communities would appear, their sole purpose to house farm workers and technicians. Feeding the UK was big business.

Above her the vapour trails of light air travel were broken by a huge transport ship descending into an airport just south of Thame. She tucked her head down and rode on. Despite her heated clothing the wind chill was starting to eat at her bones. The sun had disappeared by the time she reached Burford, smothered by dark clouds that sat ominously over the old town. She remembered the tourist attraction it had once been, thought back to her childhood when she would beg her parents to take her to the old-style sweet shop there. Even then the town had been struggling, the shops slowly closing down, the city migration already underway. Aldsworth, her destination, was seven miles ahead, but out of curiosity she turned right, wanting to see the high street again. As she dropped down the sloping hill her bike's tyres adapted to the road surface, which was potholed and uneven.

Burford was quiet. The Cotswold stone cottages lining the once-pretty descent were covered in ivy and some of the windows were smashed. She could see a few people, most of them wearing the familiar overalls of land workers. The shops she remembered were gone, closed up or converted into open-fronted garages housing machinery. The old-style country pubs she remembered were still standing, but only one appeared to be trading. It was tired looking with a cluster of street sellers plying their trade on the pavement outside.

She had heard stories of how the old towns were almost dead. They were right. This place was a ghost town. A group of workers eyed her suspiciously. Jen guessed they didn't see many motorbikes this way, particularly modern electric ones. The atmosphere here was unnerving. It felt almost lawless, like something out of the Wild West films her father had enjoyed. Bad things could happen out here and no one would know.

Her thoughts returned to the job in hand. She turned the bike around and sped back up the high street. This time she didn't look anywhere except ahead.

Just before the turning to Aldsworth, she pulled in and watched huge farming machines hovering over fields that stretched on for miles. They were the size of passenger aircraft, yet she could see at least nine. She noticed a group of men in white protective clothing hosing down what looked like a large harvester. The days of manned farming had ended years ago, but people were still needed to maintain and manage the process.

She was only three miles from home and her nervousness was tangible. Home was a place of mixed memories. She took a long, deep breath, closed her eyes and fired up her bike.

CHAPTER 20

As she pulled into the driveway, her heart sank. The entrance gate was hidden from view, tall grass pushing through its railings. The once-beautiful garden was now wild, the buildings suffocated in creeping ivy. Jen attempted to interface with the security and maintenance droid. They were built for longevity and she'd seen bots survive worse conditions.

Nothing.

Through the tall grass she could just make out the porch. She walked, crunching gravel and roots underfoot, pushing through the tough grass until something made her stop. There, wrapped in a tangle of weeds, was an old wooden sign. She tugged it free and brushed her hand across its rough flaking surface, the words BROOK MILL FARM still readable after all these years. She remembered the annual coat of paint her father would apply and how her mother kept saying they needed a new sign.

She looked up – windows smashed – the place worse than expected. Through a jagged hole in the roof a pair of birds appeared. They looked down at her before pushing off, wings cracking loudly, calling out. They flew gracefully overhead and out over the surrounding fields. The image took Jen back, in her mind, to the day she herself had flown from here.

It had been early morning, a week before her eighteenth birthday. As dawn light feathered through the wood she'd played in as a child, she stuffed her belongings into a rucksack and left Brook Mill for good. She remembered walking the driveway, crying for the lost years, closeness made distant by uncontrollable forces, a happy family torn apart by grief. Her plan of National Service wouldn't be an easy ride – her mother would have tried to talk her out of it – but Jen was determined.

That legendary Logan determination.

She'd been told many times she possessed it, her father's resolve. It was a compliment, but harder to hear in the weeks following his funeral.

She would imagine her sarcastic reply. *'I'm sure he would be pleased to hear that. If only he had been more determined to stay alive, eh? He's in the ground now, you see, so I can't tell him… oh, yeah, he was determined to get six feet down. That legendary 'Logan determination,' get right down there, Daddy…'*

She knew it wasn't fair to take her loss out on other people. It wasn't their fault. She just hated their sorrowful, pitying smiles and the 'inner strength' of it all.

Jen sighed, a thickness building in her throat. She stood on the overgrown driveway and watched the two birds until they were almost out of view. She often thought of her mother waking that day, discovering Jen gone. In her dreams she would go to her and they would hug and cry. Jen would thank her for all she'd done, tell her she understood her pain. The reality was not so kind. Jen had left her mother a long explanatory letter on the kitchen table, a neatly made bed and another empty space where love should have been. They hadn't spoken since.

Some days you never forget.

Jen shrugged and sighed again. It was a long time ago.

She approached the front door and pushed it open, the smell of urine and long-term neglect leaking through the gap. How long had the place been empty? If the rumours were true, her mother had left a few years after Jen. She'd sold every possession, every piece of furniture, locked the doors and never looked back. Jen presumed Veronica Logan made it to her precious France and settled, perhaps even found love.

Brook Mill Farm was now like most properties in the area, abandoned and practically worthless. Jen stepped into the hallway and saw the security and maintenance droid propped up against the wall. It buzzed into life, its solar backup providing just enough power to produce an activity report which read like an apology. For the first few years it had managed the property well, but then the squatters arrived and some of its parts needed replacing. Jen didn't need to read the remaining pages; she could see it for herself.

Upstairs, her mother's bedroom door was closed. Jen decided to leave it that way and entered her old bedroom. The smell of urine was stronger here, with an odour akin to sour milk sitting thick above it. The dampness would get to you after a while; even the squatters had moved on. Her eyes drank in the forgotten familiarity, eventually settling on a small black air vent in the wall next to where her bed used to be. Seeing it, cracked and dusty like the old garden sign, transported her back in time again.

She recalled how her mother's familiar sobs would drift from that vent at night and how disappointed she felt to hear them. No matter how much she tried to keep her mother's mood buoyant, some days there was no avoiding the decline. When jobs were done and friends drifted away, when the dying embers of the fire gave up hope, the night tightened its suffocating grip on Veronica Logan. Lying in bed, Jen would hear her muffled sorrow and try to pick out words or phrases in the darkness, attempting to learn the shape of her mother's grief. Occasionally the sounds would sharpen into something recognisable.

'I told you not to go.'

And then her father's name repeated over and over.

'Jacob, oh Jacob. Not you. Why you?'

Once, Jen overheard her mother confiding in a friend. She had described the darkness as *all consuming*, explaining how it was worse living out here now that people had left for the cities. The fields, the space, the peaceful garden – it had suited them once. The three of them. Her father, splitting his time between London and Cheltenham, was always home at weekends. Somehow, throughout all the troubles, the epidemics, the rationing and the hardship, their family life contained much happiness and love.

His death changed all of that. Life was never the same again. How could it be? Jen prayed that her mother's grief might eventually subside, but it wasn't to be. Instead, it settled on her, spreading like a dark stain on her heart. Jen had stopped going to her, learning from experience that any offer of comfort would be unwelcome, that her mother could no longer accept love even if she wanted to.

Instead Jen would lie in the darkness and cover her ears, and in the muffled silence, watch the shadows of trees swaying and dancing across the ceiling, waiting for sleep to take her away.

The sound of scratching in the loft space sent the past drifting away like smoke pulled through a fan. Older, but just as alone, she was left feeling vulnerable and empty, second-guessing her decision to come home.

No more looking back, Jen. Time to move on.

She walked to the gable window, dodging animal droppings on the bare floorboards, and looked out. Below her she could see the wild garden and driveway, beyond that more buildings in a similar state. Her eyes drifted up and there, dark against the horizon, she saw it. The church steeple.

Her father had buried something there, something he

wanted her to forget, something *they* wanted back. And tonight she was going to find out what.

Tonight she was going to dig.

CHAPTER 21

Nathan O'Brien raised the tranquillizer gun, took a deep breath and fired. This time his target stumbled, managed a weak groan and hit the ground hard. The man was Matthew Anderson, a news reporter for a London-based network, lured here on the promise of some dirt on a local politician. He was also the last person to see Nathan's wife alive.

Nathan looked around nervously. It was early evening and the London street was quiet, a murky half-light rendering them almost invisible even to the commuters on the overpass. Good. He ran and crouched next to the reporter, checking for a pulse, relieved to feel it banging against his fingers. He hadn't overcooked the dose after all.

'Please don't kill me,' Anderson pleaded, slipping in and out of consciousness.

Nathan had no such intention but wasn't going to share that particular piece of information.

He dragged Anderson towards a row of nearby garages knowing that the next scene, in this play of his, was going to be tough. For both of them.

When Anderson awoke he was siting, hands bound, eyes covered and mouth taped. The air was damp and smelt stale, like wet sheets left way too long. Nathan checked the blindfold before pulling the tape from his mouth. Anderson sucked the air hungrily and then coughed, his face contorting in pain.

He'd lost a tooth when he fell.

'Are you going to scream again?' Nathan asked. 'Because if you are, I'll go outside and wait.'

'Who are you?'

'That doesn't matter.'

'Are you going to kill me?' Anderson's voice cracked a little.

'That depends.'

'I'll do whatever you want...'

'Katherine O'Brien. Tell me about the night you met her.'

'Her?' Anderson's face squashed in confusion at the name. His head twitched like a bird, trying to locate Nathan in the room. 'I did exactly as I was told.'

'Told by whom?' Nathan shouted.

Anderson seemed confused. 'You – you aren't with *them*?'

'I'm worse,' Nathan whispered, desperately clinging to his tough-guy routine. 'Tell me what you talked about.'

'They'll kill me...' Anderson paused, twisting his hands against the tape binding his wrists, and then hissed, 'You as well.'

Nathan wondered if he should have played along, said he *was* with them. But it was too late for that now.

'Please.' Anderson's head flicked around the room. 'I don't know anything.' There was a subtle change in him. He didn't seem as scared.

That wasn't good.

Nathan stepped closer. 'You offered to meet her, you had information. What did you tell her? Where did she go next?'

Anderson took a deep breath, fishing for something, an idea, maybe.

'Okay. I remember her,' he admitted. 'She contacted me because of an article I wrote a few years back.'

'Go on.'

'She wanted to talk about it. There were rumours. Some conspiracy shit about Hibernation. She connected some dots, same names kept popping up. I didn't buy it.'

'Then what?'

'We met, we talked, she left. That was it.'

It was clear, just from the speed of delivery, that Anderson's story was well rehearsed. The bare minimum, not necessarily lies but nothing new. Nathan suspected it might actually be true, but time was running out. Suspecting wasn't good enough. For all he knew, Anderson could be under surveillance, the police already on their way. And of course, Nathan could have easily been spotted dragging him in here. He needed results, and he needed them quickly.

'What did they tell you to do?' Nathan shouted, closing in.

'Please. I can't.'

What are you waiting for?

Nathan took a deep breath, closed his eyes and struck Anderson, a backhand right across his face. Anderson turned back, a little too quickly, and Nathan realised with horror that he hadn't hit him hard enough. He would have to do it again, except this time, he had to mean it. Awkwardly he raised his hand, jaw clenched, determined that this time he wouldn't hold back.

Go on, you fucking pussy. Do it!

He hit him again, whipping Anderson's head to the side. The reporter let out a cry and began panting, his face contorted in pain. Nathan hadn't hit anyone before, not like that anyway, not in anger. The feeling of muscle and teeth compressing made him feel sick. It was strange, though, he could also feel adrenalin pulsing through him. His body donor was athletic and strong, something he had noticed immediately after the operation. In fact, everything was different, all of it new. His body felt charged with energy, an intoxicating reminder that this newly acquired physique came with a fresh set of rules.

Anderson spat blood. 'What the hell did you do that for?

Jesus, you don't need to do this.'

Nathan took his mind back to the night Katherine was murdered. She had called him just before meeting Matt Anderson. Two hours later, the woman he loved, the one he'd chosen to spend his life with, was stabbed through the heart.

She bled to death.

Alone.

Her face flashed into his vision and suddenly he could feel her, the pain immediate, a vacuum of loss crushing him like a can. His grief would often come like this, silently approaching and then consuming him whole. Nathan looked at Anderson, brightly lit from above like a macabre window display.

'You know what happened, you fucker,' he screamed. 'You sent her to her death.'

Anger descended in an all-consuming wave. Nathan found his hands around Anderson's neck, lifting him up off the chair, squeezing the life from him.

'Histeridae,' he screamed. 'What does it mean?'

Anderson could do nothing, any possible answers trapped inside lungs that were banging for air.

'Is it a code word?'

'I don't know,' Anderson hissed, beads of foam flying from his mouth.

Nathan had prepared himself mentally but lost track of time, his grief finally discovering a welcome and gruesome outlet. Something slapped him out of it, though. He wasn't sure, but it could have been Katherine calling his name.

Nathan. No.

Her voice again.

Don't kill him.

His hands shot open, sending the chair rocking backwards. For a moment it looked as though it might fall. But it tipped back, sending a globule of bloody spit from Anderson's mouth.

He coughed, gasping for air. Nathan knew that just a few more seconds would have killed him. He resumed pacing, babbling to himself, cursing his lack of control.

Then Anderson began to talk.

'After she contacted me' – he coughed and swallowed, blood dripping from his nose – 'I got another call.'

'Who called you?' Nathan whispered, not looking at him.

'I never met them, I swear.'

'What did they say?'

'They told me to meet her and, if she asked about Logan, to give her an address.' He was crying now. 'I didn't know they would kill her. I swear it.'

'Who's Logan?'

'Some bad shit happened, I guess. They didn't want –'

'Who is Logan?' Nathan moved closer.

'Jacob Logan. She asked about him, so I gave her the address. You know, the one where she...' He trailed off.

The one where she was murdered. Yeah, I got that part.

Nathan had checked his wife's notes a thousand times. None of them mentioned a Logan.

'Is he alive?' Nathan asked. 'Is Jacob Logan alive?'

'I don't know, I swear it.' He sniffed, sucking in three sharp breaths. 'Please, don't kill me.'

Nathan believed him; it felt right. This was how it happened. He pulled a syringe from his pocket and pushed it into Anderson's neck.

'What the hell was that?' Anderson screamed, before slipping out of consciousness.

In about two hours he would wake and have no memory of their encounter. Nathan cut the tape from Anderson's wrists and let out a long sigh. He had nearly killed him – that wasn't good – but he *had* gotten results. He had a name, one that set alarm bells ringing higher up the food chain. *Jacob Logan.*

CHAPTER 22

Jen spent the afternoon exploring Brook Mill Farm, deciding to focus on happier times. She recalled hard but fulfilling days feeding the chickens and sheep, her mother pulling handfuls of irregularly shaped vegetables from the rich soil. At the end of those days Jen would always check the battery cells and ensure the animals were secure. The Logans had always been self-sufficient, even before rationing.

Now, most of the farm was run down, but she found an old solar generator and attached it to the maintenance droid – once charged, she could programme the droid to guard the perimeter. The old church appeared at least partially maintained, which meant it would likely be locked. Jen found a shovel and some bolt cutters in the workshop and ended up in the barn, which had stood the test of time well. In her mind's eye she could see her mother driving the tractor out, her father entertaining friends and sharing the delights of home brewing.

It was dusk. Jen ate a functional, rehydrated meal and waited. Anyone watching would have seen her eyes shimmer faint purple as her active contact lenses adjusted to the half-light. Basic shapes and outlines; not full night-vision, but good enough to navigate the roads and better than a flashlight drawing attention.

The church was a short walk from the house. Just after nine, she set off. Apart from the odd solitary light dotted amongst the large houses, the village itself seemed almost deserted. She needed to be careful, though. Her tracker may have been off since the first motorway checkpoint, but they could find her if they wanted to. She just hoped they weren't as fast as Callaghan suspected.

The church was exactly as she remembered it, an unfussy stone building with a single, vaulted steeple. The surrounding gardens were wild but cut low in places, the pathway almost clear. Someone had made an effort, even if it was a token, vain attempt to control the relentless growth. Jen noticed some of the graves had been tended, little pots of dead flowers sitting at the headstones suggesting recent activity.

She scanned her surroundings again and listened. In the distance the constant thrum of farm machinery. Close by an owl announced itself, sending a buzz through her back. The moon, shrouded beneath thick clouds, meant her augmentation was struggling for light. She kept low, moving as quietly as she could on the gravel towards the church doors. The chain wrapped through the handles was feeble and, with a squeeze of her cutters, broke easily. Jen grabbed the links, stopping them from rattling to the ground, and paused for a moment before stepping inside.

Her vision adjusted to the grey shapes around her. Pews in good condition lined with dusty half-burnt candles suggested the church was still used, but maybe not often. The smell of wet newspaper and incense brought back early memories of choirs and reluctant Sunday outings.

Jen made her way towards the altar and then turned left to the only separate room in the building. With a push, the arch-shaped door creaked open. Inside, in what appeared to be the vicar's private chamber, she found what she was looking for: large leather-bound books recording births, deaths and marriages. These would also be recorded on a central database, easily accessed from her office in London, but Jen didn't want to risk a search. Her father had carefully hidden it, and the last thing she wanted to do was advertise its location by using a standard traceable search.

She pulled a flashlight from her pocket, selected the lowest setting and strapped it to her head. The memory of her father in the graveyard was somewhat indistinct. The details were fuzzy and she didn't have the time or the gear to start digging up multiple graves. She needed to be sure.

Two things she felt she did know. The first was that whatever her father had buried, he had done so in loose soil – a freshly dug burial plot – and the second was the date. That was burned into her memory. It was the last day she had seen her father alive.

She ran her finger along the books, stopped and tugged one from the shelf. Laying it flat on the desk, she opened it in the middle, flicking through the thin pages, scanning the handwritten history before settling on a name. A lady, Mrs Christine Bradley, aged 139, buried on the day her father had left: 15 July 2058.

Jen returned the book, switched off her light and snuck back out, retracing her steps to the main entrance. The moon had broken through the cloud and cast pale blue shadows across the misty graveyard. Jen pushed through long grass, working along the graves, hoping for a clearly marked headstone. She stopped at a stone that felt vaguely familiar and moved the grass aside. Mrs Bradley's name was chiseled clearly on the stone, which still looked remarkably fresh. She stood and listened for a while, her breath drifting across the churchyard, nerves biting her skin.

With a deep breath she thrust her spade into the earth, relieved to feel the ground was hard but not solid. It took over an hour but eventually, three feet down, she felt the spade hit metal.

The hole was narrow, making it difficult to see, but Jen could make out a shape, something reflecting the moonlight. She knelt and reached in, working her hands around the object, pulling at the sticky mud, trying to define its shape. She grabbed her spade and pushed at the edges, sliding the spade underneath. A box popped from the sodden soil, which burped on its release, a large clump of sticky dark mud still clinging to its base. Jen lifted it out and sat at the graveside, exhausted. She was warm but she knew that would change quickly, the sweat already beginning to cool on her back.

The metal box was shallow and unadorned, as though it might have contained tools and screwdrivers once. She eased the earth away with her thumb and noticed a latch. Resisting the temptation to open the box, she placed it, mud and all, inside her rucksack. She needed to fill the grave first. She was almost done when she heard a sound. She looked up to see a figure approaching.

'What have you found?' the figure asked. A male voice, the accent unfamiliar.

Jesus, where did you come from? How could I have been so careless?

The man inched forwards. 'Can I take a look?'

He looked to be dressed in dark combat fatigues. One thing was for sure: he wasn't local. Another sound behind her. She spun to see another figure closing in.

'I don't want any trouble,' she shouted, raising her hands. 'Here, take it.'

She placed the rucksack on the ground and backed away, trying to get both men into view. The first silhouette moved towards it.

She flicked her head torch to full beam, forcing the men to raise their hands, shielding their eyes. Jen skipped forwards and kicked one of them square in the jaw, a good connection, sending his neck snapping backwards. The second figure extended his arm, at the end of it a dark shape glinting in the moonlight. She grabbed his wrist for support and bought her raised leg down hard across his knee, creating a reassuring sound, like a hessian sack splitting at the seams. He let out a high-pitched scream and collapsed to the ground, his gun spinning off into the darkness. Jen pulled her own sidearm and flicked between both targets. The first man was out cold, the other was making too much noise. She wanted to find out who they were, but those screams would alert others. She selected a sedative and darted them both, just to be sure.

Who are they? How did they know I was here?

She had scanned herself and her bike before leaving London and was sure she wasn't bugged. She knelt and checked the men over quickly. They didn't appear to be military or police. Mercenaries, maybe. Contractors, paid to track her.

She left the men and ran back to the farm. The droid had already alerted her to multiple new targets within the grounds. She crouched against a perimeter stone wall. Flashlights flicked through the window of her old bedroom. More lights downstairs and a lone figure standing next to her bike.

Damn it.

She needed to create a distraction, something to buy enough time to get her bike. She smiled as a small blue light on the front of the maintenance droid pulsed once, unnoticed by the busy team working methodically through the farm house. Jen activated the intruder alarm setting. A deafening siren made the man nearest to her physically jump before running towards the front door, his gun tracking frantically. Pulsing strobe lights burst from the hallway and Jen saw her chance. She ran to her bike, switched to electric mode and slipped quietly away. The sound of the siren and shouting faded.

She rode fast, not looking back, and didn't stop until she reached a service station near High Wycombe. She had spent the journey convinced that an army of vehicles would close in on her, lights flashing. They would bundle her away, never to be seen again.

The service station was quiet, no cameras nearby. She killed the engine, lifted her helmet and pulled the metal box from her rucksack. Nervously she flicked the small catch open and lifted the lid. Inside, on a bed of smooth velvet, was a glass object, black and perfectly polished and about the size of a bar of soap, a strange red glow swirling in its centre. Jen was drawn to it and wanted to touch it, but decided to wait. She wasn't safe here.

Unexpectedly and without warning, a word appeared in her mind like an old friend, a name from her past, a name she might have known but had somehow forgotten. She had no idea how she knew, but this object, hidden for decades by her father, had a name.

Histeridae.

It was called a Histeridae, and Jen couldn't help feeling it was her destiny to find it.

CHAPTER 23

Nathan stumbled into the shadows of an alleyway, panting, head spinning. He raised his hands and watched his fingers dance and twitch. They were scuffed and bloody, but it wasn't his blood – it was Matt Anderson's. He paused for a moment, leaning against the chalky brickwork, the cold darkness and truth of what he'd almost done gripping him.

What is it with this body? Am I more volatile? Does this body enjoy violence?

He had heard that it could happen, your mind influenced by the host body's previous experiences. Some kind of muscle memory affecting the brain.

A young couple walked past, glancing into the gloom, realising too late that there was a man hunched in the shadows. Nathan turned and looked, his wild eyes feeding their fear. They pretended not to notice and picked up speed.

Nathan's mind drifted, lost in time, searching desperately for warmth. He tried to remember better times, looks they shared, breakfast in bed, dancing together, tenderness. He felt his hands steady and his heart rate settle and then a welcome change in the world, one he hadn't felt for a long time. For a few beautiful seconds it was as if his wife stood there with him. He could feel her warmth, the smell of her close to him, a hand on his shoulder telling him he was doing okay. He cried for a while, wracking, painful sobs that threatened but never quite took hold, until eventually her spirit faded and he was alone again. The widower, half the man he had once been, a dark figure in an alleyway.

His composure returned slowly, along with the familiar process of beating weakness from his mind. There was no way he could allow himself to slip now. *Jacob Logan.* According to Anderson, just the mention of that name had triggered his wife's murder. He waited a while longer for his breathing to settle before walking unnoticed from the alleyway.

By the time he reached the net café it was almost eleven. He paid for an hour and sat in a corner booth, facing outward. It was time to put his programming degree to the test. *If my students could see me now,* he thought, attaching a small device to the glossy terminal. The owner had needed to rummage out back for an old board. Everyone else was augmented. Nathan wanted to be as untraceable as possible, deliberately old school. He placed his fingers on the ancient keyboard. It was slightly sticky.

Right, Jacob Logan. Let's see what we can find out about you.

He began his work, hacking a local exchange and then hopping over to an internal Metropolitan Police site. From there he found a back door into what appeared to be a records database. He was already doing better than his attempts in Canada. Remote hacking was almost impossible these days. Locally bonded infrastructure was so much easier. He glanced around the café. No one was paying him any attention. He resumed, but it didn't take long to confirm what he had suspected might be the case.

JACOB LOGAN:
DECEASED.
HEART ATTACK.

He wasn't surprised. What he found more interesting was the lack of random information. Everyone had that, messy data scattered like pristine coins waiting to be unearthed. He spent another ten minutes searching before he was convinced. Jacob Logan's data was too tidy, way too neat. Nathan sat back and rubbed his right eye hard.

Tailored.

That was the word. Logan's life was trimmed and presented, professionally stitched, sifted and sorted. GCHQ would explain some of that, of course, and there were also military connections, but it was obvious. Someone had gone to a considerable amount of effort to ensure Jacob Logan was clean.

Nathan downloaded everything he could. There were encrypted files, too, but he would need more time and better equipment. He decided to get what he could. As file names flashed across his screen, one caught his eye.

Nathan flicked back. There it was. A profile image appeared, a woman. Intense green eyes and a shock of dark red hair. No wonder it caught his eye. She was striking, beautiful and yet tough looking. Nathan searched further. A name appeared.

JENNIFER LOGAN.

He smiled. Jacob had a daughter. Perhaps Matt Anderson had given him something useful after all. Nathan read quickly, trying not to think of Anderson lying on the concrete floor in that lock-up, trousers soaked in piss, face bloodied. Ten minutes later he grabbed the hacking device, wiped the keyboard down and stepped out into a thick fog that had draped itself over London.

He had made progress, but Jennifer Logan wasn't going to be easy; nothing was, it seemed. She was police, Duality Division. The last thing he needed was Duality on his back, asking questions. Like the distant buildings shrouded in mist, the truth seemed more elusive than ever. He tugged his collar and walked. His wife's spirit was still with him, warning him.

This woman might be your last chance, my love. Make it count.

★ ★ ★

After escaping Brook Mill, Jen spent the night at a roadside hotel, the kind that didn't ask too many questions and still took cash. The box containing the Histeridae – if that was actually its name – never left her side. She lay on the bed and retraced her steps. How did they know where to find her? She thought back, trying to find mistakes, but each time she returned to the dream. She hadn't told anyone, not even Mac. Did it mean Callaghan was right? Were the Government scanning people? Had they scanned her and known her plans, known she was going home? She slept with those questions tugging her subconscious like seeds of doubt finding fertile soil.

The following morning was the Sunday before Christmas. She spent it cruising the streets on her bike, searching for answers. When they didn't come, she called the only person she could trust, the only friend she had left.

'Where the hell are you?' Jim McArthur answered, the panic in his voice unexpected.

'Why? What's up?' Jen replied.

'Peter Callaghan is missing.' He spoke quickly. 'I was worried about you. I kept calling. Are you okay?'

'I just needed some space.' It was limp, and she knew it, but she was also trying to process what he'd just said.

What's happened to him? What have they done with Peter?

'Mac, we need to talk,' she said, her desperation now obvious. 'Can we meet today?'

'Yes, of course. Do you want to come to my house?' There was a pause. 'They're out shopping.'

Just the mention of Mac's wife and children sent a cold shudder through her. She knew that involving him might put them all in danger, but there was no way she could do this alone.

'Jen?'

'Yes. Sorry.' Her decision was made. 'I'll be there in thirty minutes.'

CHAPTER 24

Jim McArthur's house was set back from the road in a leafy suburb just north of Beaconsfield. Pulling onto the driveway, Jen spotted his Audi. His wife's car was gone.

Mac was standing in the doorway, and on seeing him Jen felt a pressure in her chest, an overwhelming urge to melt into his arms and burst into tears. She didn't. They hugged and she did her best to maintain her composure. When she finally relaxed a little, he pulled away, holding her shoulders and looking her dead in the eyes.

'I'm glad you called me,' he said, eyes swimming.

It helped to know she wasn't the only one fighting back tears. Mac led her through the hallway, which was covered in Christmas cards and decorated in blue fairy lights. A huge red sock stuffed with small presents hung above the kitchen door. The McArthur's home exuded a kind of easy happiness that many families aspired to, a comfortable, harmonious existence built on solid foundations. Jen sometimes wondered if this kind of life might come to her one day, but she had no experience of it, nothing she could reference or build on. For now, she just enjoyed living vicariously in Mac's version. She had always felt welcome here.

She followed him into the lounge, a large comfortable room with leather sofas and a log burner glowing in the centre. Two oriental rugs – picked up on their travels, Jen suspected – covered a pale wooden floor. In one corner was a Christmas tree with simple white lights and in the other a black upright piano. The house was tastefully decorated and ready for the holidays. Mac would often tell her it had nothing to do with him.

They sat, Mac smiling patiently. Jen wasn't sure where to start.

'Some of this is going to sound crazy,' she blurted. 'I just wanted you to know that. Okay?'

Mac collapsed back into his favourite leather chair. 'Just tell me what's wrong.'

Jen frowned. 'What happened to Peter?'

'We don't know,' he replied, a sadness coming over him. 'Literally no sign of him since last week.'

Jen took a moment to gather her thoughts. 'I saw him. The day before he went missing. We talked.'

'Go on.'

'He was scared.'

'Of what?'

'That's the thing, Mac. If I tell you, I could be putting you in danger.' The words echoed, returning from the past. 'Jesus.'

'What is it?'

'That's what *Peter* said to me. Before he went missing.'

'So, let me get this straight.' Mac smiled. 'You're worried about putting *me* in danger…'

Jen didn't smile back.

'Sorry,' he said. 'But Jen, it's *me* you're talking to.'

He had a point. Jim McArthur had been in enough scrapes, had enough threats and risked his life enough times. He was well acquainted with danger.

'You said you talked to Callaghan.'

Jen took a deep breath and told him, 'He thinks minds are being searched during Hibernation.' It was a relief to be finally saying the words. 'He found traces, "search echoes" he called them, then he ran tests.'

'Search *echoes*?' Mac asked, frowning.

'I have them too.' Her eyes met his. 'And that's when he uncovered something else, a memory, hidden away, even from me.' She pulled the metal box from her rucksack and opened the lid. 'It led me to this.'

They both stared at the Histeridae, resting on dark velvet. On first glance it was a simple, pebble-like object, glossy and circular in shape. But swirling in very centre was what looked like a piece of red silk dancing slowly. Jen had agonised all night about this moment, but Mac was the only person left she could trust.

'Does it always…' Mac trailed off, searching for the right words.

'Yes. It's always moving like that.'

'What is it?' Mac asked.

'I think it's called a Histeridae. My father wanted to hide it, even from me.'

She thought about the words leaving her mouth. He had *hidden* it from her; he had been scared that night, his pallid face burnt into her brain.

'A secret? Why?' Mac sat up in his chair. 'What does it do?'

Jen watched, almost voyeuristic as her hand drifted towards the Histeridae's surface. From the moment she'd found it she'd wanted to touch it, but hadn't felt safe. Now Mac was with her. This was the right time.

'Be careful,' Mac said sharply. 'Should you really touch it?'

She could feel its energy pulling at her fingers as they moved nearer. It reminded her of being close to a waterfall, the ions in the air charged and excitable.

'Jen!' Mac shouted.

But it was too late, her fingers touched the glassy surface, and she felt something similar to the charge of energy all those years ago. Every inch of her skin shimmered, as if her blood had cooled and then heated again, as if all her tiny hairs were lifted in a warm breeze. She was calm, the room suddenly brighter, colours more saturated and vibrant.

She looked down at her hand and tried to lift it away, but it felt as though her fingers were glued. She tried again, eventually plucking them free. The room slowly returned to a more natural colour. She sat quietly for a while, adjusting, trying to understand what had just happened. In real time, the moment of connection had lasted a second or two; for Jen, it had felt more like a minute.

'Did you feel anything?' Mac asked carefully.

Jen turned to face him. A trace of the rich saturated colour remained around the edges of his body, gently flickering. She had heard the word 'aura' before, now she was seeing one, crystal-like and yet oily. She became acutely aware of her body, as if it were separate and floating. A new feeling permeated through her, a strange understanding. It was as if her mind had roots and they were traveling, searching for sustenance. Time seemed to slow again.

Mac's face was moving but he was sluggish, his voice deep and flabby. She saw ghostlike strands stretching across the room like reeds pulled by the tide, luminescent tendrils with a life of their own. They latched onto Jim McArthur and the connection was tangible. Jen could actually *feel* it; a kind of bonding, an organic linking of space, time, earth and blood. She could see him, but also see herself. It was a unique sensation of union, as profound as it was powerful. The tears finally came, but they didn't arrive in isolation. She could hear Jim McArthur's thoughts, flowing through her, clearly separated but as strong as her own.

Mac looked at her with concern.

{*The Histeridae – finally,*} Mac told her without moving his mouth.

The two of them sat staring at each other.

'Jen?' Mac asked, worry spreading over his face. 'What is it?'

{*I need to keep her trust.*}

They were his thoughts, burning in her mind. Then a silence that seemed to last forever. Mac swallowed, frowned and without his knowledge revealed more.

{*She had it all this time. All these years…*}

'I didn't have it Mac,' Jen responded instinctively, her voice wavering. 'I didn't even know it existed!'

Mac looked confused, his mouth agape.

{*What the fuck?*}

'That's right,' she barked at him. 'I can hear you. I know what you're thinking…'

In a poisonous rush of energy, his darkest secrets flooded through her. Multiple threads, thoughts and memories, like an ocean threatening to drown her. She stopped trying to understand, she didn't need to, she'd heard enough.

'You haven't been watching over me, Mac,' Jen hissed. 'You've been waiting.'

That realisation spread, the truth piercing her heart. Was there anyone in this world she could trust?

'Jen, wait. It's not as simple as all that,' he begged.

She grabbed the Histeridae, pushed it into her rucksack and stood.

'I trusted you, Mac,' she said, baring her teeth. 'And there's nothing you can say. I know what you've done. I can *feel* it.'

Mac stood, his hands defensive, the colour drained from his face.

'It was an assignment,' he said, voice breaking. 'But Jen, you need to believe me. I do care about you.'

His inner thoughts followed those words. And the two

didn't match.

{Your father stole it, Jen. They want it back. It's a dangerous weapon. You don't know what it can do.}

Then another thought, mixed up in multiple meaning but perhaps the most common in the heads of men.

{Money.}

His betrayal was complete. Jim McArthur had been assigned to her from the start. His mission: Become her confidant, and when she finally revealed the location of the Histeridae, bring her in. Jen also sensed pain and regret. Random fragments. Not enough to make it right.

'It's too late for regrets, Mac,' she said coldly. 'I *know* what you've done.'

The sound of car doors slamming on the driveway meant his family would be through the door any second. They would bring the excitement of Christmas crashing into this terrible moment.

'Please, Jen. You're in danger.' He reached towards her. 'Give me the Histeridae.'

She recoiled.

{Zitagi won't take no for an answer.}

Jen felt as through the floor dropped an inch.

So, there it was – the link – he was with *Zitagi*. Her anger and sadness welled up and then boiled over as Mac reached towards her again. Suddenly, he was thrown violently backward, thrust back into his seat, his surprised expression that of a child deliberately tripped in a playground.

They looked at each other, unsure of what had just happened. Jen realised it was *her*; she had *willed* it to happen. The thought to push him away had been enough. She stumbled back, scared.

'Jen, don't,' Mac pleaded. 'You won't make it alone.'

'I've been alone my whole life.' The words cut her heart as they left her. 'Good-bye, Jim, give my regards to Zitagi.'

She ran from the house, tears streaming down her face, ignoring the cries of Mac's wife standing on the driveway. Jen's tears weren't just sadness, they were necessary and desperate. Jim McArthur's betrayal gripped her tightly, threatening to crush her whole. If she was going to survive, she needed to purge herself of those feelings.

She jumped on her bike and sped away, trying to escape the hurt, to somehow outrun his treachery. She had no idea where she was going or what to do next. Peter Callaghan had been right after all: they *were* scanning minds. She thought of Peter, his nervousness, how scared he would be. Her tears stopped and she focused. It was a huge risk, but before she could do anything else she needed to go back to her apartment, grab her gear and get off the grid. She needed to disappear.

Another thought crossed her mind.

The Histeridae.

If Jim McArthur thinks it's a weapon, then I need to learn how to use it, and fast.

CHAPTER 25

It was midafternoon by the time Jen reached her apartment. She waited outside the door for a few seconds and listened. Nothing. Simon was away in Scotland for most of the Christmas break. She pulled her handgun and entered carefully, covering the angles, checking her corners.

She needed to get her kit and get out of there.

Her footsteps were silent as she crossed the hallway floor. She hadn't used her implant since leaving Brook Mill, knowing it would reveal her location. It wasn't worth the risk. The apartment was open plan. To her right, the stairs led from the lounge to the mezzanine landing with access to both bedrooms, the bathroom and storage. There was also a small desk that Simon affectionately called his study.

She jogged up the stairs and into her bedroom, pressing a small keypad on the wall and ducking as a small loft hatch clicked open. Inside was a bag reserved for emergencies, something she never expected to need. Weapons, cash and clothes. She climbed the ladder, grabbed the hold-all and threw it over her shoulder.

A sound bought her to a dead stop, movement downstairs, people in the apartment. She slid out and onto the landing, crouching against the paneled balcony, her heart banging.

'Officer Logan,' a voice shouted from below. 'Don't be stupid.'

At least two, maybe three. Stupid coming back.

Jen needed to know what she was up against. She switched her Baden device on, scanning the room. Her active retinal picked up three identifiers – classified UN signatures, probably MI5. Then, in the corner of her eye, another.

What the hell?

There was a man inside her kitchen, pressed up against the door. His details appeared. David Shaw. Clean record. Non-UN Citizen, travel Visa.

Who the hell is David Shaw, and what the fuck is he doing in my kitchen?

She switched her augmentation off and pulled a white grenade from her hold-all. She flicked the pin and watched as four tiny lights blinked out.

Three.

Two.

Jen tossed it over the balcony. The men saw it roll on the ground and braced for an explosion that never came. She pinched her eyes shut, an intense flash revealing thin red veins across her eyelids. The grenade was a pulse generator, military issue and banned for use outside sanctioned war zones. It created a huge power surge and a brilliant light, rendering all active technology useless. Mind links, scanners, thermal imagers, retinals – anything unprotected would be fried. There was also the added benefit of temporary blindness and concussion for anyone within range.

Jen popped her head over the balcony and saw three men out cold. Her vision danced red and gold, bouncing blobs of colour fighting for the centre spot. She slipped down the stairs, blinking and shaking her head. The effects of the grenade wouldn't last long. She needed to get out of there, quickly, but first she needed to identify her random visitor.

As she approached the kitchen door she could see a faint

aura, like flickering oil emanating from the doorway. The Histeridae's effects were still active and she could feel that creeping sense again, as if her mind were reaching out and searching. It was a lot weaker than at Mac's. She guessed the power faded over time and wondered if the power would return if she touched it again.

Her experience with Mac had been unpleasant and invasive, but the knowledge – Mac wasn't to be trusted – had been invaluable. Hearing and feeling the inner workings of a mind wasn't natural; it felt wrong, especially when it was someone you cared about. She decided against the Histeridae. She would do this the old-fashioned way.

'Mr Shaw,' she said loudly. 'Step out with your hands raised.'

She repeated it, adding a final warning. The handle turned and the man walked forward, hands raised.

'Don't shoot,' he pleaded, looking around at the three men lying on the floor, his arms shaking. 'Jesus. Who are they?'

'Never mind them, what are *you* doing here?'

'I'm sorry,' he said, lowering his arms, 'for breaking in.'

Jen hiked her eyebrows and flicked her gun. The man's arms shot back up. He was either a very polite burglar or an unusually well-spoken Government agent. She wasn't in the mood for bumbling apologies.

'I asked you what you were doing here.'

'My name is David Shaw,' he replied. 'And I'm investigating a murder.'

'And what does that have to do with me?' Jen asked through gritted teeth.

'Honestly, I don't know, but you're somehow linked to...' He squinted and shook his head. 'I'm here about Project Histeridae. Does that mean anything to you?'

Jen stepped back. How could this man know anything about the Histeridae? Project Histeridae? Her mind was racing, but there was no time to think. Mr Random had managed to break into her apartment, so he was skilled – but there was something strange about him, an innocence that didn't match his appearance. He was well built, looked tough but was shaking, scared and out of his depth. There were a lot of questions, but one thing she *was* sure of: he wasn't connected to the team of men scattered on the floor around them.

The wail of the building's fire alarm mixed with the sound of people moving through corridors snapped her out of her thoughts. Jen considered her options. There had been gunshots, fire alarms, and now the thrum of distant sirens. Not exactly what she had in mind for her 'in and out' operation. She couldn't leave Mr Random here. He knew something about the Histeridae.

'Come on,' she shouted impatiently, already moving.

'What?' Shaw replied. 'Where are we going?'

'You're coming with me.' She turned to face him. 'Unless you have a better idea?'

Shaw looked at the three men on the floor. 'You got any more of those things?' he asked, meaning the grenades.

'No.' She shook her head. 'I've got something much better.'

CHAPTER 26

Jen strode ahead without looking back, unsure what to make of the man. Was he smart enough to know he should be scared? They were in serious trouble. But there was something niggling at her, something distant. It was as if, all along, she had been waiting for him to turn up like a missing piece.

'Why are they after you?' Shaw asked, struggling to keep up.

'Why were you in my apartment?' Jen retorted, fed up with his incessant questioning. 'What were you looking for?'

'I was planning to bug it, but someone beat me to it.'

Jen stopped abruptly, grabbed his jacket and tugged him close to her face. 'If I had met you a week ago, you would be under arrest,' she snapped. 'So I will ask you once more, why were you in my apartment?'

Shaw looked down, nodding, and answered quickly. 'I'm investigating a murder. The victim knew something about Project Histeridae, and she was killed for mentioning your father's name.'

The sound of sirens was louder now, and people were clogging the corridors. Jen processed at speed. This man knew about her father and the Histeridae.

She said, 'Just stay close and shut up.'

'I wouldn't use your tech, by the way.'

'I get it,' Jen hissed.

They continued until they reached the end of the corridor.

The fire alarm wasn't as loud here, and a group of people blocking the stairwell seemed relaxed. She raised her gun and fired three times into the ceiling. Shaw reeled backwards, his hands pressed against his ears, as the crowd screamed and dispersed. The doorway was clear within seconds.

'Let's go,' Jen said coolly.

They reached the third floor and walked out onto the now-quiet corridor.

'What are we doing?' Shaw asked.

'The gunshots will have given them our last location. That's good. Now, they will expect us down there.' She nodded to the ground floor. 'We need to find a better way out.'

She began searching. The long corridor at the side of the building was lined with windows. She lifted one and looked out. There was a fire escape, straight down – too obvious. Then she saw the adjacent building and climbed out onto the railings.

'Oh, come on!' Shaw cried.

She popped her head back through the open window.

'You want to stay here?' she snarled. 'Fine.'

The sirens were outside now, accompanied by the sound of loud hailers and footfall. Shaw sighed and followed her awkwardly through the window.

Jen mentally calculated the jump. From the fire escape, which traveled down the side of the building, they could push off and land on a flat-roofed section of the building opposite. The gap between buildings was small, the difference in height maybe eight or nine feet. She wouldn't have hesitated to leap if she had been alone. The weather was cold but clear and dry; that would help.

'Like jumping off a swing,' she said simply.

The drop between the buildings might only be a few feet, but the road below was over forty.

'You'll make it.' She stepped over the railings, hunched

down and executed the jump perfectly. A strong push, easy landing, forward roll and she was up again facing him.

'Come on, jump,' she shouted.

She realised, watching him standing there, his face white, how quickly she was having to adapt. A few short weeks ago she was a Duality police officer, enforcing a system she fervently believed in. Now, she was helping a man she had just caught breaking into her apartment escape from a building. Her building. She was on the run. She was being hunted.

'You can do it,' she shouted, knowing they didn't have long, knowing he might hold information that could help her.

He climbed over the railing, closed his eyes and pushed off from the fire escape at an awkward angle. Jen could see he wasn't going to make it before his feet even left the metal. He landed, his stomach banging hard against the side of the building, feet dangling just over the edge. Shaw panicked, scratching at the gravel, his feet kicking against the wall below, calling for help. Jen ran, grabbed him and eventually pulled him up.

Shaw coughed, kneeling on the ground, breathing rapidly, trying to compose himself.

'Thank you,' he managed.

Jen ran to the opposite side of the rooftop and looked down onto the street. She recognised the street below, reset her bearings and made her way towards a maintenance door. The door was locked. She stepped back and blasted the lock twice.

They descended the stone steps quickly and emerged in a basement car park. It was filled with auto-cars, the odd one pulling away to collect distant, demanding commuters.

'How are we going to get out of here?' Shaw asked, his voice still trembling from the jump.

Jen nodded into the distance. There, parked near an exit ramp was her bike. She walked, he followed. She began replaying the last ten minutes in her head. The men, the grenade, finding him in her apartment.

'They'll know who you are by now,' she said.

'How?'

'There are cameras all over my building.'

'I disabled those before I went in,' Shaw said, almost as an aside.

Jen stopped and looked him slowly up and down. 'What are you, some kind of hacker?'

'No. Well yes. *Some kind* of hacker I suppose. I teach people how to stop them. Well, at least that's –'

'Get down,' Jen whispered, pushing him and pointing towards a cluster of parked cars. 'Hide, over there.'

In the distance a figure walked down the exit ramp, silhouetted against bright sunlight, gun tracking. Jen pushed Shaw into the shadows, then ran, pressing herself against a large concrete pillar. She was too late.

'Don't move!' The man shouted, tucking himself behind a row of cars. She leant around and listened. He didn't verbally communicate with his team, and she hoped – because of the pulse grenade – they had been ordered to disable all comms in case of another blast.

What now, Jen? Shoot your way out? Then what?

A second man crept up behind her. 'Hands in the air.'

She knew there was no point trying to spin and shoot him. She thought of the Histeridae and wondered how often she could use it.

'Gun on the floor.' The man inched forward. 'Do it.'

She placed her gun down, raised her arms and turned. The Histeridae was in her rucksack. Too far to reach. The gloomy car park brightened suddenly, not by much, but it was noticeable, a bloom of radiance. She had thought about touching the Histeridae's surface, imagined its energy pulsing though her. She thought of it again, and as she did the colours returned, vibrant and heavily saturated.

A feeling began in her gut. It traveled up her hips and out through her shoulders, bringing with it images and fragments of light, joining them together, creating a singular flickering halo around the man in front of her. Blues, purples and reds shimmered and danced around his outline. Jen could see a spinning tunnel of light pulsing between their minds. She was connected to him and saw his expression change, felt his breath quicken as he struggled to keep his gun raised. She could feel his will, battling her own, a very different sensation to Mac's. This man was attempting to push her back, to fight her.

They were mentally at war.

He wanted to shoot her, to put her down. Jen felt nauseous and realised, with horror, that she was losing the battle. She felt herself physically shaking, panic gripping her. The man had raised his gun again. She gave it everything but it was impossible.

He was going to fire, and there was nothing Jen could do to stop him.

CHAPTER 27

Time slowed to a near standstill, the Histeridae allowing her longer to process the situation, to realise she was in trouble. Connected with her assailant, wrestling with his mind, Jen tried one last time to get him to lower his gun. In the end, all she managed was to move his hand a fraction to the left as he fired.

The bullet shot just past her right temple.

Jen seized her chance, grabbed her gun and fired back. The white blast lifted the man off his feet, dumping him hard onto the concrete. The man who had originally spotted them had relaxed slightly. That was a mistake. From a distance he fired but was too slow. Jen dropped onto her left knee, fired back and deposited him awkwardly onto the bonnet of a nearby car. He slid down, crunching to the floor. Shaw crept out of the shadows.

'Jesus, are they dead?'

'No,' Jen crouched, checking the nearest man over. 'Just stunned.'

'Should we take their guns?'

'They're DNA-linked and tracked. Useless.'

She noted his use of *we*, walked past him and examined the wall.

'What are you looking for?' His voice was shaking.

'This,' she replied, pulling a chrome-plated dart from the

wall. 'Silent and instant. They attack the nervous system; if they pierce your skin you can't move. Very effective.'

'At least they aren't trying to kill you,' Shaw offered.

Jen was certain it would only be a matter of time.

Shaw frowned. 'He had you dead-on. I could see his hands shaking. How could he miss you?'

Jen ignored the question. 'You need to get out of here.'

'What?' he said. 'After all that, you can't... you can't just leave me.'

She turned to face him. 'Until about ten minutes ago I didn't even know you, so yes, I *can* leave you.' She sighed. 'And besides, I can't trust you, David Shaw. If that's even your real name. I can't trust anyone.'

'But what about Project Histeridae?' he pleaded. 'Maybe we can help each other. Share information. Figure this out.'

'Look, we can meet up again, talk more, but for now you're going to slow me down.' She paused a beat. 'I'm sorry.'

'I told you I was investigating a murder.'

Jen nodded, but her attention was elsewhere.

'It was my wife,' he said quietly. 'They killed my wife.'

Jen looked back at him. 'I'm sorry. I truly am. But I've got bigger problems to worry about right now. I'm better off alone.'

'The minute you use any technology, they'll find you,' he said quickly. 'I could help, keep you under the radar.'

Jen had started to walk away but stopped. She looked him up and down again, considering her options. He *had* managed to disable the cameras in her apartment building. She knew better than anyone that if the Government wanted to find her, they would. Maybe she *could* use him. Either way, this was all taking too long.

'Okay. Listen,' Jen said. 'We leave here separately.' She almost accessed her neural network to send him the address but stopped. Not using mind interfaces would take some adjustment. 'Go to 46 Ladbroke Grove, Notting Hill. Ask for Thomas and then wait for me.'

She didn't like involving Thomas. It was a risk, a weak plan, but it was all she could think of given the time.

'You'll be there?' Shaw asked.

'Yes.' She was off and running. *I hope so.*

They were nearly at her bike when three more men appeared. They ducked down. Jen thought it through. She might make it up and out onto the street, but outrunning the police was almost impossible once they had a sighting. She could use the Histeridae, but then what? Up there would be more police, an endless stream. She couldn't control them all.

She turned and looked at Shaw.

This man she had only just met. He looked back at her, the fear in his eyes obvious and real. He clearly had no idea what to do. As if on cue, the vapour-like tendrils appeared again, creeping towards Shaw's head. If she willed it, they would encase him, revealing his aura, and she would hear his thoughts, find out for sure if she could trust him. Before she had time to think, she asked him a simple question, deep below the surface of consciousness. She asked if she could trust him, if his intentions were good. The most basic of questions.

The answer came, not as words but as a feeling like a heaving swell of deep water. This man wasn't with Mac or Zitagi or any Government agency. He was like her, alone and vulnerable and against people like them. The Histeridae delved deeper and Jen could feel her questions probing further into his mind.

She stopped, the tendrils pulling back suddenly like delicate silk in a freak gust of wind. The men were closing in; she had no time or chance to focus. That was reason enough not to use it, but there was another: this new power, this invasive ability to enter people minds, was scary and most certainly unethical.

She wanted to be careful, didn't want to abuse it. She had found out enough. She could, for now at least, trust him.

Shaw was pointing, his face like ash. She followed his finger line and saw a heli-droid, about the size of a dinner plate, skimming past the three figures. It would begin scanning the area any second, and it was armed. Her decision was made. She tugged the rucksack from her back and faced him.

'You need to take this,' she whispered.

'What is it?'

'Just don't lose it. It's what they're after.'

He pushed it back, shaking his head. 'Then I don't want it.'

'It's too late to *decide* what you want. Take it to 46 Ladbroke Grove and tell Thomas I sent you.' She began creeping around the car.

'What are you doing?'

She glanced back at him. 'They don't know who you are, they haven't seen you. I will draw them in. When they follow me, wait a few minutes and then walk out. Don't look back and don't run. Just walk out. Okay?'

Shaw nodded reluctantly. In the distance a red laser projected out from the heli-droid. The beam spread, triangular, from floor to ceiling and the droid began its sweep.

'Then will you tell me what the hell is going on?' Shaw asked.

'Yes,' she assured him, crawling towards her bike. 'If you make it, I'll tell you everything I know.'

The men spotted her first. The droid stopped its scan, locked onto her and flew, its speed frightening. Jen made it to her bike, jumped on and started it up. With a high-pitched screech of tyres she rode straight towards the group of men. They scattered as the droid took aim. She squinted, concentrating. She would have to rely on her ability to aim manually. In her younger days she would spend hours shooting manually at the range but had backed off in the last couple of years. There just didn't seem much point in practicing.

She cursed that decision now. Lifting her hand, she shot five rounds at the droid. Thankfully the last one connected, spinning it, disrupting its hover. The droid shot wildly, spraying bullets in an arc. One of the men screamed before dropping silently to the ground. Twisting the throttle, Jen sped between the other two, up the ramp and onto the road above. She felt the Histeridae's power diminishing as she rode, the iridescent glow fading gradually from her vision. She'd had no choice but to entrust it to a man she hardly knew, and it had all happened so fast.

Mac's face flashed through her mind.

Trust, she thought with sadness.

What does that really mean now?

CHAPTER 28

Jen weaved through traffic at speed, the last afternoon sun bleeding low across the skyline. She'd managed to outrun the first heli-droid, but it wouldn't be long before more arrived. She knew this game; she had played for the other team many times. Now it was her turn to be hunted. She calculated Thomas's house to be a fifteen-minute ride.

Need to lose them first.

Above her two mobile cameras detached from their rooftop mounts and descended rapidly. They weren't armed, but they were fast and hard to shake off. She knew that somewhere, across town, a surveillance team would be coordinating the chase, multiple screens displaying her speeding bike from every angle.

The traffic parted – a rare sight – and Jen passed irate passengers complaining inside their vehicles as they were pulled, automatically to the edges of the road. Ahead, cutting through the thin mist, she saw the blue and red glow of police lights. A roadblock. There would be an electronic spike on the road, and of course, gas. Targeted pathogens were widely used now; you could gas an entire shopping centre and only take down the individuals you wanted to. No need for multiple units, no need for fuss.

She craved the chance to think, but that was a luxury she didn't have. She jammed the rear brake and kicked the back of her bike off to the right. A plume of thick grey smoke billowed up behind her as she leant hard, sliding the back end across the road. She twisted the throttle, dropped a gear and accelerated. For a second it felt as though she might lose it, the bike bucking against her, but the tyres gained traction. She was now heading southbound. Not the right direction, but that was the last thing she could think about now. Surviving. That was all.

In her mirror, another drone, this one bigger and clearly armed. She now had three drones in close pursuit; two cameras and an armed heli-droid. She saw a thin red laser target flash across her. She leant left and right, ducking and bobbing.

The droid fired, rapid shots. Jen heard them whistling past and saw the flash of ricocheting shells across the road surface. Too close. She mounted the curb on her left, her bike's suspension banging loudly in protest. People scattered as she screamed along the pavement. To her right the drones appeared like flashes between the parked vehicles. She would never outrun them. Ahead, a large bus. Decent cover.

Jen braked aggressively, her bike tipping forward in a thick cloud of black smoke. She leapt from it, leaving it to slam down onto its side, and ran to the bus. Inside, startled commuters pressed against the glass, watching the show in fearful amazement. Jen locked eyes with a girl, maybe eight years old. She was pointing at Jen and tapping a woman next to her. Jen leant against the back of the bus and craned her neck, looking down the empty street.

The drones arced high into the air before spinning back at speed, tracking their target. Grabbing her pistol, Jen leant out and fired, concentrating on the armed heli-droid. It flicked vertical each time she fired, avoiding her bullets, and within seconds was firing back. Jen dived to the floor as it screeched past, the sound deafening, then popped back up, managing another couple of shots as it twisted away in a near vertical ascent.

This time she connected. A small spark followed by a brief cough of blue smoke. The droid faltered briefly before completing another – this time awkward – aerial loop. The two smaller cameras were hovering above her like curious bees. She looked up at them, knowing her image would be filling screens across London. The temptation to flick her finger didn't last. She could hear the whirring rotors of the armed droid. It was damaged but functional and was closing in. It would have adjusted its attack and be on her any second, shooting through the gap.

Jen scrambled out of the bus, lifted her bike from the pavement and jumped on. In the distance she heard the familiar hum of police bikes and sighed heavily.

Welcome to the party, boys.

She joined the road as two bikes appeared. The police riders tucked in as they spotted her, their bikes gaining fast, and were either side of her in seconds. There was no negotiation, no request. They began firing. She did the only thing she could and slammed hard into the bike on her left. She caught a glimpse of the rider's expression, his bike spinning out of control and leaving the road. In the confusion she managed two shots into the front tyre of the other bike, deflating it, sending the rider into a lurching rhythmic dance as he tried to regain control.

Jen accelerated, not seeing the tyre reinflate automatically. The rider fired back awkwardly, his shots narrowly missing her leg, bullets dinging loudly from her metalwork. She looked ahead. The road split in two. Again she braked hard, but this time the rider stayed with her. He shot twice into her fuel tank which instantly belched fuel. Jen took the road to her left, the pursuing rider maintaining his position beside her.

He didn't fire again, and Jen was just starting to wonder why when she felt the sharp sting of darts peppering her back.

It was the heli-droid. The expected paralysis didn't come, and Jen realised with relief that her back protector must have taken the brunt of the impact. Her relief was short-lived. It fired again, this time skimming the edge of her back plate and piercing her skin.

There was no pain, just an immediate loss of sensation in her right arm, as if it were no longer hers. The rider to her side gestured for her to slow down. She was struggling, her right arm numb, and she watched helplessly as her gun fell, clattering on the road behind her.

She came to a weaving stop on a low bridge, another street beneath. The heli-droid was approaching. She ran to the edge of the bridge and jumped, her left arm grabbing the railing, where she dangled for a few seconds before letting go. Her short fall was broken by a gathering of people below, their bodies compressing beneath her weight.

She staggered up. Two people remained on the ground, a man and a woman injured by her sudden and unexpected fall. Jen looked around, her vision beginning to blur. She was in the middle of a busy street market, the pungent smell of fish and fresh vegetables helping to cut through her hazy mind. Around her people were shouting and in the distance the wail of sirens. Jen began to run as best she could, ignoring the complaining bystanders. That's when she heard another sound. A distinctive metallic whirring. A sound she didn't want to hear. An armed police droid approached.

'Do not move,' it bellowed in its processed, authoritative tone.

Jen was cold and breathing heavily, big gulps of air, desperately searching for an escape route. She backed underneath the curved bridge, aware that the rider above would shoot if he could see her. Again the droid warned her. She decided to run for an alleyway.

As she turned and ran, the droid ejected three small devices, sending them skimming through the air like polished metal plates. They passed her, descending quickly before gripping the road in a triangular formation. With a sudden burst of green light they snapped open, creating a six-foot-high wall of light around her. It was a targeted trap shield. Jen slowed, stopped and fell to her knees, cradling her limp right arm. People around her were screaming, running freely through the glowing green force-field surrounding her. She inched forwards and felt the terrible, sharp needles of energy coursing through her body like broken glass in her veins.

Jen felt a ball of fear push up from her gut. She was caught, her unique DNA betraying her. She'd used the traps herself. They were perfect. The droid closed in and the street filled with police and lights.

CHAPTER 29

'We've got her,' Jim McArthur said, surprised by how tired his voice sounded.

'Excellent,' Zitagi replied. 'And the Histeridae?'

McArthur paused, leant his head back and sighed. A headache had been banging through him all day.

'Do we have it?' Zitagi asked, impatiently.

'No, we don't.' He imagined her pursed red lips tightening.

When she spoke again, her voice was slow, calm and controlled. 'Then find out where it is.'

McArthur processed the facts. Jen was captured, that much he had expected. But without the Histeridae? That was bad. Not for them – they would find it eventually. It was bad for Jen.

'McArthur?' Zitagi's voice reminded him of a school headmistress. 'Find out where she's hidden it.'

'Okay. I understand.'

'Do you?'

'Yes.' He understood, alright, perhaps too well.

She continued, 'One of the agents in the car park incident was exposed to the Histeridae. We can use him.'

His mind was racing to keep up. 'How?'

'It's been over twenty years since the Histeridae was last used. With current tech we should be able to create a way of blocking it.'

Of course. When Zitagi suggested she could *use* someone,

it was never for their benefit. The agent would be collateral damage. And if the benefit involved mind extraction, so be it.

A sudden realisation chilled him. He swallowed.

She used the Histeridae on me too.

'I will be there tomorrow.' Zitagi barked her orders, interrupting his thoughts. 'See what you can get out of her before then.'

McArthur told her he would do his best and was surprised when she remained on the line.

'Oh, and by the way,' Zitagi said absently, before hanging up. 'Peter Callaghan is dead.'

★ ★ ★

Nathan arrived at Ladbroke Grove, a red brick terrace in Notting Hill, just after dark. His legs had only just stopped shaking, the shoot-out in the car park fresh in his mind.

Jennifer Logan.

She had made an impression, alright: she'd taken out a bunch of armed guards in her apartment – some kind of flash grenade – and then two in the car park, three if you included the one the droid took down.

After watching her speed off, Nathan had waited, found a stairwell and then walked from the building as if nothing had happened. Exactly as she'd told him to. Had he really only met her today? His hand instinctively reached for the strap of his bag.

He walked the drive, scanned the tabbed list of numbers and pressed the buzzer next to 46. All he wanted was to do was get off the street and ditch the bag.

A man dressed in a smart suit answered the door. His hair and skin were immaculate. 'Can I help you?' he asked suspiciously, looking Nathan up and down.

'Are you Thomas?' Nathan asked.

'Who are you?'

'I'm a friend of Jennifer Logan.'

The man frowned, raising an eyebrow at Nathan's appearance. 'I don't think so.'

Nathan realised it had been a while since his last shower and his beard was a few days in. 'She told me to come here and ask for your help. She's on her way here now.'

'She wouldn't do that.' The man shook his head. 'She would call me first.'

'Not today,' Nathan said coldly. 'She's in trouble.'

Thomas took a step back, his hand on the door handle. Nathan leant in, making the most of the height advantage.

'She said you were the only person left she could trust. She'll be here soon.'

Thomas edged out of the doorway and eyed the corridor nervously.

'What kind of *trouble*?' He used the word like it was contagious.

'The kind you hide from.' Nathan said, watching Thomas intently. 'Now, *please* let me in.'

The corridor had been quiet, but there were voices now.

Thomas closed his eyes and sighed heavily. 'Damn it,' he whispered before stepping back and making way.

Nathan stepped inside, closing the door behind them. The house was minimalistic, tasteful and expensive. Nathan smelt burning oils and coffee as he passed the kitchen. Thomas gestured towards a small room.

'You can put your bags in there.'

Nathan dumped his rucksack and Jen's hold-all. To his right was a single bed. Nathan could feel it calling him. Not yet. He returned to the hallway and thanked Thomas, who looked unimpressed.

'How long will she be?' Thomas asked. 'It's nearly Christmas, and believe it or not, I have plans… a life.'

'She just said soon.'

An awkward silence followed, eventually broken by Thomas. 'What's your name?'

'David Shaw.' Nathan replied, remembering to lie just in time.

'And how do you know her?'

'We worked together for a while.'

'Oh, right,' Thomas said, unconvinced.

Another silence.

Nathan said, 'Look, I'm not here to cause any trouble.'

'I'm glad to hear that.' Thomas folded his arms. 'What kind of trouble is she in?'

Nathan thought about her warning. Whatever was in that bag was pretty important.

'I don't know,' he lied again. 'But I'm trying to help her.'

That part was true. He did want to help her, if he could, but also hoped she could help him. If she ever made it back here, of course. A chill came over him as he remembered. It had been bad. A team in pursuit, police drones, the works. He wondered if he would ever see her again.

What's so important? What do they want so badly?

Thomas stood watching him. Nathan decided he would wait, but knew that when the opportunity arose, he would open that bag and find out for himself.

★ ★ ★

Jen wasn't in a usual holding cell. This place was cold steel and reinforced glass. Military. In every corner she could feel cameras on her, focusing, watching, recording. She sat on a metal bench that was bolted to the floor, her ankle swollen slightly, sprained but not broken. Not that it mattered. She had been captured.

Going back to her apartment had been a risk, she had known that, but without supplies, identity or weapons she wouldn't have lasted an hour. It had been a calculated risk, but one she'd made before knowing how far the deceit went. Mac and Zitagi were just the tip; the iceberg went deep.

She thought of David Shaw and how, in a moment of madness, she'd given up the Histeridae, been forced to trust him. Her father had stolen it with the sole purpose of keeping it from them, and she'd let him down. She wondered if he was captured, held in a cell like her, the Histeridae lost forever.

Hours passed, giving her time to think, which wasn't a good thing. The lights were low, the room specifically designed to give no stimulus. She felt like she was underground but it was impossible to tell. They could keep her here for as long as they wanted to and then they would kill her, she knew that, but somehow losing the Histeridae was worse. She had become convinced that it was her job to expose the truth, whatever that was.

The door lock activated and Jim McArthur entered the cell, followed by two armed guards.

He stood and waited until eventually Jen faced him. He was pale, his eyes drawn, but she knew it wasn't because of her. They hadn't found Shaw, he didn't have the Histeridae and he was in deep trouble.

'You need to tell us where it is.' His voice was rough but clear.

On hearing his voice, Jen felt as if cold steel had filled her throat and she fought back tears. He was now her enemy. It didn't matter how much she wished it wasn't so.

'Fuck you, Mac,' she said quietly, her eyes burning into him. 'I trusted you.'

'Where is it?' he said angrily. 'Where have you hidden it?'

She looked down at her hands, which were cuffed to the bench, and tugged, the metal clinking loudly.

'Tell me something,' she asked, void of emotion. 'Where's Peter Callaghan?'

McArthur walked to the corner of the room and faced away from her. 'He's dead.'

'Oh, Mac.' Jen released a painful sigh, her heart calling out to him in spite of her fear and anger. 'What have you done?'

She couldn't help the tears now. They came and she let them.

'You bastard.' She spat the words like venom. 'You'll pay for this. All of you.' She looked round the room, eyeballing the various lenses.

McArthur approached her. 'If you don't tell us where it is, then we will *make* you.' He paused, then whispered, 'You *know* what I mean.'

She knew exactly. She'd had the last few hours to think about just that. Mind extraction. She'd heard the stories but bit back on her fear. She didn't want to give him the satisfaction.

'You're her little puppy now.' She smiled as best she could. 'Run along, Mac. Do as you're told.'

McArthur raised his head and drew a long breath. 'I tried,' he said finally.

'You did more than that,' she shot back at him.

'This isn't how I wanted it to be, Jen.' He twisted his neck against his collar. 'I warned you and you still ran.'

As Jen watched him walk away, it felt like another one of her dreams. Like Mac was somehow playing a character, bound by a destiny that didn't belong to him, one she was powerless to change.

Mac instructed the surly guards to prepare her for transfer and left without looking back.

Jen felt hope pour out of her like oil from a punctured drum. Soon they would extract the information they needed and her life would be over. And then, with her gone, they would find David Shaw and kill him too.

She thought of the Histeridae again. Would he use it? Would he even try?

CHAPTER 30

Two hours was a long time for her mind to stew. When the guard entered the cell, cuffed her and ordered her to stand, Jen was strangely relieved. In silence they walked the sterile corridor, passing identical doors, twenty or so before she stopped counting. She wondered who might be held behind those nondescript walls. David Shaw, the mystery man, perhaps? Maybe even Thomas by now?

After various security checks, the guard pushed open two large steel doors and they were outside, the sun bursting over them. Jen barely had time for her eyes to adjust before being pushed into the back of an armoured vehicle. Blinking against the harsh light, she saw a runway and tall fencing in the distance. It didn't help; she still had no idea where she was. The thick doors sealed her in darkness. No windows. Just the rhythmic dings of rain starting on the metal roof. The rain had turned into a downpour by the time the doors opened again. Jen was surprised when Jim McArthur entered the car and sat opposite her, shaking the rain from his jacket.

She scowled at him. 'Come to babysit me?'

He didn't make eye contact. The guard banged the side of the vehicle and it pulled away. She studied Jim McArthur in the artificial interior light. He looked uneasy.

'Peter Callaghan.' She winced at his name, the thought of him gone. Murdered. 'My God, Mac.'

Her thoughts turned to the Duality Division. A group of dedicated officers she had worked alongside for years. The unit had been specifically created to support and uphold new laws, legislation that she believed was going save mankind. What did that mean now?

'Ravenscroft. Richards.' She was trying to figure out where everyone fit into this secret world of his. 'Are they all in on it?'

'Everything you thought you knew.' His voice cracked like thick ice. He leant towards her. 'It's all lies.'

'Your family? That was a lie too?'

The pause was enough. They were part of the façade.

Jen thought back to summer days, barbecues on his patio. His wife bringing a plate of salad, tender, loving exchanges between them. It was like a dream in which you could sense a bomb was about to go off but you couldn't warn anyone.

They traveled in silence for a while until the road sounded different and the armoured vehicle sped up.

'Where are you taking me?' she asked.

McArthur looked noticeably uncomfortable. He tapped at a small console on the side panel of the truck. It looked like a map.

'What's going on?' Jen asked. 'You need to tell me.'

McArthur reached inside his jacket and pulled a gun. Jen felt the pit of her stomach sink. He was going to kill her. Shoot her, right here in the back of the van. Dump her body somewhere. She felt like glass, heavy and immovable. It would take all of her effort to launch herself at him. She wanted to go down fighting at least and was busy planning her first move when he spoke.

'I'm going to alert the driver,' he said quickly, his face chalky white. 'We're getting you out of here.'

McArthur pressed the intercom and explained that the prisoner was having a seizure. The truck came to a swift stop and they heard the driver exit, walk around the truck and open the side door. McArthur fired, shooting the driver square in the chest, knocking him backwards. This time when Mac spoke, he sounded like the man she'd known all those years. Her friend.

'You've got about fifteen minutes before they start looking for you.' He handed her a small pouch. 'Retinal blockers,' he explained. 'At least you can walk the street. If you're scanned it will flag you as unknown, so you need to be careful. Two alerts and they will close in.'

Jen was struggling to process all the information. Jim McArthur had been with her from the start, throughout her career. He'd always been there. His betrayal had shattered the foundations of that world, yet here, now, he was somehow trying to put it right. She looked at him and he smiled with a heavy sigh that bought his whole chest down. She reached over and placed her hand on his.

'What about you, Mac?' she said softly. 'Can you come with me?'

'I messed up, Jen,' he said, his expression flat and cold. 'I'm sorry.'

'Why? Why did you do it? What do they want it for?'

He looked round nervously. 'We don't have time for this.'

'I have to know, Mac.' Her look was enough.

Jim McArthur's resolve deflated. In a matter of minutes half the British Government would be on her, but that didn't matter. She wanted to know, and he had to tell her.

'After your father stole the device, I was assigned to you, a sleeper mission. It was never supposed to go on so long. Jen, I never –'

'But what made him steal it?'

'The research your father conducted changed everything, and when Baden got hold of it... let's just say he didn't agree with their direction.'

'Baden?' Jen was missing the connection.

'Government bought them lock stock. Not common knowledge, but they did, and some people made a lot of money. Your father could see it going wrong. That's when he stole it, to stop them.'

'From doing what? What did Baden want to do?'

As the question left her mouth she knew the answer. Baden technology permeated society, their name a part of the accepted fabric of modern life, but Jen was drawn back to one place specifically. A place where that logo had been etched on almost every piece of equipment.

'The Hibernation chip,' Jen whispered. The answers were banging at the base of her skull like small grenades, sending shivers through her. It didn't yet make sense, but there was finally some truth to what Mac was telling her. A tuning fork was humming at last.

Mac was nodding. 'Your father's research into the Histeridae – it unlocked the human brain in a way no one could have imagined.'

His words lingered in the air between them.

'Can you forgive me?' he asked her eventually.

Jen didn't hesitate. She hugged him tightly and the tears came again.

'Fucking hell, Mac,' she sobbed, squeezing him hard before he gently guided her away.

'You need to go,' he said firmly. 'I did as you asked, now go.'

'But what's going on? Callaghan believed they're searching us, searching our minds – did you know about that?'

A radio crackled into life and a voice drifted up from the guard lying on the ground in front of them. It was asking for an update on the alert they had just received.

Jim McArthur held her shoulders and spoke firmly. 'Jen,

they don't tell me everything. All I know is that it involved your father but starts and ends with the Government and Baden.'

The screen next to him began flashing red and the vehicle alarm started shrieking. Jen jumped out of the truck. They had stopped on a gravel lay-by just off a main road. It was outer London somewhere, she wasn't sure where exactly. In the distance, layers of circular roads towered above the city. Jen grabbed the guard and dragged him out of the view of the traffic streaming past, each commuter a potential witness, their minds imprinted with the scene and ripe for scanning. McArthur was out of the truck and leaning against the side.

'Come on, Mac,' she pleaded, grabbing a fob from the guard's belt and clicking open her handcuffs. 'You can come with me, we can figure this out!'

'There's no point running.' He was smiling, but his eyes were glazed. 'No point. I've been doing that my whole life. Calm on the exterior, running like crazy underneath. Well, not anymore.' He sighed heavily. 'I'm done. You're stronger than me. You always have been.'

'I'm sorry.' It was all she could think to say, and in that moment she both loved and hated him. He was right. If she stayed any longer they would catch her again and all of this would have been for nothing. Jen kissed his cheek. Jim McArthur was always right.

She inserted the retinal blockers, turned and ran.

Jim McArthur watched her, as he always did, until she disappeared from view. His body felt weak and he had a pain in his right shoulder. Stress, probably, or perhaps – he hoped – death would be kind enough to gift him a heart attack. He imagined Zitagi's face when she heard the news of Jen's escape. That flawless face would be rigid, teeth clenched tightly, eyes trying to contain fury. Zitagi hadn't authorised the transfer; she knew nothing of his intentions to help Jennifer Logan escape. He smiled again. He'd managed to keep it from her, to help Jen, to give her another chance. Of course, it didn't make it right – he knew that – but at least he had tried to make amends.

An incoming call appeared, Zido's name blinking in the corner of his vision. *Right on cue,* he thought and ignored it. That woman. She'd had enough of his time.

Finally managed to stand up to her.

He looked down at the gun sitting heavy in his hand and wished he could have done more. He wanted to tell Jen everything, the whole plan, but they had run out of time. Always seems to be the way, he thought. We have our whole lives to tell people how we feel, and yet still we run out of time. He thought of his family, another part of the lie. He was very fond of them, as he was many of his colleagues. What a mess it had all become. He raised the gun to his head and decided his last thought would be Jen. She had been like a daughter to him. He hoped more than anything that she would forgive him. Her face filled his mind, moments they had shared.

Tears welled up in his eyes. She was a good girl.

CHAPTER 31

It was the afternoon of Christmas Eve. Thomas heard the knock again. He approached the door, nerves biting. His initial relief left quickly as Jen pushed past him, entering the apartment. The smell of sour sweat and fear accompanied her. She hunched over, hands pressing heavily on her knees.

'What's going on?' Thomas asked.

'I'm sorry.' She was clearly exhausted. 'Is he here?'

Thomas sighed and nodded. His fear was overtaken briefly by a pang of sadness. He only had a couple of clients like her, women he genuinely enjoyed spending time with. He supposed the sadness was a form of acceptance. She was in trouble and that meant their arrangement was over. It was a shame.

'Yes, he's here,' Thomas replied quietly. 'But this isn't part of our deal, Jen, you know that.'

'I know.' She regained her breath and placed her hand on his shoulder and attempted a smile.

Nathan stepped into the hallway.

'I wasn't sure you were coming,' he said, his tone cold. 'Where have you been?'

'Is it safe?' Jen replied.

'Yes, it's in there.' Nathan tipped his head towards the spare room.

Jen walked to the spare room and returned clutching a handful of credits.

'What's going on?' Thomas glanced at the money and then back to her. 'Are you kidding?'

'It's only for a couple of days.' She pushed the money into his hand.

Thomas calculated it was roughly what he made in a month. It probably should have been more, considering what she was putting him through, but he liked her. Silence confirmed his reluctant agreement.

'Can you give us a few hours alone?' Jen asked.

Thomas glared at them both, his anger rising up. 'This is fucked.'

He pushed past Nathan and grabbed a long coat from a rack behind the door. 'I'm going to my parents' for Christmas. Whatever you've done, I want you out of here in three days.'

Thomas lifted his packed suitcase and left.

Jen could tell Thomas had wanted to slam the door. It wasn't like him to be so upset; he was always so careful and considered in everything he did. She felt bad for him. He was innocent in all of this. Not exactly a good man, but certainly not a bad one.

She turned and looked at David Shaw, who attempted a weak smile.

That feeling again. Something not right about him, something that didn't fit. It had bothered her earlier but it was really nagging now. He was tall and muscular, attractive, yet seemed completely unaware of himself. Like he was wearing a mask. For all she knew he could be another of Zido's goons, but even that didn't add up.

'When we were in that car park,' he spoke in a sombre tone, his expression suggesting this was the first of a thousand questions bubbling under the surface. 'That guy had you in his sights.'

He was right, of course. Her escape was impossible. Anyone

watching would have known that.

'Follow me,' Jen said and walked towards the dining room.

In the hours since her escape, she'd planned her next move. Nothing was simple of course, there were so many things to consider, but one decision had come easily.

Trust no one. Literally, from now on everyone was under suspicion.

'Wait a minute.' He stumbled after her. 'You need to tell me what the Histeridae Project is. That was the deal. Remember?'

They entered the dining room. It was bijou, small and beautifully decorated. Dark red walls lit by studded crystal lights, a gold circular mirror dominating the main wall. In the centre of the room was a dark mahogany table with facing chairs. Jen asked him to sit.

'What are you doing?' he asked nervously.

'I'm going to show you.'

'Show me what?'

There was only one way she could trust him. She placed her bag on the table.

'You wanted to know what Project Histeridae is?' She said, matter-of-factly, lifting the device on the table. 'Well, here it is.'

Like anyone seeing it for the first time, he was immediately transfixed by the gentle rippling movement coming from within.

Jen said, 'Now trust me and stay calm.'

Before he could respond she accessed the Histeridae, and its creeping tendrils appeared and began their search, drifting naturally in the direction of his active mind. The thought strands had come quickly this time, stronger, and she felt calmer, too. He couldn't see the beautiful lights, the private showing her eyes were being treated to.

'That's the Histeridae?' he asked, the fear in his voice obvious.

'Yes. It wasn't just a project name,' she replied, learning to split her focus between talking and searching, her eyes fierce with concentration.

His aura, purple and blue, flashed brightly as the tendrils latched around him. She could feel his uncertainty and confusion. In the car park she had asked one simple question – and he hadn't even known she had been there – this time she would go deeper and was determined to control the exploration.

'What were you doing in my apartment?' she asked, her voice like a choir in his mind.

She concentrated. Unintelligible chatter came first, as it had with Mac, inner monologue spilling from his mind in random bursts. Slowly ideas emerged, thoughts she could latch on to. She was right. Under his tough exterior he was scared and pedaling hard. The truth came like a child's confession, a monologue without breaks.

< *Until now, he hadn't known what the Histeridae was. He was in her apartment to try and find out more about her. He wasn't working for them, he was working alone, had been for some time.* >

She could feel his heart racing and instructed him to close his eyes, to try and relax.

'I can't move,' he said, his voice shaking and uncertain. 'What are you doing!'

He tried to stand. She stopped him.

'I need to be sure I can trust you.'

'What the hell is this?'

Jen pushed a wave of calmness over him, trying to steer his emotions. He seemed to respond, closing his eyes. Jen did the same. It was dark. Not pitch black, though. There were flashes of red, of shapes.

Like a womb.

She began to see things, fragmented visions, as if remembering them for herself. They were his memories, flickering through her like Polaroids scattered in the wind. It was too much to take in, and suddenly feelings were surging through her, too.

Jen frowned and concentrated, trying to slow down the manic carousel of imagery. It was important to stay calm, but that wasn't easy. He mumbled something, this time sounding really scared.

Was he feeling these emotions with her?

The murder. The one he had said he was investigating.

It was his wife's. She was beautiful. His true love.

Jen felt a sickening, crushing sense of loss. His loss. It echoed her own, but had different characteristics, not necessarily deeper, but Jen was sure she hadn't felt anything like it before. There was anger, too. He didn't like to show it.

Nathan.

That was his name — his real one. He was Nathan O'Brien, not David Shaw. Another rush of understanding, as if his mind were a hissing, pressurised container filled with details desperate to escape. The knowledge didn't arrive in a familiar way, instead it came in waves. Tidal. Yes, that was it. The process was like the surf on a shoreline rushing in and then back, revealing hidden messages on the foaming sand. Nathan was afraid, scared all the time.

Jen's heart was pounding. The deeper she went the more likely it felt she would lose herself. Her plan to ensure she could trust him had become a strange, invasive form of voyeurism. She wanted to release him, to pull away from his mind, but was struggling to differentiate her thoughts and emotions from his. She took a deep breath, trying to avoid the panic that was biting at her guts. She focused and tried to visualise leaving his mind, tried to bring back the feeling of entry but in reverse.

A vision arrived. She found herself looking up from the ocean floor at the distant sparkling surface above. She hated diving. For her, the relief of breaking the surface was tangible, of being back in a world where you belong after visiting somewhere forbidden. Escaping Nathan's mind felt similar to that, except she couldn't breathe. Panicked, she began to rise, ignoring the danger of the bends, leaving his thoughts, returning to her own singular state. Rushing, bubbling water became a single tear traveling down her cheek. Sucking in a gasping rush of air, she was back. She shivered and wiped the tear away. She wasn't sure how long the process had taken, but the natural light in the room had dimmed. It could have been hours.

Nathan stared back at her, his eyes glassy.

'What happened?' He was shaking, too. 'What the hell did you just do to me?'

'Do you know how dangerous a body relocation is?' she asked, her anger a welcome way of ignoring her fear. 'What the sentence is if you're caught?'

Nathan's face transformed from upset to completely shocked in an instant. He spaced each word in his response. 'How do you know that?'

How do you tell someone about a device when you don't even understand it yourself?

'The Histeridae reads minds.' It was all she could think to say.

Nathan stood, his legs threatening to buckle, and backed away from her. 'Jesus,' he said, the panic clearly building. 'Are you doing it now? Are you in my head now?'

Jen had to know the truth, know that she could trust him, but the guilt was sitting heavily within her already.

'Nathan,' she said, trying to calm him down. 'It's okay.'

'You know my name!' he screamed, stumbling back against the wall.

'Yes. And a week ago I would have arrested you on the spot for mind relocation and body swapping.' She paused and realised with some certainty that before this was over she might need to do the same. She might need to relocate, to body swap.

It was a sobering thought.

'Whatever that thing is, it's not right,' he said.

Nathan was obviously struggling to accept what had just happened. She could understand that. The Histeridae could do incredible, dangerous things. Invasive things.

He continued, 'There's one thing you seem to be forgetting here. Something you're missing.'

'And what's that?' Jen replied.

'After what you've just done to me, how am *I* ever going to trust *you*?'

CHAPTER 32

'Explain it to me again, Doctor?' Zitagi asked.

The doctor looked uneasy. He walked across the room and took a sip of water. He had been in charge of the Government-funded medical facility for over two years, and in all that time he had never once met anyone from *upstairs*. Now, suddenly his entire department appeared to be doing her bidding. Projected in front of him was an image of skull and brain with red dots, spread like a virus, showing recent activity. 'When used, the weapon leaves a trace on the victim's mind.' He paused, knowing his words would have dark consequences. 'There were signs of something unusual here, but nothing we could use.'

'How long did it take him to die?' she asked.

'Seven minutes.' The doctor sighed. 'It must have been hell.'

Zitagi flicked the lights back on and faced him.

'Hell is where *we* will be if we don't find a solution to combat this threat.' She fixed her stare on him. The doctor knew it was pointless discussing the options; he just needed to do as he was told.

She stepped towards him. 'We need this information.'

The Doctor nodded. 'Yes, I understand, but if we do another extraction there is no guarantee it will give us any more data.' His throat clicked as he swallowed.

'Prep the second subject.' Her voice seemed almost jovial. 'I have every faith in you.'

The Doctor felt his stomach curdle. The patients had been brought in yesterday: Government agents, exposed to some of kind of new mind weapon. That was all they would tell him. Initially, aside from some cuts and bruises, the agents appeared to be in good health. Both had been shot with an energy pulse round, but the effects of those wore off within hours.

Their brain scans, however, told a different story, revealing evidence of some form of neural attack. The weapon – device, whatever it was – had left a clear imprint. It was unlike anything the Doctor had seen before, but a second scan revealed something even more surprising: the imprint was fading. His initial fascination had turned to horror when the woman ordered an immediate mind extraction in order to harvest the information.

'The person who did this to them is a terrorist.' Zitagi spoke quietly this time. 'We have to understand how it works. Sometimes that means collateral damage. Hard decisions.'

The Doctor understood. He had heard this lecture before. Leave the hard decisions to the people who were cold enough to make them.

'The way the brain is accessed,' he said. 'I've never seen anything like it. Yes, I can see a consistent pattern, but all this is new...' He trailed off.

'It's better if you don't think too hard about it. Your job is to extract the data and then focus on the challenge ahead.'

'Challenge?' he asked nervously.

'Yes. Doctor,' she replied, her tone somehow managing to emphasise his lowly position in the overall hierarchy. 'You are going to figure out a way of blocking the device. So it can't be used to harm people again.'

He frowned, his mouth hanging agape.

Zido's face returned to its default granite state and the Doctor knew then that the conversation was over.

'Just find a way to block it.' She walked towards the door and, without looking back, added, 'You've got two days.'

CHAPTER 33

The following day, as the late afternoon sun bleached through Thomas's apartment, Jen watched Nathan's fingers flash over a holographic keyboard, filling a projected screen with lines of code. He was obviously still upset and the mood was heavy.

'You need to accept this connection,' he instructed, accessing her mind augmentation.

Jen saw the request. Admin level. The last time she'd seen one of those was during the set-up procedure six years ago. Everyone had some kind of mind implant. Hers was standard, a small network chip that enabled her mind to access the world and all its devices.

She accepted.

'Try using it again,' he said without looking up.

She attempted to access the local network and shook her head. 'Nothing.'

He pressed a small cube in the centre of the table and the floating screen and keyboard were gone. 'Okay. It's disabled.'

'Do I need to get it physically removed?' she asked nervously.

Nathan stood and stretched. 'No. I've disabled all connections. They can't locate you unless you actually jump onto a network.'

'What about the Hibernation chip?'

'That's passive. It literally gets used once a year to knock the brain into Hibernation. They can't use it to track you.'

There's a lot about that chip we don't know, Jen thought, but decided to keep that to herself for now. He was probably right. She doubted they could track anyone with it, but they *were* using it to search minds. How was she going to tell him that?

Nathan began snooping along Thomas's bookshelf. He picked up a book and leafed through it angrily. He had every right to be upset. The experience of mind searching had been a profound one, for them both. Getting to know a person was supposed to take time, a natural process that humans accept and understand. The Histeridae short-circuited that entire notion. And she hadn't just *seen* inside his mind, she had felt his pain, his grief, his love. Perhaps the biggest problem of all? It was one-way. He hadn't felt or learnt anything about her. It was an unnatural invasion and had left her with a lingering and consuming sense of guilt.

'Thank you,' Jen offered. 'For bringing the Histeridae here safely, for disabling my comms.'

He looked at her blankly. 'You'll get used to it eventually, by the way.'

'What's that?'

'Being cut off.'

It would take some time to adjust. Mind augmentation was everywhere, the only way to access some devices and networks. She removed her contact lenses and felt disconnected, alone.

Nathan picked up a photograph of Thomas. 'How do you know him?' He turned the picture towards her. 'Ex-boyfriend?'

'Er. No,' Jen mumbled, caught off guard. 'Well, kind of.'

Nathan shrugged again; he was doing a lot of that. She watched as he continued nosing around the room. There was so much she wanted to ask but decided to take things slowly. She needed to gain his trust before bombarding him with questions about his wife or the procedure.

Body swapping. Did he really understand the risks? Perhaps

he did. She had felt his determination and loss, those feelings still fresh in her mind. His mind relocation seemed to be holding well. No signs of splintering. That was good. And, he had managed to disable her network chip. He might just be useful after all.

'Where did it come from?' Nathan asked, staring at the Histeridae, its shiny surface radiant in the early evening light, its magic drawing his attention ever inward.

'I don't know, but I'm going to find out,' she replied. 'Nathan. Listen, I am sorry.'

He nodded blankly.

'Really, I am,' she said, more firmly this time. 'But I had to be sure.'

'It was a violation,' he snapped at her, shuffling his feet, embarrassed. 'Sneaking about in someone's mind. It's not fair.'

'You're right.' She was almost pleased to get a response, even if it was anger. 'I won't do it again.'

'It's personal stuff.' He frowned hard, not ready to let it go. 'My wife. My feelings.'

Jen sat quietly, allowing him to vent, finding herself agreeing with him.

'I had a friend,' she said eventually. 'A colleague. His name was Jim McArthur. I trusted him completely, had known him for twenty years, and all that time, he was working for them. The Histeridae showed me that. Without it I would never have known.'

Nathan walked to the window and stared out at the street below. 'Still doesn't make it right though, does it?'

'No. It doesn't.'

There was silence for a while.

'Can I ask you a question?' Jen knew she needed to be gentle, to tread carefully. 'What was your wife's name?'

Nathan stared at her suspiciously.

'I just want to try and do this properly,' Jen offered, 'Start again. Get to know you the normal way.'

She watched him. It seemed like he was physically preparing himself to talk about her. It was a long time before he spoke.

'Katherine,' he said. 'Her name was Katherine.'

'And do you think you could tell me what happened? What she was investigating?'

'I kind of figured you already knew everything.' He tapped the side of his head sarcastically.

'I stopped the minute I knew I could trust you.' She waited, seeing his defences lowering. 'Just start at the beginning. You told me she was investigating something.'

'Yes.' He spoke slowly. 'Links between the Government and Baden Corporation. She had a nose for that sort of thing.'

'What did she find?'

'She'd had a tip-off. Some of the early deals were suspect, huge sums of money. She started digging – she was good at finding that stuff.' Nathan smiled, but there was an obvious pain. He swallowed and continued. 'A few weeks before they killed her, she managed to get a reporter to talk, all off the record, fragments of information, rumours. That's when she first heard about the Histeridae project. She was convinced she was onto something.' He rubbed his hands up and down his face. 'She was right.'

Jen nodded. 'Mac told me the same thing. The Government *own* Baden. Did you know that?'

Nathan shook his head.

'My father's research started it all, helped Baden develop the Hiberchip, and now they're searching us when we hibernate, using the chip to read our thoughts.'

Nathan continued to shake his head.

'What?' Jen's voice was higher than she expected.

'I'm sorry,' he replied. 'But you sound like a crazy conspiracy theorist.'

'I do.' Her thoughts turned to Callaghan. 'But it's true. I've seen it. Search echoes. They're monitoring our thoughts, searching us, and it's all linked to Hibernation and the Histeridae.'

'And Baden.'

'Yes. And Baden.'

'What about data privacy?' Nathan countered. 'The Symbiosis Act? How the hell could all this go unnoticed?'

'If they're all in bed together then the policymakers create their own rules, they cover their tracks. Think about it; after the troubles, the UN were given exclusive powers of governance. Within years we had identity cards, new immigration laws, travel permits, neural facial recognition, you name it.'

'Why though?'

'Why what?'

'Why do it? Why search? The world's going to shit – why do they want to know what we think about it? What difference does it make?'

Jen sighed, it was a good point. 'People were scared. Maybe the UN just saw their chance to make some new rules. "*We need to make the word safer.*"' She was mocking a political debate. '"*Protect ourselves against the global threat.*"'

He nodded towards the Histeridae. 'So, it's served its purpose, then hasn't it? The Hiberchip was developed, and now it's searching away. Why do they want that thing back so badly?'

Jen said, 'It's still a weapon, and they don't fully understand it.'

'Maybe they want to destroy it. Cover their tracks,' Nathan suggested.

'Maybe.'

Now it was Jen's turn to stare out the window. She stood

and looked down on the City, a curious feeling growing inside her. She had never believed in fate, or destiny or any other manmade attempt to make sense of the world. Yet, the events that led them here were accompanied with a sense of interconnectedness; some strange, hidden meaning. The Histeridae, her father, Nathan's wife. A thread, perhaps linked.

'Why did you start all this?' she asked him.

'To find out who murdered my wife,' he answered easily. 'And then…' He stopped himself, frowned and clearly changed what he was about to say, 'Find out the truth.'

'I think they're the same thing. The reason people keep dying is to hide the truth.'

Nathan stared at the floor and shrugged. A few minutes passed. He seemed uneasy, agitated. Here was a man who had started with a single objective: revenge. He had almost said it. Find out who murdered her and kill them. Now it was muddied, confusing, multiple threads threatening to distract him from his goal.

'I won't stand in your way,' Jen said carefully, acting on her hunch.

Nathan looked up. 'How do you mean?'

'If we find out who murdered her, I won't stop you.'

Nathan took a long, deep breath. 'Thank you,' he said finally.

Jen didn't take that lightly. They could take her badge and set her on the run, but deep down she was still a police officer. And yet, here she was telling Nathan that she wouldn't stop him enacting his revenge.

Adaptation, she supposed. It would be necessary if she was going to live through this.

'One will lead to the other,' she said. 'I'm sure of it.'

'And then what?' Nathan replied.

She turned to him, realising that for the first time in as long as she could remember, she was glad for some company, thankful that this strange man, who had appeared out of nowhere, was going to be part of all this.

'Nathan, I think it's up to us to blow this whole thing open,' she said, her determination returning.

The vague hint of a smile crept along the edges of his lips. 'Where do we start?'

Mac's words echoed back through her mind.

'Whatever it is, however deep it goes, it started with your father but it ends with Baden.'

'You said your wife managed to get someone talking. Someone who knew about the money, the dirty deals.' Jen placed her hand on his shoulder. 'We start with the Baden Corporation.'

Nathan nodded and then said, 'By the way.'

Jen looked at him quizzically.

'Happy Christmas.'

CHAPTER 34

The search team were close. Owen Powell gripped the cold railing and peered over the edge of the metal walkway. The water below was rising. Soon the tops of the data servers would slip beneath its silky black surface. He estimated its depth to be about twenty feet now, the rotating yellow security lights only just visible below the surface.

'For God's sake, get me out of here,' he screamed at a panel on the wall, his eyes darting frantically around the steel chamber. A voice answered, young and filled with confidence and reassurance.

'Mr Powell, we are working to locate you. We'll find you.'

Powell made a sound in his throat, an involuntary childlike whimper that scared him even more. How the hell did he get himself into this? A leaking server room deep underground. He found himself staring at his expensive shoes, felt the sweat on his back soaking into his perfectly pressed shirt. He was going to drown in here, locked in, alone. He was the fucking CEO, for God's sake. He was important.

'Sir?' The voice again.

'I'm here,' Powell replied. *Where else would I be?*

'Sir, I need you to look above the door and confirm which server room you are in.'

Powell looked up at the large stenciled letters above the thick steel door.

'457B,' he screamed, 'I'm in 457B.'

Something below him groaned, the sound of steel complaining. It was the kind of sound he associated with ships cracking in two, or submarines about to implode. He leant over the balcony again to see a sudden belch of water and steam followed by a rush from one corner to the other, creating a swirling, pale green foam on the water's surface. The main lights blinked out and the security lights kicked in, bathing him in a hellish red. He imagined himself floating silently in the freezing water, those red lights magnifying his terrified expression, eyes wide open, mouth agape, a bubble dancing from his nostril.

'Get. Me. Out of here.' The desperation and pitch of his voice was increasing.

He heard the distant sound of men and machinery and drilling. Perhaps they were opening the door manually, by force. How long would that take? His mind offered images of his family, his wife. His life outside of the company, one he knew he had ignored. All these years, given to Baden, seemed so pointless now. For what?

Another huge bubble of water surged up from the centre of the room below. A thin mist of water sprayed over him.

'Mr Powell,' the intercom said. 'There is a panel in front of you. Can you please enter your unique ID for me?'

'My what?' His voice was higher than it should be.

'Your identifier pin. We can drill through the locks, but we need to deactivate the security first.'

Powell felt the chill of real fear grip him. He didn't know it. He hadn't needed it for years.

Oh Christ.

The water pushed up through the square grating of the walkway and over his ankles, sending a sudden shock through his legs.

'Sir, we have a team on the other side of the door, we can reach you, but you need to be act quickly.'

'You think I don't fucking know that!' His teeth were banging together uncontrollably, the water almost at his knees.

Think, Owen, for God's sake think.

He began punching numbers. His daughter's birthday.

Red light.

His birthday.

Red light.

Room filling with water. Red lights. Floating dead. Red lights.

'Oh Jesus. I can't remember it.' He thumped his hand against the wall, tears welling up in his eyes.

Wait. Wait! It was the day he became CEO, wasn't it? The most important day of his life.

He pressed it into the console, his finger almost slipping on the last digit. Green light.

'That's it!' he screamed, chest tightening against the cold. 'Get me out of here.'

'The team are drilling now. Stand by.'

The water pushed and swirled, threatening to drag him sideways and under. He looked around the steel room, filling up, black, freezing. There was no way they were getting through the door. It was twelve inches thick. He felt the water lifting him and gasped against its harsh chill, screaming out, begging for escape. His head bumped against the ceiling of the server room. He pressed his hands against it, part of him hoping it might move, that something would happen, something would give. He panted, crying out as the water filled the space. Owen Powell, CEO of Baden Corporation, screamed and thrashed, drowning in a mass of silvery bubbles.

He thrust himself forwards, taking a massive gulp of air, his scream suddenly finding a sound in the blackness surrounding him. Then, a hand, touching him, warm and dry.

'Darling, it's okay.'

Powell's heart felt as though it was about to pop from his chest. He was soaked in sweat but otherwise dry, surrounded by air, not water.

His wife held his shoulders. 'Darling, it was a dream, it's okay, you're safe.' She flicked on the sidelight and he saw their large bedroom. Expensive, plush and as described: safe. He exhaled loudly, his body heaving one singular sob. The relief was huge, but he couldn't recall ever crying in front of his wife; he certainly wasn't going to start now.

'Are you okay?' his wife asked.

I thought I was dead, I really thought I was dead.

'I'm fine.' He stood and walked to the bathroom. 'Bad dream, that's all. Go back to sleep.'

Facing the mirror, trying to compose himself, he fought the urge to cry.

Red light. Drowning.

He swallowed hard, rubbing his face, not wanting to close his eyes. He shuffled out of the bedroom, deciding on a glass of water. There was no way he was sleeping, not for a while.

Walking the stairs in darkness, bare feet padding on the soft carpet, he chose not to activate the interior lights. He stopped in the hallway and approached the window, pressing his face to the glass, breath creating clouds. All was quiet. Tall trees swaying, lit from below, surveillance, cameras, an eight-foot-high perimeter wall. He and his wife had lived here for three years without incident. Security was tight and it seemed people got the message. This was private property; keep out. He walked across the hallway and into the kitchen, the dream still bothering him.

Jen was rigid, pressed up against the exterior wall of his house. As Powell walked away she closed her eyes, breathing out heavily, heart thumping. Accessing him during his sleep, without alerting him, had been difficult. She had been about to tell Nathan they would have to come up with a new plan when she'd managed it. Suddenly, like a key clicking and then twisting in a stubborn lock she was inside his dreams, inside his mind. Then it was simply a case of suggestion, of creating the right dream, or in his case, nightmare. Convince him that he was trapped inside the Shiryaevo Vault, fill it with water and let panic do the rest. The plan had worked. She had Baden Corporation's vault number – where they kept their dirty secrets – and also Powell's manual override code to get inside.

His sudden jolt awake had left her with a strange sensation, though, as if she were stuck in a layer somewhere between the dream and the reality. Strange, floaty. She needed to concentrate, release Powell and slip away. If anyone knew she had been here, then the whole plan was screwed.

As she struggled to focus she heard a voice. It was distant, but it made sense to her somehow, muffled words forming a recognisable sound. With increased urgency the voice ripped through the fabric of her state. It was Nathan. She tapped her ear and heard a short blip followed by some interference.

'I'm here,' she said, not knowing how long she'd been standing there in a daze.

'Where the hell have you been?' he barked. 'I've trying to reach you.'

'What's up?'

'We've got trouble.'

CHAPTER 35

Jen saw them: two men emerging from the long shadows, cutting across Owen Powell's well-maintained lawn. His warning had hit her like a slap on cold skin. Her body began to shake as clarity returned in a mixture of nerves and adrenalin.

'Why are they here?' Jen whispered.

'I missed an outgoing alert,' he replied. 'They're security. The house wasn't breached so they haven't alerted the owners. Not yet, anyway.'

Nathan had deactivated the security systems but obviously missed something. It didn't bode well for the tasks that lay ahead.

She tried to think. The guards would perform a scan, meaning they would pick her up any second. She needed to get across the lawn and back over the wall.

The dream. It's fading.

Jen knew it was critical she remembered, but like any dream, the clarity was shifting, becoming something else, something hazy.

The guards were close now. She didn't dare speak again.

427B.

No wait. 457B. 457B. The date he became CEO.

She repeated it over and over in her head. Powell had delivered, shown her where Baden kept their secrets. Jen had recognised it instantly, hidden under snow-covered mountains, wrapped by a silver river. The Shiryaevo Vault. Now she knew the vault number and code – but there was more. During her search, Powell had revealed something else. Something unexpected. As he drowned, believing he was about to die, he had revealed his biggest secret, something he would never tell a soul.

Powell knew what the Hibernation chip was *really* designed to do.

'Don't move,' one of the guards said.

Jen raised her hands but concentrated on the Histeridae. Inside her bag, unseen by the guards, it glowed, its intense power flowing through her. She wondered if it worked that way for everyone, some kind of bond that grew stronger each time. The men became outlines in the darkness, unaware of the beautiful light show Jen was seeing. Like the roots of a luminous tree in search of water, the whispery thought tendrils began their work.

Jen let them guide her, marveling at their organic beauty as they shot, swirling across the porch and out towards the men. Spinning tunnels of light gripped the first guard's mind before jumping across to his companion. Jen let out an involuntary gasp, a mixture of relief and triumph. Her power over the Histeridae was increasing. She was now connected to three minds; she had created some kind of neural network.

'Fuck me,' she whispered.

'Say again?' Nathan replied, confused.

She ignored him. Her vision, a kaleidoscope of images, her mind filled with voices, concerns and thoughts, all rallying for attention. Mental stimuli poured in from all three men. Powell in the kitchen, drinking water, watching the box, and the two guards approaching the house. She could see what they were seeing, through their eyes.

No, no. Stop!

It was too much.

Something was wrong.

Jen's heart was banging. *I'm overloading,* she thought. *I can't do it.* The men in her newly formed neural network were breathing fine, but she had stopped. Finally gasping for air, as if she'd just surfaced from the bottom of a pool, she understood. The key was relaxation – not easy considering her situation – but she needed to stay calm, keep her heart rate down and concentrate.

The effort was mental, not physical. The two guards were held, fixed, but she could feel them struggling against her. She focused, the crackling purple streams around their heads glowing brightly as she concentrated. She reassured them, working on simply holding them still as she slowed her heart rate. She then shifted her attention to Powell. He was watching the screen in his kitchen and eating cereal now, unaware of the silent battle taking place on his lawn. Jen carefully retreated from his mind, the thought trails drifting like cinematic mist played backwards through the corridor. Jen tried to split her mind, to separate the information she was receiving.

Two security guards.

She managed to block out their visual input, tuning purely into their minds. Once there, she began an orchestrated form of conversation between them, discussing the fact the grounds appeared to be clear.

They both agreed.

They nodded.

She assured them it was okay to head back to base. They relaxed, turned and walked away.

As the gates closed and the final glimmering strands dissipated, Jen allowed herself a smile. She wasn't sure if the fake conversation between them had been verbal or not, but that didn't matter. She had managed to control the situation and couldn't deny that right now she felt unstoppable.

Nathan was parked two streets away. By the time she reached him, that confidence had faded. She didn't feel well; her heart was pounding in her ears. She dropped to the pavement.

'Are you okay?' Nathan crouched beside her. 'What happened?'

'I'm fine,' she said, gasping for breath.

He helped her up, guided her into the passenger seat and waited until her breathing settled.

'It's the Histeridae.' Her voice was thin and scratchy. 'I controlled three people, like a network or something, but it takes it out of you.'

He nodded and waited.

Eventually, he couldn't wait any longer and asked, 'So, did you find anything?'

She smiled, remembering the secrets Powell had revealed, what the Hibernation chip was designed to do. 'Yes. More than I was expecting. We hit the jackpot. Seriously.'

'Go on.'

'Searching was just the beginning.'

★ ★ ★

Nathan drove, the wipers working overtime against a downpour that had been hammering for the last twenty minutes. Jen hadn't talked much since leaving the mansion. Half an hour ago she couldn't even move.

'Shit.' He sighed, looking ahead at the long queue of traffic, searching for a reason, a roadblock or checkpoint. He couldn't see anything. 'As long as they aren't scanning, I'll stay on this road.'

When they finally crawled past the large construction site, the traffic jam made sense. It was one of many Hibernation centres being built across London in preparation for the universal rollout. Men in hard hats clambered around, glistening in the inky wet night. Huge machinery hammered and welded. This building would be home to city dwellers during their twelve-month cycle. Functional and practical. Human resource reduction, intrinsically linked to your location, to services, to the power grid.

Jen looked past him, into the darkness. 'I found out something tonight,' she said cryptically. 'Something important.'

Nathan nodded, his eyes following hers as she watched the men moving around the site like ants; organised and focused. 'Tell me.'

'They want control.' Her voice was slow and distant, heavy with the weight of information and what it meant.

Nathan turned to her. 'How do you mean?'

'It isn't about searching,' she said, her voice trembling with raw emotion. 'That was just the beginning.'

'The beginning of what?'

'They don't just want to know what you're *thinking*. They want to *tell* you what to think.' Her voice was getting louder. 'During Hibernation. Don't you see? They want to put ideas *in*.'

Jen squinted out over the building site, her distant expression giving way to one of stoic determination. Nathan was suddenly struck by her beauty, a timeless quality that went beyond the obvious allure men experienced on meeting her.

She turned to him, reflected raindrops streaking down her face.

'The Hibernation chip works both ways,' she said. 'That's what Hibernation is all about. They're brainwashing us.'

CHAPTER 36

The rain finally stopped around 3am. The roads were practically deserted. Another ten minutes and they would be back at Thomas's. Jen wasn't in the mood for any more challenges.

Nathan stared straight ahead, his expression unchanged. 'All I'm asking is how much of this did you get from him, and how much of this is your idea?'

'What are you implying?' She frowned.

'I'm not saying I don't believe you.' He flicked an eyebrow and shrugged a little. 'I'm just saying that we need proof.'

Jen laughed. 'You think I don't know that? I'm a police officer.'

Her words hung between them and Jen was reminded that her life as a Duality officer was over.

'I *was* a police officer,' she corrected herself.

They passed over a crossroads. Green lights all the way.

'Look, I know it sounds unbelievable —'

'You're talking about Hibernation,' Nathan growled. 'It's going to save mankind, Jen. Our backs are against the wall and it's our only chance. Everyone knows that. And now you're saying it's all about mind control, about brainwashing?' He raised his voice, the frustration clear. 'Why the hell would they do that?'

'I don't know,' she said, flatly.

Nathan continued, 'People are hibernating because they

know it's right. They don't need to *make* us. Everyone knows it's our only chance.'

'I don't know,' Jen said again, 'but I'm going to find out. With or without you.'

Nathan tutted, 'Oh, let's just waltz into GCHQ or MI5 or something and ask them to hand over their dirty laundry. Just ask them to spill their guts on this great conspiracy.'

'You're tired,' she said. 'You don't know what you're talking about.'

'Oh, fuck you,' he replied sharply.

They spent the rest of the journey in silence. Truth was they were both tired, and whilst Jen didn't like to admit it, the less said now the better. Her thoughts wandered. The Hibernation chip. He did have a point. Why go to such lengths to control people when there were clearly bigger problems? People were already united. Accelerated warming was a global threat, a common foe. They didn't need control – did they? Her thoughts moved to Callaghan. He had sounded crazy, but he was right, and now he was dead. She shook it away. Sleep would come soon. She needed it. Nathan was still scowling, gripping the wheel, knuckles white.

Interesting, she thought. *The schoolteacher has a bite after all.*

★ ★ ★

Jen awoke. It was midmorning and the smell of coffee and bacon hung in the air. She sighed and rubbed her face. It had been a while since she'd eaten and she was starving. She could feel an aching in her bones like the first few days of flu. The Histeridae, she supposed, must have drained her. She lifted the sheets and pulled herself out of bed. As she stood in her pyjamas and stretched, a worrying thought crossed her mind.

Could it be harming me? Maybe even killing me?

She heard Nathan's voice and felt bad again. He'd told her to fuck off. She smirked at the memory. It had been quite funny, actually, and it was good to know he had some fight.

'Jen, get in here.' Nathan's voice was raised and clearer now. 'Quickly.'

She walked into the lounge. Thomas was back and stood with Nathan watching the box.

'What is it?' she asked.

Nathan was shaking his head. Jen approached and saw her face on the screen. She ascertained two things quickly: they were watching the news, and it was bad.

'Oh, shit.' She began to process what the news reporter was saying.

Jennifer Logan, a long-serving Duality officer, is wanted for the murder of Peter Callaghan…'

Her image moved to the side as two more images appeared.

'…and James McArthur. She is armed and dangerous and police are advising, if you see her, not to approach her directly. Contact them immediately…'

Thomas turned the volume down. 'People might have seen you,' he said, his face ashen. 'They might have seen you coming *here*.'

Jen stared at the screen. Peter's picture was an old one, Mac's recent.

Mac. Dead.

She'd seen it in his eyes when she'd left him, had suspected he might take his own life, but decided instead to focus on seeing him again. That day would never come.

She noticed beads of cold sweat on Thomas's forehead as he began pacing the room.

'Did you kill them?' he snapped.

'Please, Thomas. Of course I didn't.' She took a step towards him. 'Calm down.'

'Calm down?' he screamed. 'I could go to prison for this.' He stopped as if considering what that actually meant, a confused look washing over him. 'To prison, for *you*?'

Jen searched for the right words, but they never came, perhaps because there weren't any. Thomas marched off and a few seconds later could be heard crashing around his bedroom. Probably packing. Again. She felt sorry. He was innocent and now implicated in this mess. Thomas had meant something to her once, back in a previous life. He had been her window into another world, one that she could never truly inhabit but loved nonetheless. They'd had fun, but that all that was over now. She would offer him more money and persuade him to disappear for a while.

Turning to Nathan, she said, 'I'm in serious shit.'

'I know,' he replied, stone-faced. 'We both are.'

The moment for saying sorry about the previous night came and went. Instead Nathan just smiled lamely and said. 'It's going to be okay.'

Jen couldn't see how. It had been hard to move about before; it would be almost impossible now. She felt trapped and frustrated, and later, as she watched Thomas leave his apartment, despair joined the chorus.

Peter Callaghan, Jim McArthur.

Dead.

She needed to figure out her next move, and quickly – before their names were added to that list.

CHAPTER 37

It snowed solidly for three days. Jen woke on the last day of December to an icy grey London cut in two by a blood-red sunrise. It was below freezing, but that didn't bother her. She had known real cold. National service had made sure of that.

It was times like these when climate change could seem like a distant problem. It was hard to imagine in the fresh chill of winter that some regions were now uninhabitable dustbowls. She sighed. Of all the things she was questioning or doubting, accelerated climate change wasn't one of them. There were enough independent accounts across the globe to reassure her it wasn't part of the conspiracy. Temperatures were screwed at both ends of the spectrum. Mankind had been on the brink of extinction. Until *the answer* arrived. Until Hibernation.

'Shit,' she said into the empty room. She dressed quickly. 'If Hibernation is the answer, what's the *real* question?'

She joined Nathan. He was at the lounge window enjoying the silence only a heavy deluge of snow can bring. On the dining table sat a steaming cafetière and two cups. She was amazed at how much coffee he drank in a day. The news was still on, but the volume was down. Her face was appearing less frequently now. Hard to keep a story alive without something juicy to add each day. Laying low wasn't really her style, but it had been necessary. Until now.

'I know what we need to do,' Jen said.

Nathan walked to the table and poured some of the coffee. 'Good morning,' he said, demanding manners.

'Yes, sorry.' She smiled and joined him. 'Good morning.'

They sat for a while and Jen waited until Nathan seemed happy for her to start.

'You said we needed proof that the Hibernation chip is being used to control people. I think I know how to get it.'

'Go on,' Nathan said, pouring yet another coffee.

'Powell knew their chip could be used to search and manipulate people. Baden Corporation turned a blind eye, took the money. The Government paid them off and some people got very rich, very quickly. So, inside the CEO's dream, I *suggested* he could help me find evidence, maybe even locate my father's original research.'

Nathan lowered his cup and stared at her. 'And what did he say?'

'He didn't say anything, he showed me. In his dream, his nightmare, he showed me a place where Baden keep *all* their secrets – their *dirty laundry*, as you put it. And I know where it is.'

The location was the Shiryaevo Vault, a privately owned facility in Russia. Jen had spent some time there early in her career, and it had taught her many things, the most important of which was the value of useful land. Russia had plenty, and when the world went to shit, they delivered year-round farming on a scale previously unimaginable. Russia had become powerful again, but it wasn't just because of agriculture. Large-scale data and computing operations required huge amounts of energy and needed to be kept cool all year round. The vault was the biggest of them all. As she filled him in, it became clear that he wasn't convinced.

'There must be an easier way,' he protested.

'There isn't. I saw it. It makes sense.'

Nathan paused, drank the remainder of his coffee, and eyed the kettle. 'Putting aside for a second that the Shiryaevo Vault is one of the most secure installations in the world, it's in *Russia*, Jen. I mean, how the hell would we even get there? Especially now.'

'Okay,' she said, doing her best to sound confident, knowing he wasn't ready to hear her unorthodox travel plans. 'Let's just say we *can* get to Samara and I get inside. We get the evidence we need, Nathan. We can take them on.'

'But there is no way we can do it.' He was almost shouting. 'It's imposs –'

'I accept you can't hack a place like that from the outside,' Jen argued, 'but we have the Histeridae. If I can get inside, I can give you local access. Thanks to Powell, I know the vault number and I have his access code.'

Nathan shrugged and looked at the floor. 'I'm not that good. I wouldn't even know where to start.'

'You said you wanted proof.' She was up and pacing. 'Well, this is where we find it. Powell was scared of what Baden have hidden down there. My guess? We find evidence that proves the Government are using Hibernation to control people. Don't you see? Then we have a chance!'

Nathan locked eyes on her. 'I get it. We need evidence, and maybe, just maybe, it's down there, but there's a really big fucking problem. I'm not a professional hacker and you're wanted by every camera on earth.'

He was right: her plan, this crazy idea, all hinged on their ability to get to Russia and hack one of the most secure facilities on the planet. She could easily forget that Nathan hadn't been specifically assigned to infiltrate this target. Her days of Government teams and drafted experts were over. He was just some guy who knew his way around interfaces – handy enough, she supposed, but also sloppy. The mansion security guards were a good example of that. She thought again about the Histeridae. Perhaps it alone would give them a fighting chance. Breaking into the vault, eluding armed guards… she could feel fear lurking, trying to push its way to the surface, but did her best to hide it from him. This *had* to work. They didn't have any other options.

'My father managed to break the Histeridae out of GCHQ. I'm learning how to use it, getting better each time. Stronger. I controlled three people at once. We can do this.' Her eyes tightened. 'We have to.'

Nathan was up and making more coffee. Jen knew she needed to tread carefully. Getting to Russia would require a fake identity and the correct travel permits. That meant becoming the kind of person she used to hunt. She needed to become invisible.

She took a long deep breath, knowing her only option was Lynch Taylor.

And he wanted her dead already.

CHAPTER 38

A taxi stopped near a cluster of tall warehouses in London's dockland region. Jen paid and stepped out, cramping against the bitterly cold air. Like most of the people she would see this evening, the driver wasn't augmented or chipped. The criminal underbelly of London had chosen to remain device-free.

A smart move, she thought with some irony.

She hadn't told Nathan she was coming here. Managing his mental state was important now and tonight's meeting was a dangerous move. If Nathan had known what she was walking into he could easily melt down, and although she didn't want to admit it, she needed him – perhaps more than he needed her.

She looked around. It was January 3 and the snow was gone, replaced by patches of depressing brown slush pushed up against mounds of grey ice. Large storage facilities towered around her, dark and deserted. In the distance she could hear the muffled thudding of a bass drum. The Docklands, largely ignored during the extensive redevelopment, now consisted of low-quality storage, underground clubs and rundown bars. The perfect place to exploit the needs of your average man. She found herself wishing she had the Histeridae but knew she couldn't risk bringing it here. She would have to rely on good old-fashioned greed and bribery. She walked towards the muffled music, hoping her contact would show up – and that she would make it out of here alive.

She arrived at the agreed meeting place, a small red sign fizzing in the damp air above her. She checked the time: 9.49pm. She was early. There were a few people, heads down, moving quickly. This wasn't a good place. It was for drinking and vice and you didn't linger. She was relieved when a man approached her, heavy set, middle aged and smartly dressed. His hair was white and thin and lay scraped over his head like flattened candy-floss. He looked her up and down, and when he spoke his lack of dental hygiene was obvious.

'Follow me,' he said in a deep, gravelly voice.

'Where are we going?' Jen asked.

The man didn't reply. He looked around, his puffy yellow eyelids seemingly accustomed to the gloom.

'This way.' He shuffled off, mumbling something under his breath. Jen decided not to attempt any further conversation. They continued in silence, the hunched figures around them thinning out. The man took a left turn into a narrow alley that smelt faintly of moist ash and rotting vegetables. Her senses were wound tight, working every sound, shadow and angle. Although the alley appeared deserted, Jen could feel eyes watching them.

The man was only slightly ahead of her. She played various scenarios through in her mind. There were many ways to break a limb, and she was ready if he made a sudden move towards her. The man stopped outside two dark blue steel doors. Old posters had been ripped from the brickwork around it and there was music coming from inside.

'This is it.' His voice was impossibly low. 'I'll wait here.'

Jen thanked him.

'Oh, and you'll be quite popular in there.'

She looked at him quizzically.

'You being a woman,' he added. 'With hair like that.'

The man lingered too long on her breasts and then banged loudly on the door three times. As it opened, Jen found herself walking in.

She entered the dimly lit bar, eyes adjusting to the gloom. The place was a nauseating hybrid of American truck stop and Italian restaurant and smelt like sour beer and ashtrays. In the corner, an antique jukebox, its florescent tubes, once vibrant, now succeeded in framing it like some kind of infected rainbow. Jen counted ten people spread amongst the circular tables. The establishment felt big but it was too dark to tell. Jen approached a steel bar that ran the length of the furthest wall. The barman eyed her with suspicion.

'Double whiskey with ice,' she ordered, sitting on a faded leather bar-stool.

'On the rocks,' the barman corrected her.

She nodded, raising an eyebrow. *Just get me the fucking drink. Asshole.*

She'd been given no further instructions, so she began memorising the room, planning her escape if it all went south. She missed the security that Duality bought to a situation like this and considered the policewoman she used to be. And there it was.

Used to be.

Her job had been her life. The barman placed the drink in front of her and she knocked it back, enjoying the harsh burn on her throat. *I'm not a policewoman anymore,* she thought with bitterness.

There was a mirror behind the bar, just below the inverted optics, and she used it to study the room behind. She could see at least two men watching her. She turned as another man approached. He asked her to follow him and they left the bar, the man ducking under an archway in the corner of the room and entering a smaller, private area. Jen scanned her surroundings. In the centre a circular table, surrounded by tall, purple velvet seating, a gold chandelier hung above. It reminded Jen of a cheap strip club. A thin man sat in the middle, flanked by two others. Jen was frisked thoroughly. The thin man stared at her, eyes shadowed in deep sockets.

'Thank you for agreeing to meet me,' Jen said, as confidently as she could manage. The man looked bored and flicked his bony fingers towards the seat in front of her. She sat down and he continued.

'How could I not?' His faced curled inwards. 'You've got fucking nerve coming here, that's for sure.' He paused and smiled, his red lips stretching over his teeth. 'But honestly? Jennifer Logan? Needing my help? I'm intrigued.'

The man opposite her was Carl Taylor – or, as he was more commonly known, Lynch – and Jen didn't take her eyes off him. She'd been part of the team that convicted Lynch of human trafficking. He'd done eight years. The case had also exposed two crooked police officers and unraveled an elusive, organised crime network in the Central London area. Lynch had every reason to hate her and even more reason to want her dead.

'I need transit to Russia,' she said loudly over the music. 'Can you do it?'

The two men on either side of Lynch eyed their boss carefully. Lynch smiled, his white skin almost translucent under the lights.

'There's no fucking way, Logan,' he said, his London accent attacking each word. 'You're one hot package right now, and the reward on you is too good.'

The men looked back at her confidently.

'Give me just one good reason why I shouldn't hand you in,' Lynch said playfully, clearly enjoying his moment. 'Or why I don't just kill you now?'

Eight years inside and Jen could feel the hatred leaching from him.

'I can get information on Conrad,' she said, her lips shaking into a smile. 'I can tell you where he is.'

Lynch frowned, leant forward, resting his chin against his long fingers, and began stroking his lips inwards. 'You're full of surprises, aren't you.'

Conrad Fowler had been Lynch's right-hand man for years, but when caught and pressured, he cut a deal that put Lynch and the rest of his crew behind bars. For that kind of betrayal people expected retribution to be swift, but Fowler had somehow managed to evade Lynch and disappear. The money ploughed into finding him had become almost legendary in criminal circles.

Lynch seemed to drift away mentally for a moment, until finally he let out a long, deep breath.

'And I thought I was going to get to play with you tonight.'

Jen didn't want to think about what that might mean. Lynch gestured for his men to leave, and when they were alone, Jen asked him again. 'Will you do it?'

Lynch shook his head, tutting, his outstretched finger flicking from side to side. 'Now, now, Logan,' he said, mocking her. 'Not so fast.'

'I need ID and transit to Samara. In return I give you Fowler.' She added, 'You've got nothing to lose.'

'Maybe. Maybe not.'

'Get me to Samara,' she said, 'and you have my word. I will deliver Fowler to you on a plate.'

Jen knew what was important to people like Lynch. He might be a slippery, evil son of a bitch, but shit-suckers like him valued trust and honour above all else. He wanted Fowler more than he wanted her dead. That was the gamble, and it seemed to be paying off.

Lynch tipped his head back and screamed. 'Fuck.' He was laughing but was clearly annoyed. 'You got me good, Logan. Rock and a hard place.'

'No maybes,' Jen said clearly.

'Okay. Okay,' he said, flapping his large hands around. 'It's more than you deserve, but I can get you to Moscow.'

'No good. I'm taking all the risks.' She realised with unease that he *wanted* her to persuade him. He wanted to play games. She could see him searching for a way to kill her *and* get the information on Fowler. She said, 'And you get him. Finally.'

Lynch chewed his tongue, his black eyes glistening and cutting into her. Playtime was over.

'I can get you on a cargo plane of farm workers,' he said dryly. 'It flies into Ufa.'

'Ufa?' Jen said doubtfully. 'Never heard of it.'

'It's the closest I can get you,' he snapped. 'Take it or leave it.'

'What about Kryazh Air Force Base?' It was small, near Samara, and the one she'd had in mind all along.

'Sure. If you want to get caught, go there.'

Jen couldn't visualise the distance between Ufa and Samara. Traveling across Russia would be difficult, especially in January. Icy conditions and her inability to travel via conventional routes increased the chance of failure exponentially. Jen swallowed, unsure of her next move.

'How far from Samara?' she asked, knowing his response wouldn't be helpful.

'Jesus, Logan!' Lynch hissed loudly, spraying small globules of spit over her. 'Beggars. Choosers. It's the best I can do.'

Jen closed her eyes and nodded slowly.

'And it won't be cheap, either, a fake ID and retinals. Plus, I'll need to pay people off on both sides. It will work, but it's going to cost you.' He paused, enjoying his moment, reveling in her desperation. 'It's going to cost you a lot.'

'How much is a lot?'

'Sixty,' he said quickly.

'Are you joking?'

He smiled, sat back slowly and folded his arms. 'It would have been cheaper if I hadn't done eight years, Logan.'

This was payback. It was the best she was going to get.

'When?'

His wide, sickening grin was back. 'Three days,' he said, clearly pleased with himself. 'Be ready.'

★ ★ ★

It was early. Nathan stared at his screen and cracked his fingers. 'Hacking' was an ugly word, something his students would use at the start of their course. He guided them towards more elegant terms, ones that suggested grace and some level of artistry. Hackers hacked, and often their motives were monetary or just plain malicious. What he had taught – in a life before this madness – he considered an art form.

Most of his students would go on to be security experts – white hats, as they were known – and they, of course, would fight the black hats. The terminology was oversimplified, something invented by people in suits who needed a simple analogy to describe a complicated world, but it was true. It was chess. A game. Good against bad. Sneakers against criminals.

He thought back to a challenge he had once given his students, something he called 'Gap Assembly.'

On that occasion, the brief had been to 'assemble' detailed plans for the recently built Stadium of Light in Copenhagen. It had been constructed to celebrate the 2076 Olympic Games and was a terrorist target from bid through to completion. Each plan, document, blueprint, quote and signature had been logged, encrypted and securely stored.

The claim, at the time, had been that all data connected to the project was impossible to hack. A few years later, his team – albeit in complete and glorious secrecy – had proven them wrong.

He likened it to an artist he had seen once. The man had created an artwork on a huge canvas using the tiniest of dots. Stand close and you could see the technique, the individual presses of a pen, but take a step back and a landscape appeared, an illusion rich with depth and texture.

Assembly was similar; it involved the gathering of tiny packets of information. For every secure document, there was always a trail, something that wasn't secure, a sketch, a proposal, a tweak to a piece of construction. Each piece of data formed a picture that made sense as a whole, the gaps often a case of simple guesswork. Nathan hoped the blueprint for the vault would reveal itself in the same way: an architectural drawing bought together using skill, technique and old-fashioned gut instinct.

The cursor on his screen winked, taunting him to start.

He got to work, deciding to hit a multitude of possible sources but spread it out over the next few days. Within hours he saw two files connecting and smiled.

The assembly was underway, dot by dot.

CHAPTER 39

Zitagi stood outside the office and calmed her breathing.
Summoned.

She had sped across town meticulously preparing her answers, her mind trawling the facts. Nothing happened without reason; each singular act was connected to another, even if sometimes it was hard to see. Logan had been to Owen Powell's house. That meant she had made the connection between Baden and the Histeridae. She was better than Zido had expected, a worthy opponent. She checked her dress and shoes and knocked confidently three times.

'Come,' his voice bellowed from inside.

In a world of buzzers, passes and security systems, Victor Reyland was a man who liked to keep things simple, old-fashioned even.

She entered his office, a large corner suite with high ceilings and huge windows spanning the length of two walls. The hum of the air conditioning fought to maintain the low temperature he seemed to prefer. Reyland stood looking out over the city. He was a tall man and at seventy-two considered to be middle-aged, which was laughable. He was fitter than most fifty-year-olds. His rank no longer had a title within the agency, and like any good leader, if you stepped out of line he wouldn't correct you. You would do that yourself.

'Zido, it's good to see you.' His voice was warm but he

didn't turn to greet her. She joined him by the window, her mouth dry.

'It's beautiful, isn't it?' he said, not moving an inch.

She looked out and studied the huge buildings towering almost a kilometre high. Airships and transporters blinked across the late afternoon sky. Beauty wasn't something Zido could appreciate easily. It felt like weakness.

'It is, Sir,' she answered obediently. 'Very.'

She could feel that something was wrong, a hairline crack of doubt within him, and knew how important it was to fix that before it grew into something that couldn't be repaired.

He continued to stare out of the window. 'When we bury a problem, we don't expect it to come back and haunt us. And if it does, we control it.'

'I will get it back,' she said confidently.

He turned looked at her. 'I don't doubt that.'

Zitagi hid the surge of relief that washed over her. Reyland walked over to a small chrome table and invited her to sit. She obliged and Reyland stared at her, his eyes unblinking, paused in time. He waited for her to swallow and then poured a glass of water.

'You are still confident of retrieving it?' he said, handing her the glass.

She nodded. 'Yes, Sir, I am. Absolutely.'

'Good.' He paused, eyes like liquid steel. 'Tell me about Logan. What's her next move?'

Zido needed to reassure him, and quickly. 'She's working alone but she'll want to make connections. She will need to. The next time she surfaces we will be ready.'

He smiled a little. 'Ah, yes. Your little experiment.'

'We are close, Sir. A few more days and we will have a way of blocking the Histeridae —'

'Callaghan, the chase, the guards and now McArthur. It's a

trail, Zido,' he said. 'You know how these things can unravel.'

'I assure you, I will find her and this will all be over. Soon.'

He leant forward, smile gone, his expression like stone. 'I'm getting heat from upstairs. *I* know you can handle this, but they want to team you with Phillips, turn things up a notch.'

Zitagi nodded and cleared her throat, unsure she had heard him correctly.

'Phillips?' she said calmly.

That fucking idiot. Over my dead body.

Something buzzed, Reyland's secretary reminding him for the third time he was late for an appointment. They stood.

'Don't worry about Phillips,' Reyland said, grabbing his jacket. 'I will stall them. Just don't mess it up and keep me informed.'

She nodded.

Finally, just before he left the room, he added, 'The body count. Keep it low.'

Their meeting was over. Zitagi entered the executive elevator elegantly and with a calm demeanour, but by the time she reached the ground floor her anger was boiling.

Jim. Fucking. McArthur.

She blamed him for most of this mess. He had been weak, unable to make the tough decisions when it mattered. And now Phillips? That weaselly little shit had been snapping at her heels for years. The very fact they were even considering him made her seethe. The anger passed, as it always did, and by the evening her familiar cold clarity had returned. She knew what she needed to do. Reyland was putting his faith in her and she wasn't about to let him down. When she pledged her life to the cause, she'd meant it, *unlike some.* Her remit was more important than anyone would ever know, and Jennifer Logan was not going to stand in the way of that.

Zitagi would be ready, and this time she wouldn't waste

energy trying to capture her. This time she would kill her and take back the Histeridae. Murder. It was easier sometimes. And then, when that was done, she would ensure that nobody, especially Phillips, got close to her affairs again.

CHAPTER 40

Jen had never been good at staying in one place too long. Hiding at Thomas's had been particularly difficult, the atmosphere a disconcerting blend of functional and distrustful. She had tried to explain to Nathan why she hadn't told him about Lynch, why she met him alone, but he remained angry. As she watched him stuffing clothes and equipment into a hard-shell case, she realised what she had done was wrong. Whether she liked it or not, they were a team and she needed to be more open with him, needed to trust him. He was standing now, arms folded, studying the map that was opened up on the table. She joined him.

'When I'm done, we meet here, on this road,' she said, tapping the pickup point. 'Just North of Kurumoch.'

He nodded. 'And then we hide and wait.'

There was a pause, as if he were about to say something else. Instead he rolled the map roughly and continued packing. They had been over the plan a few times but decided not to torture themselves anymore. It was full of holes and unknowns that no amount of planning was going to fill or make right.

They would travel separately. Jen would fly into Ufa Airport posing as a farm worker. Security at Ufa was an unknown, but workers were shipped out quickly and regularly to the various food production plants in the area. She would need to avoid detection, stay away from conventional routes and make her way north on foot, picking up a train on the trans-Siberian route to Samara. From Samara it was a ten-hour hike across the Zhiguli Mountains to drop straight down onto the target: the Shiryaevo Vault. The plan required improvisation at nearly every step. It was dangerous, but the only plan that offered a chance of remaining undetected – and also, importantly, the only plan that retained an element of surprise.

For Nathan it was simple: take a commercial flight into Kurumoch International and find a hotel in the nearby town of Tolyatti. He had assembled basic floor layouts of the Vault, and once Jen was inside he would be able to guide her using close-range communication. She would enable him to hack from the inside.

'You know we might not find anything, right?' he said carefully.

'We have the number of the server room and the code. We'll find *something*.'

Later that evening, bags were packed and there was nothing else to do but wait. Nathan pushed the remaining food around his plate. They hadn't talked much during dinner.

'What was it like?' she asked, 'leaving your life behind?'

Nathan curled his lip and shrugged. 'In the end I didn't have much of a life to leave, I guess.'

Jen cast her mind back. Was it really possible that only a month ago her life had seemed so on track? So full of purpose? He looked up at her, his right eye bloodshot, and it seemed again as though he might say something but then thought better of it. He frowned, looking tired.

'We've got an early start,' he said, scooping up the dishes suddenly. 'We should get some sleep.'

Nice going, Jen, she thought, and spent the rest of the evening wishing she hadn't asked about *before*. She wasn't good at talking, particularly not about matters of the heart. She took her time cleaning the apartment, convincing herself it was for Thomas's eventual return and not to shake the feeling that the walls were closing in on her. In the end there was nothing left to do but sleep or wait.

'Up at 4am,' she said to Nathan, who was standing in the doorway.

He nodded, the kitchen light bleaching his face. Jen sighed and turned to leave.

'I'm sorry,' he said quietly.

'For what?'

'I was happy once.' He spoke quietly and with sadness. 'I try not to think about that anymore.'

Jen nodded gently. 'I can understand that.'

Nathan stepped towards her and she could see a determination within him. She'd seen it the night of the break-in, too, like a fire glowing under the surface.

'I'm going to find out what happened to her,' he said defiantly. '*And* we're going to find out the truth, about Hibernation, about your father. All of it.'

Jen realised, perhaps a little late, that he was attempting a motivational speech. She was shocked. Not by his attempt – that was actually pretty good. She was surprised by her apparent need to hear it.

Sometimes maybe that's all we need, she thought. *Just one person to care, to try. Someone to believe in.*

Without warning, her mind was thrown back in time. She became lost for a moment, transported back to her childhood. She was maybe eight or nine and had been watching a family of tree sparrows build a nest for weeks, excited by the chance to see the birds hatch and eventually fly. A few days later she caught a large crow eating the eggs – that was a feeling that would never leave her. Nature at its most brutal, tiny birds that would never hatch, never get a chance at life.

When she discovered one single egg had survived the attack, there had been no debate. It was her duty to give that single egg a fighting chance. She camped out all night in the garden, and as dawn was breaking, the morning dew soaking her blanket, she saw her mother walking from the house, lamp in hand. Jen expected to be gently reprimanded or marched off to bed, but was instead handed a mug of hot chocolate. Had a drink had ever tasted so good? Steaming and sweet, but more importantly full of love, a sign of support, of belief. Her body and heart had been warmed by her mother's gesture of solidarity. Jen could still remember her triumphant cries when the crow returned to an empty nest. The bird had hatched, the crow defeated.

The following day her mother had brought her a gift, a simple, inexpensive ring. She had said that it was for Jen's determination, that even if you could only save one life, it was still worth it. Jen had worn it with pride until her finger grew too wide and could no longer take it.

'Are you okay?' Nathan asked, pulling her back into the present.

'Yes,' Jen replied, confused, still consumed by the power of past. 'You bought back an old memory for some reason.'

'Of what?'

Jen stared past him, her eyes unfocussed, a frown spreading across her face. Nathan placed his hand on her shoulder. She looked up and shook her head, smiling limply.

'I'm okay,' she reassured him. 'I'll be happier when we're moving.'

'You and me both.'

Later that night, in the privacy of her bedroom, she pulled a small pouch from her bag and tipped the small ring into her hand. It was way too small for her now and had been dulled black and purple over time. She threaded a thin bootlace through it and tied it securely around her neck. Sleep eluded her for a while and she lay there in the darkness, working her fingers over the makeshift necklace.

She didn't think of her mother very often. After she left Brook Mill they hadn't spoken much, and their relationship had eventually been severed completely. Memories before her father's death, like the one about the bird she had experienced earlier, were nearly always good. Afterwards was a different story. For the first time in years, Jen wished she could go back and start again. Make things right. It wasn't her mother's fault. As she slipped through the invisible membrane of consciousness, her last thoughts were of her mother, of home, of happier times. Questions drifted, tugging at her as she descended into the depths of sleep.

Where did she end up? Was she happy? Was she even alive?

Hours passed, lost in a heavy dreamless sleep. When her alarm sounded, Jen was surprised to feel unusually refreshed. She dressed in what she hoped would pass for typical farm workers' attire and checked through her kit. If last night had been about her mother, then this morning her thoughts were with her father. He had inadvertently given her this chance and she wasn't going to let him down. She wrapped the Histeridae in a small black cloth and pushed it deep into her bag before joining Nathan in the lounge.

'Your car's here,' he said, nervously looking through a crack in the curtains, the morning sun on his face.

She looked him over. He was dressed smartly in warm, expensive-looking clothing. His reason for travel should stand up. Samara could be beautiful at this time of year and a freelance photographer traveling alone for a few days was believable. They hugged briefly, neither of them wanting to prolong the good-bye. Thomas's place had been their home, a sanctuary and a prison. Both of them were glad to be leaving, even if they were heading into the unknown.

'Good luck,' Jen said.

'And you. Be careful.'

Nathan watched her leave, waited until her car disappeared from view and checked his watch. His flight wasn't until midday, but he went through his kit one more time. The night before he'd asked Jen how cold it was in Russia.

'It's minus thirty,' she had said with a wry smile. 'And for the record, that's *really* fucking cold.'

CHAPTER 41

The taxi dropped her off a couple of miles short, as planned, just after 5am. It felt good to finally be outside again. Jen pulled her cap down and walked, keeping her head low, aware that a strategically placed camera could expose her at any moment. After an hour, she saw signs informing her she was nearing Lyneham. The airport was a major European hub, transporting food, machinery and workers, the bulk of them destined for Russia. She heard a vehicle approaching, its lights casting a deep shadow along the pavement. A charge of adrenalin fired through her. If this was her ride, it was bang on time.

The vehicle passed her and stopped, brake lights bathing the road. She heard the tug of a handbrake followed by a door slamming and footsteps. The driver appeared and without any acknowledgement opened the back of the truck.

'Get in,' he ordered.

Inside Jen could see hundreds of identical steel containers and, blinking in the darkness, eyes peering back at her.

'I said get in,' the driver's voice was forceful and impatient.

Jen jumped up and found space, aware of the souls around her even if she couldn't see them. They traveled in silence for about ten minutes before the truck slowed to a stop. Jen presumed they had reached the airport entrance and wondered how Lynch would circumvent the security checks. As they pulled away, Jen let out a sigh. The usual weakness, she guessed.

People and money.

After a number of slow, weaving turns, the truck finally came to a stop. The driver killed the engine. Jen heard the sound of doors slamming and then the truck's iron shutters flew up, bathing them in brilliant artificial light. The driver gestured impatiently for them to get out. Jen jumped down and three other stowaways followed her, squinting against the sudden brightness. The truck was one of many parked in a large refrigerated hangar, crates and boxes piled high around them. The driver gathered them together, pulled a scanning device from his jacket and individually checked them, ensuring the ID's and retinals read correctly. Each one a green light. He looked around nervously before herding them into a nearby portable hut. It was dark and smelt of sweat and rubber. Jen could see overalls hanging on the walls.

'Wait here,' the driver said, looking at his watch. 'In less than an hour the trucks arrive, and there will be a lot of people. Join the crowd.' He eyeballed them individually. 'Then you're on your own.'

The man left and Jen picked a corner to sit and wait. The group consisted of a man, a woman and a younger girl. The man looked Polish, the woman and girl Indian, perhaps. Wherever they came from, they were clearly scared.

Conversation didn't come and Jen was happy with that. She pulled her cap down and closed her eyes. She didn't sleep, just listened and waited. Her thoughts turned to Nathan. There were no guarantees they hadn't linked the two of them together by now. Zitagi and the agency were resourceful, way better than Jen could probably imagine. Nathan. He'd seemed distant when she left.

Coming from the queen of distant.

She shrugged at the irony. In the past she would have considered him an idiot for undergoing a body swap. Now, she admired him. It must have taken a lot of guts. More importantly – having seen splintering first hand – was that it seemed to have worked so successfully. When all this was over, she would need to disappear like him. She couldn't deny it, a fresh start sounded good.

Would he come with me?

She allowed her mind to drift into the future. It would all depend on what they found hidden in the vault. Right now that felt like a million miles away. She tried to focus on the task ahead: getting on the plane.

The door handle rattled heavily. Jen's eyes opened immediately and she saw the Indian woman's expression, wide-eyed and afraid. Voices now, the handle moving again and then a fist banging on the door. Jen shuffled over to the huddled group and placed her finger to her lips before positioning herself to the left of the door. If they came through, she would grab them and hope they weren't armed. Thankfully the voices sounded jovial and after a few minutes they gave up and left. Jen hadn't needed to use the Histeridae. That meant she could conserve her strength.

She stayed by the door until the trucks came, which were on time to the minute. The four of them left the hut without discussion, joining the sea of people streaming from the vehicles. She could feel the sudden heat of hundreds of bodies around her and the smell of dust and leather. Up ahead there was a checkpoint, two guards scanning people, and beyond that a huge aircraft. So far the plan was as agreed. He might be a slimy bastard, but the money spent on Lynch had been worth it.

Jen cleared pre-flight boarding and looked up at the huge Boeing AirHaul Freighter, the smell of aviation fuel burning her nostrils. The aircraft, which could take off vertically, was circular in shape and capable of transporting 640 tonnes of cargo over huge distances. She climbed the steel steps, made her way to her seat and buckled in. Above her, four windows cut into the domed fuselage bathed passengers below in warm morning sunlight. In front of her, a screen showed the runway and surrounding area as well as data on the journey. Flight time would be approximately two hours and fifty minutes.

The doors closed, and after the brief safety announcements the huge aircraft lifted vertically from the ground with a roar of its huge engines. Jen watched the sunlight move across the interior as the aircraft banked and gained altitude. She closed her eyes, deciding to catch up on some sleep, knowing it might be her last chance for a while.

She awoke suddenly.

The plane was shaking and lurching, fighting a strong westerly headwind. The seatbelt sign flashed on. She could see mountains on the screen in front of her. Russian mountains.

Forty minutes later the aircraft descended into Ufa International Airport, below them the unmistakable precision agriculture Russia was now so famous for. Massive biodomes glowing red, stretching on for miles, so many she lost count. Her thoughts returned to Zido Zitagi. She had known the feeling of outrunning her wouldn't last.

They might be onto me already. Waiting for me when I step off this plane. What then? What about Nathan?

She clutched her bag tightly. Whatever happened, she had the Histeridae and would go out with a bang. The thought made her smile.

She needed to remember that.

Dig deep and that old Logan determination was still there. She would fight – to the death, if she needed to.

CHAPTER 42

The Boeing taxied to a halt. Jen disembarked and shuffled forward, glancing up occasionally at the dark shapes surrounding her, people with faces covered, outlines softened by fur coats and hats. The cold was instant and crushing, breath bellowing out in clouds from the mass of bodies. Ahead she could see a tower lighting a checkpoint and at least four armed guards. Beyond that, large buildings and hangars. She estimated there to be at least two hundred people around her. It wouldn't take long before she was scanned.

She felt a hand grab her and turned. 'Come with me,' a solider ordered.

Lynch had promised her a contact on arrival, but she had no way of knowing if this was it.

The soldier tugged her aside and walked her towards a single-storey stone building that looked like a barracks. Jen could feel the Histeridae now, tempting her, asking to be used, offering to check the soldier's intentions. She glanced at the soldier and noted his side arm, as well as an assault rifle slung over his shoulder. Both would be genetically linked to him and useless in her hands, but with the Histeridae, that didn't matter – if she had to, she could use his hands instead. The thought made her shiver even more than the permeating, bone-numbing cold.

They reached a door. 'Inside,' the man said. 'Quickly.'

Jen entered the still blackness of the room and faced him. Even in the low light she could see that he was younger than she had originally thought. He looked nervous, his cheeks reddened, veins split by the harsh conditions.

'Over there.' He pushed a key card into her hand and pointed. 'That's the stores. You can get supplies and sleep there tonight. Changeover is at 4.30am. Supplies come in and out. It's your best chance.'

Jen took the card and nodded, straining to see any detail in the inky darkness, let alone the stores he referred to. When she turned back, the soldier was gone. The steel door banged shut, silencing the howling wind in a whistling rush.

Above her a small window allowed a little moonlight into the room, and she waited for her eyes to adjust. Eventually, across the room she could see the shape of a door and the familiar red dot of a wall-mounted card reader. She walked over, swiped the card and with a flash of green heard the heavy lock click open.

She caught herself thinking, *They don't make them like they used to.* It was old technology and that was her father's voice. She smiled and entered the stores. Inside were steel lockers stacked in neat rows along the edges of the room. In the centre, wooden benches with a hanging rail, and to her right, large metal cupboards. Ahead, she could see racks of uniforms and clothing and snow gear. She let out a huge sigh of relief. Traveling with the necessary clothing and equipment would have aroused suspicion. Finding them here was critical.

She began sifting through the rack. Snow boots, jacket, mask, and then the best find of all, an active thermal base layer. She hunted around for overnight equipment and found a tent and sleeping bag, not the grade she was hoping for, but they would have to do.

As long as she could stay hidden overnight, she might at least have a chance of surviving the hike over the mountain range. She opened a cabinet and inside, arranged in a neat shiny row, were automatic weapons. Even with the Histeridae as her ally, she couldn't deny the feeling of security one of those would bring. It pained her to leave them but she knew they required DNA pairing to work, and that wasn't something she could activate alone.

She spent the next hour carefully packing her gear, ensuring each item would be easily accessed when needed and that clothing would remain dry, and then settled into her bag. She didn't expect to sleep but would at least stay warm. The sound of people had faded. Outside she could hear the wind howling ghoulishly between the buildings and the constant idling drone of aircraft engines. She tucked herself away behind a rack of uniforms and covered her head as best she could. If someone came in, they wouldn't see her straight away. It would have to do. Within minutes she was asleep.

★ ★ ★

The sound of aircraft thrusters woke her. Jen pressed her face against one of the tiny storeroom windows. It was snowing outside, thin flakes darting playfully in every direction, searching and joining together before bursting apart again. When the trucks came she grabbed her gear, zipped her jacket high around her neck and crept outside. It was 5.11am. In the darkness, long lines of arctic trucks were parked in multiple rows, their red tail-lights blooming through the flickering layers of falling snow. She could hear the sounds of men and machinery, loading and hauling.

Hugging the wall, Jen crept away from the noise, crossing two buildings before arriving at a small perimeter wall. She vaulted the wall easily and began to run, staying out of the light, hoping her white combat fatigues would hide her from view. It felt good to have her body moving again, feel her heart pounding. The snow wasn't too thick here, but it was hard going and within minutes her lungs were burning against the cold.

She cleared a kilometre or so before daring to look back. The airport glowed in the darkness like a jewel, its Cyrillic rooftop letters silhouetted clearly against a cluster of brilliant lights, its buildings colouring the snow with warm amber light. She checked her GPS before continuing. Her target was north, a freight train traveling the southern route of the Trans-Siberian Railway. It was scheduled to pass through Dema Station at around 8.am. Jen would use it to travel the 450 kilometres to Samara, arriving just after sunset.

That was the plan.

Ahead was only darkness. She pressed on over humps and mounds, the creaking snow underfoot amplified by the soundless landscape. The journey was broken only by the occasional hedgerow or low stone wall. By seven, the threat of sunlight was building, an inevitable force that would soon beat the all-consuming greyness surrounding her. Jen could ascertain the difference now between land and sky, and make out shapes from the previously blank canvas. She could feel the frozen river underfoot too, solid and easier to walk on. A path through the hills opened up in front of her. When she reached the singular train track, nestled at the base of a hill, she knew that Dema Station couldn't be much farther. Passing a small industrial plant, she saw the lights of traffic up ahead and jogged along an underpass tucked beneath the busy main road. As she approached the station her heart sank. The train was huge, over a kilometre long, but it was already moving through the station.

Her train.

Jen berated herself for not covering ground quickly enough but then stopped. This wasn't the time. If she was going to catch that train – and there really wasn't any other option – she needed to run. Now. The station was an oval-shaped network of lines, maybe ten, some of which were filled with parked carriages and trains. All the lines eventually filtered down to two and all left the station to the west. Jen pushed herself forward. It didn't take long for her thighs to scream, fighting against the heavy snow. Luckily the train was on the nearest line but was at least 100 metres away and accelerating fast. There no way she could match its speed and jump up with snow this thick hampering her approach.

Don't panic, she commanded her racing mind. *Think!*

She spotted a line of carriages parked behind it and made a mental calculation. Jen dipped her head and ran as fast as she could, diving over the tracks and in front of the powerful engine. As she tumbled to the ground she glanced back, hoping the driver hadn't seen her. She didn't see anyone, just the grinding power of huge wheels howling past her.

She was up and scaling the ladder of one of the stationery carriages. She reached the top and looked along the line of parked trucks. There were at least twenty of them, evenly spaced with gaps small enough to jump. On her left now the moving train streamed past, picking up speed at an alarming rate. A few more carriages and it would be gone for good. The next train was due in three days. Not an option.

Looking ahead, she was reminded of school, of long jump, of that feeling just before the event. She didn't hesitate, didn't allow fears to pollute her vision of the perfect jump. She leant down, took a breath and sprinted forward, hopping over the gaps, doing her best to maintain speed. It was impossible to gauge the distance, so when she reached the last parked carriage she just jumped. As her feet left the stationary carriage she couldn't help but imagine how it would feel to tumble, thrashing like a rag doll into the hurtling wheels below. The weightless moment ended and the vision of being sawn in two was shattered by her landing, her body suddenly accelerating, the momentum carrying her further and further towards the edge of the moving carriage.

Adrenalin rushed through her as she slammed down, arms thrashing wildly, searching for grip on the slimy tarpaulin. She cried out as she slipped over the edge of the moving train, clinging by her fingertips to the ice-cold metal of the carriage, scrambling for a foothold, boots sliding desperately against the carriage's surface. Somehow she managed to un-sheath her knife, stabbing the blade through the canvas on the side of the carriage. Suddenly she was pushed flat by a compressed rush of air and all around her saw flashes of steel and lights. Again she cried out before looking back along the carriages and realising she had almost been plucked from the train by a signaling station. It winked playfully in the distance. Still the train accelerated.

Fucking hell, Jen, come on. Move!

Her right hand, solid with tension, was gripping the hilt of her blade. It had ripped the canvas open, torn along a few feet and come to a hard stop at the edge of the metal carriage. With her left hand she grabbed the flapping fabric and managed to swing her body, pulling herself up. The wind was deafening now, biting and burning her face, the snow heavier and more aggressive at this speed. She lay flat, face down for a few seconds, the tremendous roar of the train vibrating through her. The wind was so fierce she couldn't open her eyes.

As she dropped through the ripped hole, Jen hoped – in fact, Jen prayed – that whatever was below would offer a soft landing.

CHAPTER 43

The aircraft made its final descent into Kurumoch International Airport just after 8am. Nathan peered out at the steam rising from tall buildings into the early morning sky. Street lamps, dotted like white suns, appeared against a blanket of snow. He disembarked and an hour later found himself facing an armed security guard.

'What is your business here?' the guard asked, his thick Russian accent hacking the words. He was overweight, bald and very pale. Nathan stared at him without blinking.

'I'm a photographer,' he answered calmly. 'I'm here for the view.'

A steady stream of passengers walked by, heads down. The guard took Nathan's equipment and spread it out over a black faux-leather table, taking a particular interest in one item – the access interface Nathan favoured so much. Bringing it was a risk but he couldn't do the job without it. He nodded when asked to explain its use, managing to enact its necessity for light readings and such. To the uninitiated, the device could just about pass for camera equipment. The guard seemed tired and not overly concerned. He repacked the case badly and ushered him on. Nathan thanked him, and his luck.

It was nothing compared to what Jen is going to have to do, he reminded himself, unsure if the chill passing through him was coming from the exit. A red sign above the automatic door assured him it was −21 degrees Celsius outside, normal for the time of year. He tugged his hat, zipped his coat and stepped out into the icy air.

His vehicle was a standard hire car. Small, economical and more importantly for him, inconspicuous. Tomorrow he would check the meeting location, buy food and then hole up in Tolyatti, a town about 50km east of the Vault. Shared power lines would be his best way to hack in and pretty much everything in the area was powered by the nearby Zhiguli Hydroelectric Station.

As he left the airport, the car's navigation system informed him the journey would take twenty minutes. Nathan leant back and peered out of the window. In the distance he could see huge factories, their tall, smoking towers and yellow lights cutting through the morning mist. The accelerating climate change had been tough on Russia in the early days. Now there were obvious signs it was doing better. He thought of Canada again, as he often did when he arrived somewhere new. It had been his dream once; it too had felt like a country on the brink of something positive, another place on the rise. Canada's independence from the UN had been brave and empowering, especially at a time when most countries were clamouring to meet the criteria.

Independence.

A smart move, as it happened. The trust people placed in the UN and its role of global governance seemed increasingly misplaced. He wondered what he and Jen would do if they found something tangible. Something big enough to rock the foundations. Where would they go to break the story? Would they ever be safe again?

Probably not, he decided, realising that he should try and remember that. His life had a bigger purpose now. Yes, he would find out who killed his wife and he would get revenge, but there was more: the truth, all of it linked and stitched into his own story somehow.

If you're going to light a match, you might as well fetch the petrol.

Nathan shrugged. His life? Future plans? Might as well forget it. He wouldn't ever be safe and he shouldn't cling to any such hope. He'd heard it said that soldiers died that way, desperately believing they would make it out of a war zone alive. The ones who lived were the ones who accepted that they were already dead.

Later that night, his idle mind had him pacing his hotel room. It wasn't the cold that bothered him. It was the time on his hands. How would he manage for two days with nothing to do? The earlier news bulletin hadn't helped. There were numerous reports of a blizzard coming in.

A blizzard. That's not good, not good at all.

He pulled open a large sliding door and stepped out onto a narrow balcony. It was like walking into a freezer. He felt his body tighten, gut twisting to stay warm, face burning against the icy air. Below him a busy street and all around him sandy-coloured block stone buildings. It was a hard place, cold and depressing.

He looked east toward the foreboding ridge of the Zhiguli Mountain Range and the Shiryaevo Vault nestled beyond it. He thought of Jen and prayed she would make it in before the blizzard hit. He wasn't sure who he was praying to, but he pushed the request out into the universe anyway. They needed all the help they could get.

★ ★ ★

Jen's fall had been short, the train's carriage filled nearly to the top with large sacks of grain. It was so cold that the sacks had begun to freeze, and Jen was starting to wonder how long it would be before she did too. The one blessing, she supposed, was being out of the wind. She listened to it whistling through the gap in the ripped tarpaulin above her.

Hours later she clambered up over the hessian sacks, covered her face and popped her head out. It felt as if someone had slapped her, the cold wind ripping at her skin. In the distance she saw what she needed. The Zhiguli Mountains, their jagged peaks cutting the skyline, steep slopes dropping sharply into the frozen Volga River. They were an unusual sight. At under four hundred metres some wouldn't consider them mountains at all, but seeing them towering in front of her she could understand how they had captivated people's imaginations over the years. Local folklore included unexplained fireballs in the sky and transparent ghostlike creatures appearing from the ground, often attributed to the work of aliens bending the Volga River to their will.

Jen ducked back inside the carriage and checked the time. Soon the train would arrive in Samara; she needed to be off before then. She tried to keep herself moving but could feel the dreadful numbing pain in her hands and toes returning. The active base layer she'd found in the airport storeroom was only just maintaining her core body temperature; her extremities were less fortunate. When the train lurched and slowed she was actually relieved – at least she could start moving again, give her blood a chance to warm up.

As the train made its way around the Southern tip of Samara she climbed up again and lay flat this time, managing to open her eyes. To her right Samara city, its towering buildings cutting the horizon; to her left a frozen blue river and beyond that woodland, covered in a thick blanket of snow pricked by black trees. The train slowed again. This was her chance. The deep snow could offer a soft landing, but without knowing what lay underneath it was too dangerous to just jump.

She climbed to the edge of the carriage and slid over the side. She hung, lifted her knees and walked her feet up the cold steel where she waited until the tracks were lined up with nothing but flat deep snow. She pushed off, releasing her hands and spinning in the air as best she could. The feeling of weightlessness reminded her of leaving a swing as a child, the delicious fear and trepidation of the landing to follow. The ground came and she rolled, tumbling to a stop. Sitting in the deep snow she watched the train thunder past and then crawled to a nearby corrugated iron hut, powdery snow creaking under foot.

She crouched and checked her handheld GPS. It estimated the trek would take ten hours but it was snowing heavily now and the wind – a constant force – was more aggressive and threatening to knock her over. Jen had felt worse, but considering she wasn't even in the mountains yet, it was bad news.

She put her head down and pressed on. One step at a time.

CHAPTER 44

Jen shielded her eyes and surveyed the area. Towering above all were the Zhiguli Mountains, their colour flattened to a hazy blue. Ahead the Volga River bent and twisted abruptly in on itself, forming an almost-closed loop, commonly known as the Samara bend. Jen wasn't surprised the locals had their folklore. River curves like this were extremely rare and such places always had their stories – all, of course, to be taken with a generous helping of salt.

Jen stepped onto the frozen river, its dusty white surface cut by thousands of manmade lines, and made her way towards a small island in the centre. Whilst the Volga would remain frozen for at least another month, its centre was already thin and dangerous. The tiny piece of land would offer a safe crossing point.

The wind howled and rose up, threatening to knock her sideways. She steadied herself and pulled a set of goggles from her backpack and tightened her hood, the muffling effect creating an unnerving sense of separation. She put her head down and stepped out onto the ice. It took all her strength now to ensure she was moving forwards. Her plan was to cross and then follow the river's edge, climb the Western tip of the mountain and drop down onto the target.

She had experienced a blizzard once before. Her well-equipped unit had holed up and waited for the storm to pass. This time she was alone and woefully unprepared, her body temperature plummeting. Jen was finding it increasingly difficult to judge the terrain, and there was no denying it anymore: she was in trouble. She had turned inland and begun her climb up one of many ravines cutting into the mountainside. Darkness descended quickly and Jen felt hope slip away, along with the glow of her GPS.

Approximately a hundred metres above sea level she lost her footing and fell, tumbling and barreling down the side of the mountain before landing hard, knocking the wind from her lungs. She lay for a while, convinced she wouldn't be able to move, that she would die there, the warmth of civilisation a distant dream. She felt the blizzard pulling and tearing at the snow on the ground around her and screamed, her voice drowned by the ferocious wind.

Eventually she stood, wavering like a drunken sailor, her body so numb that she couldn't be sure she hadn't broken something during the fall. She realised with a sickening wave of panic that she couldn't open her eyes. Using her teeth she pulled off her right glove, warmed her hand under her armpit and placed it over her tender eyelids. She felt a thin layer of ice melt, and then pain as blood returned momentarily to her skin. After a quivering struggle her eyes finally clicked open, but visibility was zero, her hands lost in a haze of dancing snow. There was nothing more to do. She would camp here the night, wherever *here* was.

If I live through the night, maybe I'll find out.

Her tent didn't require pegs or poles. Placed on the ground, it locked into position, inflated and self-assembled. She grabbed her bag and collapsed inside, zipping the entrance shut against the fierce storm. Relief wasn't immediate. First there was pain as her body began to thaw, then a dullness in her nose and fingers, a numb feeling that might lead to frostbite. Slowly she warmed up, gradually and evenly, managing to avoid the urges to rub the affected areas. That wouldn't be good. The fact she felt tired and irritable *was* good. Mild hypothermia – she could live with that.

She clicked a small lamp, illuminating the orange innards of the tent. Its thin fabric was billowing like lungs in spasm, the edges almost touching each other. Using a small stove she melted thick lumps of snow and drank, warming her core, thanking her decision to pack it. Outside the wind was increasing in ferocity, wailing like a thousand banshees. Again and again it felt as though she would be pulled into the air and smashed back onto the mountain, where she would lay broken and buried for weeks.

In that moment of solitude, small and insignificant, she wondered what the hell she was doing halfway up a mountain in Russia. For what? A hunch?

She was shivering again, but there was no change of clothes. Instead she peeled off a layer and slid into her sleeping bag, her thoughts settling on her parents again. It was weak to turn to them now, but she didn't care. Not tonight. Jen held her necklace, clutching the ring her mother had given her, and prayed. Not to any God, or any ethereal being. She prayed simply to fate or destiny. She prayed she would find something hidden in the mountains, something even the locals wouldn't believe, something worth dying for.

★ ★ ★

The gift of exhaustion granted her some sleep, but around 6am Jen woke, freezing, the storm threatening to disembowel the tent. If she didn't move soon she would die. She packed her things, dressed in her icy clothing and emerged from the tent, like a calf being born, steam rising up and out of the entrance. The blizzard had actually weakened and she was just able to make out the incline of a ridge up ahead, and her own footsteps in the snow behind her. One step at a time, she reassured herself.

The storm retreated. Gone was the recognisable foe, replaced by a stealthy killer, an all-consuming cold the like of which Jen had never experienced. It felt as though her blood were being filtered through ice-cold steel. Her body leeched warmth. Her teeth chattered uncontrollably, her skin bonding with the frozen scarf wrapped around her head. She cursed as the GPS unit fell from her hand, its cracked screen fixed forever on minus thirty nine. Above her the peak of the mountain, majestic and distant, seemed to taunt her, its voice whistling through the trees.

You were never going to make it.

Jen whimpered, dropping to her knees, hope spilling out of her like fuel from a bullet riddled aircraft. She was punctured by solitude, her body shutting down against the terrible, permeating cold. She heard voices, demons scratching at her sanity, more and more of them, their questions swirling and joining together. Questions that demanded answers.

What about love?

You've been played your whole life. All of it lies.

You've denied yourself love. And now you're going to die here. Alone.

For what?

She growled like a wounded dog and pulled herself up, staggering through the icy woodland. Silver birch trees surrounded her like an endless maze, the air still and calm. She realised the pain was leaving her, along with those nagging questions, dissipating like her breath drifting away in clouds of steam. She was tired, could feel a weight pulling her down, could hardly breathe. She'd been searching for the truth for so long. Now, death was near. She twisted around, flinching, half expecting to see death himself – a dark figure come to take her, to make it all better.

I'm going to die, she thought calmly.

She was holding the communicator Nathan had given her, single channel and short range. He had assured her it would work, but she wasn't near enough to him. She'd tried it numerous times and received only static. Their last conversation came back to her. She replayed it in her mind.

'You can use this to contact me,' he'd said, handing her the radio. 'It's a communicator.'

'I haven't seen one of these in years.'

'I know.' He was holding an identical unit. 'It's retro.'

Jen had noted his excitement, his innocent, boyish expression, and smiled.

'What?' he'd asked her.

'You would never know to look at you,' she had said, smirking, 'but you're a real geek on the inside. You know that?'

A real geek on the inside.

Nathan O'Brien *was* a geek, but she would never see the real him. She'd only ever *seen* David Shaw, an imposing figure of a man, not Nathan. It was hard to get your head around sometimes. She realised, as she lay there dying, that she wished she could see him again, to tell him that. Tell him he should be honoured, that she didn't bestow *like* on many people, that he was one of the good ones.

Too late now.

She collapsed again, down to her knees and then forward, until the side of her face lay flat against the snow. She smiled. It felt warm. How could the snow feel so inviting?

My mind.
It's telling me that.
It's giving in, letting me go.

She saw a bird. Small and grey.

It was looking at her from a branch, twitching its head as if trying to understand. She watched it for a while, her eyes struggling to stay open. An intoxicating, flickering purple aura began to circle the bird. The Histeridae. Jen smiled as she lay dying.

The Histeridae.

She had never considered it might be possible to link to animals. She was surprised when she saw herself lying there in the snow. As the tiny bird lifted into the sky, Jen gathered what little energy she had and began searching. She could see the land below through the bird's eyes. It took a while, but something happened, something different. She had a flash, a vision, a mountain hut, stone and wood, built up against the mountain. The connection to the bird broke suddenly, leaving her alone again.

Jen raised her heavy head to see coloured tendrils, leading through the trees and down the mountain. She crawled, eventually managing to stand, each footstep like heavy lead. It was something beyond effort, digging deeper than she knew, but the vision of the hut had bought fresh hope. The Histeridae was guiding her to safety.

When she finally reached the wooden shack, its roof buried under impossibly thick snow, she realised what was actually happening. It wasn't guiding her, it was simply finding the nearest mind. The wilderness hut, built specifically for trekkers and people stranded, was occupied, light bleeding from the small windows. She smelt the aroma of warm, salty food and felt her stomach cramp and throat tighten. She fought against a sudden swimming exhaustion and realised, as she opened her eyes, that she must have passed out.

A man was approaching. She tried to move, to escape, but her body no longer responded to her unreasonable demands.

She moved her lips but words didn't come. The man rolled her roughly onto her back. He was large and bearded, the smell of fish and fire poured from him. Jen could feel his heat and was aware of being lifted, and then an unexpected sense of shelter, of real warmth. Her eyes opened briefly, long enough to see large wooden beams and the shadow of an open fire dancing on the walls.

She felt safe but knew that was unlikely.

She passed out again, drifting down into the blackness where her demons lay waiting, their questions unanswered, their appetite for despair insatiable.

CHAPTER 45

Jen's mind danced on the edge of consciousness, vaguely aware of time slipping away and a dull throb in her hands and feet. Hours passed. She opened her eyes and blinked a few times until her vision gained some focus. Above her were thick oak beams, to her left an open fire, still smouldering. The hut's rough stone walls were warmed by a morning sun. She'd slept through the night.

Rolling her shoulders, she felt her neck and upper spine pop and winced as she swallowed, her mouth dry and sour. It didn't take long for her memory to come rushing back. Her fall. The man.

She sat up suddenly, peeling back the fur bedding that had kept her so warm. The shelter was basic, designed to save life on nights like the one she'd endured. Next to her pack, propped up by the door, was another bag, canvas and heavy-looking.

I need to move, I need to get out of here.

She was still dressed. That was good. Her dreams had been filled with unpleasant imagery and fear, the man and the mountain taking what they wanted from her. She stood and felt nauseous, her head swimming. She would need to take things slowly. That's when the door handle twisted and the man stepped in. He boomed something in Russian, and before Jen could react, slapped her hard on her right shoulder. She felt her whole body lift.

Jen stared at him blankly, wishing she had studied Russian. He was big and heavy with dark leathery skin covered by a messy grey beard. He looked to be smiling but it was hard to tell. Spinning a bag over his shoulder, he emptied a pile of logs and began throwing them into the corner of the room, restocking the shelter.

Jen helped, and although her fingers were numb, she was relieved to see they weren't frostbitten. She guessed the man was a local hunter who had been trapped by the blizzard and holed up in the shelter for the night. He glanced over and smiled, his eyes glimmering purple in the bright sunlight. Jen took a step back and swallowed.

He was augmented with active contact lenses.

As soon as this man was off the mountain and back onto a network, they could search his mind for imagery. They would see his memories of her and, once they knew she was in Russia, would make the obvious connection to the Vault. Questions circled, making her feel weaker still.

Should she tie him up? Leave him here? What if she didn't make it back? He could die.

She eyed a branch, nestled amongst the bigger logs. It was just thin enough to wield, long and hard enough to use as a club. She picked it up and for a brief moment imagined striking him. The man turned, frowned, shook his head and continued to throw logs like they were made of paper. It was amazing how much connection could be made through simple body language.

She knew it was pure luck that he'd found her. If he hadn't come along she would be dead, buried in thick snow. She sighed and added the potential weapon to the growing pile, knowing her decision might have serious repercussions.

It was a risk she was willing to take. She wasn't a killer.

She wasn't like Zitagi.

★ ★ ★

The news report echoed through the only occupied room in the Zvezda Hotel, Tolyatti, like a lone transmission drifting through deep space. The correspondent's voice became choppy as the picture sliced through the middle and then disappeared completely. There had been another attack on a Hibernation zone in Italy somewhere, a resistance group known as The Liberation. Nathan stared at the blank screen, watching his breath travel slowly towards the window, which was covered in swirling crystal patterns of blue and white ice.

The blizzard, which had hit Tolyatti two days ago, had frozen the place solid. Since then the power had been intermittent and a cluster of electric heaters, strategically positioned around him, worked just long enough to keep him alive. That morning, dreams of happier times had been stolen by the burden of waking. He'd been holding his wife, hugging her, telling her she would be okay. Some days it just didn't make sense. All their history, the world they had made together, was his now. His alone. They would never look back on it together. He'd woken in the cold silence and allowed himself a few minutes to cry before wiping the tears roughly from his face.

The day before he'd visited the kitchen to order food and found it deserted, that staff nowhere to be seen. He searched and in the end managed to make a cheese sandwich. Sitting in front of the bar heater, defrosting it just enough to eat, he'd considered whether he could drag a generator up to his room.

Room? More like a tomb.

He had spent the day testing equipment and trying the radio, a close-range, encrypted transmitter. Old technology that would only work when Jen was near. Every hour on the hour, nothing but static. He didn't want to consider what might have happened. She would make it somehow. He thought about what to say when she did make contact. How would he break it to her? That without power he could do nothing?

He checked the temperature again – minus forty – and told himself not to think too much. The power returned, briefly illuminating the room before flickering out. It came again and then remained constant, the orange bars glowing on the multiple heaters surrounding him. In distant rooms he heard the whirring sounds of frozen machinery struggling back to life. It was surprising how quiet a hotel could be without the forces of energy running through its metal veins.

Making the most of the sudden power, he accessed his computer. Hacking the Shiryaevo mainframe would only be possible from the inside, but he could do some preparation. Local networks all led to a single exchange point. He could at least be ready, crouched, like a sprinter waiting for the gun.

He checked the Vaults blueprint again, and Jen's route marked out through its multicoloured wireframe corridors.

Nothing to do now but wait. He checked local weather reports. The blizzard was subsiding but temperatures were set to remain, not quite the coldest the area had known, but close. *Close enough to freeze to death,* his mind assured him. The fear of failure washed through him again and he thought back to Brazil. The oppressive, dusty heat seemed strangely appealing now and he imagined just a few seconds of it, burning his lungs. It would be worth it, he decided, wondering if he would ever see his old body.

Suddenly the radio buzzed, three vibrating alerts sending the device dancing across the tabletop in front of him. Nathan let out a shocked, guttural cry and grabbed wildly at the radio, sending it crashing to the floor. He leapt up, relieved to see it intact, and entered the passkey.

'Are you there?' he shouted.

Nothing but static.

'Jen, are you there?' he asked again, desperate this time.

'I'm here,' she replied.

A huge sigh escaped him. 'Are you okay? You're late.'

'I ran into some trouble.'

'I was worried. Where are you?'

'Near the entrance, freezing my arse off.'

The sarcasm was obvious and he was relieved to hear it. He hadn't wanted to admit it, but the idea of losing her had been gnawing away at his loneliness since arriving in Russia. Some of his dreams had been about her, about them.

'When do we go?' he asked, praying the power would remain constant.

Her answer came without hesitation. 'We go in now.'

CHAPTER 46

The freezing fog finally lifted and Jen could see the ridged peak of the mountain and the snaking silvery river Volga in the distance. The Zhiguli hydroelectric dam supplied the majority of the Vault's power demand and its distant hum assured her she must be close. It was a relief. The terrain was treacherous underfoot and she wasn't sure her legs – stiffening horribly against the cold – would last another day.

She descended awkwardly down the west face of the mountain, kicking up clouds of dusty snow into the ravine behind her until she reached her target: a large heat vent, around twenty feet in diameter, belching thick clouds of steam into the air like a boiling kettle. She scrambled down and knelt beside it for a while, enjoying the heat prickling her skin, breathing life back into her hands.

Leaning over the edge, through a cross-hatch of thick metal bars and barely visible, she saw an access shaft and a ladder wrapped inside a safety cage. There was no way to open the vent from here; she would unlock it later from the inside. After a brief rest she stuffed her rucksack beneath a nearby rock, making mental notes of her location. Her plan was to exit here, retrieve her bag and slip away undetected. Warmed and lighter, she continued, the strength returning to her legs along with a quiet optimism. The sun finally cut through the basin below her, revealing what she had come so far to see.

The Shiryaevo Vault, its glistening stone structure rising from the white mountain, bathed in glowing security lights.

Jen calculated her position. The visitor centre was clearly visible, surrounded by a high-gated fence and intersected by roads and car parks. Vehicles inched in convoy towards the main entrance and people, tiny and scattered, made their way in the misty morning gloom. The vault was a huge installation, the biggest of its kind in the world, and the majority of the facility was buried deep inside the mountain. What could be seen from here was just the tip of the iceberg.

The vault operated a three-tiered security protocol; the deeper you went the more secure it became. Tier one: numerous guards and patrol droids – they would require authorisation before firing – as well as scanners and motion sensors. Security checkpoints dotted every hundred feet or so. Tier-one guards would be friendly, carry sidearms only and be used to dealing with the workforce. Inside would be technical administration, home to hundreds of civilian workers and analysts. Beyond that was tier two security, heavily armed guards patrolling the miles of tunnels and corridors and automated systems protecting the data chambers. Finally, tier three, the critical zones. Government level. Where the secrets were kept. Here, the guards would shoot to kill and ask questions later, doors would be timed and security systems compartmentalised with safety lock-outs. Armed military droids would be programmed to make life-or-death decisions. It was the kind of security you could trust, the kind megacorporations and governments paid big money for, the kind terrorists would never get near.

Jen had been involved occasionally with counterterrorism units, and it always impressed her how organised and aware these teams appeared to be and yet how seemingly unprepared they were when a new threat arrived. Even with all the planning and preparation and vigilance, terrorists always seemed to manage to circumvent their countermeasures. Jen hoped that the Histeridae was another example of that: something this facility was never designed to cope with, something they never could have imagined. For the Histeridae to give her an edge, the vault's weakness needed to be human. That's how she would get inside, and once there, Nathan would do the rest.

Fifty feet from the road she heard the sound of trees being pushed aside by something big, something gathering speed. A red dot flashed through the branches in front of her and then settled on her chest.

'I've been picked up as expected,' she said to Nathan.

'Okay, good luck. Talk again when you're inside.'

'You're sure they can't hear us?'

'This tech is nearly thirty years old. They stopped listening for it a long time ago. And even if they did, it's all secure, all encrypted. Trust me.'

Even though being found was part of the plan, Jen couldn't help feeling technology could let them down. A droid appeared hovering above her, twice the size of a person, its dark orange jets melting the snow into pools of water below. It explained that she was in a restricted area and must be processed immediately.

She followed the droid along the perimeter fence, noting the less-than-expected number of personnel. Passing trucks were only half filled and the car parks the same. The conditions, it seemed, had reduced the vault to a skeleton crew, and whilst they were shipping people in, it was a slow process. Jen smiled. The weather might have worked in their favour after all.

★ ★ ★

Ahead Jen could see two guards approaching, side arms still holstered but body language that suggested they wouldn't be for long. The taller of the two – the one who appeared to be in charge – was shaking his arms, instructing Jen to stop. He spoke quickly in Russian while the smaller, stockier one eyed her suspiciously. With language augmentation she would have understood them immediately. Without it, she had no idea what they were saying.

'Do you speak English?' she asked, feeling antiquated.

'Of course,' the tall guard replied sharply in a thick Russian accent. 'Stand still and be scanned.'

The droid moved closer. 'Remove your scarf,' it instructed, in a deep metallic voice. 'Prepare for scanning.'

A retina scan was to be expected, but Jen had hoped to get nearer first, to maybe give Nathan access to the security systems, a chance to change her results. It was earlier than planned, but there was nothing else she could do. She took a deep breath and accessed the Histeridac.

The short guard growled something in Russian, obviously confused and uncomfortable. Jen ignored him. In some ways it was a relief to be using the device again, to finally be on the offensive. She networked the guards together and began persuading them.

< *I am with a team of technicians here to complete routine maintenance, but we became lost in the storm.* >

The droid moved closer and repeated its request. Jen could feel the humming vibration of its metallic body. It would have a concealed taser.

'No, is okay,' the tall guard said, overruling the droid in broken English. 'Follow me. I get you to security desk. You need to check in.'

The droid pulled back and immediately continued its designated patrol accompanied by the stocky guard, who only looked back once.

Jen followed the taller guard. He seemed relaxed, unfazed

by her use of the Histeridae, and Jen was aware of her growing ability to control and function simultaneously. She wondered if perhaps her experience with the bird, albeit brief, had taught her something. If she concentrated, she could see through the host's eyes, in this case *see* what the guard was *seeing*. It was a form of split concentration that was becoming easier the more she practiced.

Ahead was the main entrance, an ugly lump of construction built directly into the rock with a revolving steel doorway in the centre. Jen instinctively slipped her hand inside her pocket and felt for the data transmitter. Presuming she could get inside, it would give Nathan access to the security system.

She turned to the guard accompanying her.

< *I'm going to need a security pass,* > she explained silently.

'We arrange that inside,' the guard replied, apparently not realising she hadn't spoken.

Jen continued walking. There were more people now, and cameras, scanning and watching. Two armed guards stood at the doorway checking the odd pass as people flooded in and out. She knew if they became suspicious things could get complicated very quickly.

<*Why don't I just have yours?* > Jen suggested.

The guard stopped and handed it to her.

< *You can forget about this now, it doesn't matter. Okay?* >

Jen watched him until he was back at the perimeter fence and then carefully retracted the Histeridae's tendrils from his mind. Ahead she could see a short queue of people disappearing into the building, swiping their passes across a panel to the side of the main door. She joined them, her face still covered. It was fast and there was no time to think before it was her turn. She swiped her stolen ID card across the reader, her heart pounding. The panel flashed green. She walked past the guards, through the rotating glass door and into the building.

The lobby reminded her of airport security, cold and clinical with paneled steel walls and a polished stone floor. The sound of heels and voices was mixed with polite announcements and the whir of scanning machinery. Ahead she saw a row of turnstiles, and beyond that a number of larger scanners where a group of people were being processed. It looked to be retinal scans and breath tests. To her left, a long reception desk, and to her right, a canteen with corridors leading off in various directions. She estimated there were about twenty people in the reception area, another thirty or so in the canteen, and spotted at least six armed guards: four covering the scanners and two more ahead.

She heard Nathan in her ear, his voice making her jolt. 'I have access to the security desk. I'm going to switch your stolen card with a fake ID.'

Her stomach tightened as the two guards approached, pointing and raising their voices.

'Quickly,' she whispered, guessing what they were asking her to do. Her face was covered with a scarf and they wanted her to take it off. She nodded but did nothing, her mind battling the urge to run.

'Nathan, do it now!' she hissed, her mouth still covered.

Surely they can hear us. This isn't going to work.

The guards became agitated and repeated the order.

'Nearly there,' Nathan said.

Jen saw one of the guards reach down and place his hand on his sidearm. If he pulled it, the others would too, creating a scene that would likely trigger an alert. It could all spin out of control quickly.

The guards inched closer, barking orders.

Jen began unwrapping the scarf, knowing that in seconds her ID would be confirmed by recognition software that was already piecing together the unique shape and contours of her face. She tugged the last of the fabric away and faced them. The moment seemed to stretch out, faces frozen, the atrium eerily silent, seconds feeling like minutes. A droid slid between two guards, stopped close to her face and scanned her.

CHAPTER 47

The nearest guard waved a small handheld device across her body, jabbed at it a few times and looked her up and down. The device beeped. A good sound.

'Miss Jade Savoretti?' the guard asked, as if confirming the delivery of a parcel.

Jen nodded, letting out a careful and private sigh of relief.

'Sorry about that. We need to be careful, I'm sure you understand.' The guard finally smiled, it was thin and brief but it meant she was safe, for now. He walked towards the body scanners. 'Follow me.'

'You're a technician.' Nathan's voice in her ear. 'Routine maintenance on chamber four servers.'

Ahead, people were placing bags on a conveyor and walking through full-body scanners. Jen knew that a technician would only be allowed to carry specific and pre-authorised equipment into the vault. There was no way she could smuggle it in. It meant she would need to control the guards on duty.

She took a deep breath in through her nostrils and relaxed, rolling her shoulders gently back. She imagined she was on her rooftop, gliding through movements and lost in her own world.

Relax, she told herself, *breathe.*

She controlled four guards this way, passing through the initial security checkpoints. Each time a screen highlighted a suspect object or doubt crept into a nervous mind, she silently and expertly controlled the situation.

The guard – the one who had scanned her in the lobby – stood waiting. He was young with a bony face and fingers that seemed too long for his hands. He needed to grow into his body and, like most people she'd met since arriving in Russia, looked like he needed a few days of real sun. Jen noted his name tag. Silver uppercase letters on black. LOSEVSKY.

'May I use the bathroom?' she asked.

Losevsky pointed to a corridor on her right. Jen entered, locked herself inside a cubicle and attached a tiny camera, the size of a grain of rice, to her lapel.

'Jade Savoretti?' she whispered.

'Jade. Like your eyes,' Nathan said. 'Took me hours, which to be fair was a pleasant distraction. This place is bloody freezing.'

Jen screwed up her lip. 'I sound like an Italian pop star.'

Nathan grunted and she could hear him tapping. Eventually he spoke. 'Okay, I have visual from your camera and I can see your location.'

'You sure they can't hear us?'

'Relax, it's fine.'

'Easy for you to say. I was surrounded by guards in the lobby with you chatting away in my ear. I felt vulnerable.' She paused a beat. 'Exposed.'

'Trust me,' he said again and Jen decided she had no choice.

'Nathan?'

'Hmmm?'

'Talking of exposed, I do actually need the toilet,' she admitted.

'Okay, but Jen?'

'Yeah?'

'Lone technician, difficulty getting to the vault. Split from her team. The plan worked.'

She heard a click and hoped it meant he was gone. Her

cover story had been his idea and he was clearly pleased with himself. She smiled, sat and urinated. It was a relief. Her nerves felt electrified, she was buzzing all over and wondered if the numb tingling in her fingers might actually be frost damage. She stood and looked down into the bowl. Her urine was dark; she was dehydrated.

'A doctor would probably tell me to rest for a week or so,' she whispered to no one and flushed. 'No chance of that.'

She rejoined Losevsky, who escorted her through the first of the administrative areas within the vault.

'Chamber four is quite a long way in,' he said, his English good. 'I can take you some of the way.'

Apart from the obvious scale, the admin area appeared to be a fairly standard office set-up. Hundreds of civilian workers sat at consoles, drinking coffee, tapping away, taking support calls. It was noisy and chaotic. Rows of identical booths, each decorated and individualised with pictures and personal items.

Losevsky led her through a large steel door and into the first of many corridors. Jen felt the temperature drop. The tunnel was about fifteen feet in diameter with white ceiling lamps reflecting onto a shiny laminate floor. The limestone walls, irregular in shape, had a luminescent quality not dissimilar to the face of a glacier. Jen thought it was like traveling through the centre of a huge ice sculpture.

They reached another steel door, this one thicker, with a small circular window at eye level. Once through, the next corridor opened up into a large cave roughly the size of a sports hall. Jen felt her body twitch and cramp against the icy coldness creeping back into her bones. Her diaphragm was raised up and her breathing more shallow. It was her body's way of warning her, the deathlike state of yesterday still fresh in her mind. Inside the cavern, lined up in six neat rows, were servers encased in clear Perspex.

Above them, steel struts crossing like an impossible railway network carried cabling and blue lights that pulsed every metre or so. At the end of each stack a single red security light was blinking.

Jen could see hundreds of similar lights, tailing off into the distance like a landing strip. There were literally thousands of boxes. All active, all alive.

'Have you been to the vault before, Ms Savoretti?' Losevsky asked, striding the black vinyl floor towards another doorway in the distance.

'No, never,' Jen answered, taking in the scale.

'This is one of nineteen data halls,' he explained, brightening up. 'Most of the world's conversations are stored here.' He turned to her and smirked. 'Bet there's interesting stuff in here, eh?'

Jen looked back at him. He was clearly excited to be showing a girl around. She understood that, but she needed to be careful. She didn't want to make a connection, and especially didn't want to be remembered.

'Level four is…?' She didn't break a smile.

Losevsky's face dropped a little. 'This way.'

'Okay, you're passing through the last of the level two areas.' It was Nathan's voice in her ear again. 'He's right, you know. There are nineteen of those data rooms, 25,000 square feet each.'

'You're a geek,' Jen said, quietly.

Losevsky turned and looked confused. Jen looked the other way until he started walking again.

'I admit it. It's true.' Nathan's smile was obvious. 'Right, you're going to take a lift and then more security. Levels three and four. You'll need to do your *persuade* thing and hope your ID holds up. You work for Synergy, one of the companies on their list of approved suppliers. It should be okay.'

Losevsky didn't speak again until they approached the security gate.

'I can't go any further than this.' His voice was flatter than before.

Jen thanked him and smiled. He returned the gesture happily, like a puppy. She watched him go. He seemed to have regained some of the spring in his step.

Nice kid.

Jen decided not to think about the trouble he would be in soon. She turned and faced the next corridor in the underground maze. It was smaller than the others, a long tube-like structure, around 30 metres long, with a separate clear section in the centre like a glass room, with four guards, two either side. The nearest two were eyeing her closely, the farthest two were sitting on plastic chairs. It was obvious they didn't get a lot of traffic down here.

'It's a scanning chamber,' Nathan explained. 'You step in, they scan you, let you out if you're cleared. Those doors could withstand a huge blast, you know, wouldn't even knock a hair out of place on any of those guards.'

'Thanks for the info.'

Jen approached and connected with the first two guards. She needed to ensure they would allow her into the airlock. They frisked her and only stopped momentarily to check her bag. The other two guards beyond the scanner were up now. A large screen displayed the outline of her body as she entered the chamber. Once inside, the clear doors sealed with a rush of air and deep thumping sound, popping her ears. Machinery kicked into gear. Through the clear wall she could see the guards on the far side processing her scan, which would of course show discrepancies. Jen switched her focus to them, releasing the guards from the entrance.

Something felt different immediately.

Of the two guards, the one on her right was going to be a problem. She knew it straight away. He looked up and frowned at her, fighting, reminding her of the agent in the car park when she had first met Nathan. Jen was surprised by how long ago that felt. Mac had still been alive. It felt like a different life.

Jen concentrated. The 'problem' guard explained to his colleague that Jen was carrying unauthorised equipment. She closed her eyes.

Don't panic. Stay calm.

She felt her heart swelling against her chest and her lungs being squeezed as if under pressure. This fatigue appeared to be cumulative and dependent on the target's ability to fight the Histeridae.

Jen was inside their minds and seeing with their eyes now. She could see herself standing in the chamber, eyes closed, and the screen with the offending objects highlighted in red. To her right a large red button, a panic button… which was begging to be pressed. The 'problem' guard wanted to hit that alarm. *This woman isn't authorised,* he was shouting in his mind. *Something's wrong!*

Jen pushed the breath from her lungs and concentrated. The guard's name was Andrei Shulga and he was very strong-minded. Always had been.

< *Andrei, there's nothing wrong,* > she told him, guiding his thoughts. She went deeper, to a place beyond suggestion, a place where she could become his thoughts. It felt like diving into the ocean and the water was darker here.

< *This woman isn't here to do any harm. She is a technician and has full clearance.* >

She turned Andrei's head toward his colleague, who looked confused and worried.

'Are you okay, Andrei?' the guard asked, his voice sounding slow. He was speaking Russian but Jen could understand him somehow, the Histeridae working at a deeper level of her brain, deeper than language.

Andrei Shulga finally spoke.

'I thought something was wrong, but it's fine,' he said and felt better as the words left him. Andrei knew that if he said something, then he meant it, he didn't waste his breath otherwise. He worked the situation through in his mind again, unaware that it was Jen planting the seeds and controlling the outcome.

The storm and the lack of staff are making me twitchy, Andrei thought. *Yes, that's it. It's fine. It's all fine.*

'She's clear,' he said confidently.

Time returned to normal. Jen stepped from the chamber and nodded at them both. She asked for directions. In Russian. With the route explained, she continued past them. Although her locks of red hair were pushed under a black cap and she hadn't worn makeup for days, the guards watched her a little longer than they would most technicians.

It was quieter down here, the kind of silence that only exists deep under the earth. Even the machines were quiet, tucked away inside sealed rooms, the place deserted. Five minutes went by and she didn't see anyone.

'Not far now,' Nathan said suddenly, making her jump.

Not far. Owen Powell had been drowning down here. A dream created by Jen with one purpose: reveal where Baden kept their secrets. Chamber 457B held the answers – Jen was sure of it – and she was close.

'Nice work, by the way,' Nathan said.

'Thank you.'

'When did you learn to speak Russian?'

Jen shrugged. 'Until today, I didn't know I could.'

CHAPTER 48

'You're close now.' Nathan watched the small red dot move across his screen. 'You should see the chamber just up ahead.'

The large, cavernous server rooms and manned security checks were way behind them now. Nathan was relieved. There was only so much he could do if they raised the alarm. Since then he had watched her dot move through what seemed like miles on his three-dimensional blueprint. The final *assembly* was still incomplete in places, chunks of rooms and corridors missing or sketchy, but it wouldn't matter – her route was clear.

'There's a door.' Jen's voice was calm but accusing.

Nathan beamed the blueprint into the room. It appeared, its glowing lines reaching up to the ceiling and out to the walls. He stepped into the projection and began exploring, zooming into the tunnel and looking for clues.

The map was cobbled together from millions of sources, each one assigned and colour-coded, a kaleidoscopic depiction of weeks of work. He positioned himself in her exact location, bringing the map to almost life-sized. There, right in front of him, was a missing section of wall.

He frowned. The assembly was incomplete.

'Nathan?'

'I don't see the door,' he replied.

'I can assure you, it's here. Big, solid and locked.'

Nathan spun the map again, looking for alternatives. There

wasn't another obvious way through.

She spoke again. 'Can you open it from there?'

'I'm going to try,' he said, doubt buzzing through him. 'I'm sorry. I must have old data for that area.'

There was a pause. 'Listen, Nathan. You've done really well getting us this far. Just do what you can.'

Jen looked at the door. Solid steel. Next to it was a flat, red scanner. There was no way she was getting through. Nathan needed to get it open. He'd messed up once before when they had broken into Powell's house, missing an alert and putting her in serious danger. She wasn't angry at him – she meant what she'd said, he had done well – but this wasn't good. Even if they made it though, what about her escape route? What if they hit a dead end again? She looked back down the corridor, miles of white vinyl flooring and doorways stretching far into the distance, and prayed she wouldn't have to go back.

'Did it work?' Nathan asked.

Jen's heart sank and then the door clicked open loudly.

'Never doubted you,' Jen said, laughing. 'Not for a second.'

Ahead were more corridors with large black numbers stenciled above doorways. It was a welcome sight and finally an indication of progress. They started at 400. Jen jogged, heart pounding, until Nathan's voice told her to stop. She looked up.

457B.

Red light. Drowning.

She shuddered at the memory and entered Powell's code into the keypad next to the door. *The day he had become CEO of Baden Corporation.* She closed her eyes and hoped. When she opened them again, there was a green light.

She stepped through the doorway and into a glass tunnel, suspended above a limestone chamber of servers – at least ten white rack units – each with an attached monitor. At the far end of the walkway was a circular room and a console.

She walked, boots squeaking against the polished surface, breaking the otherwise perfect silence. 'I'm inside now.'

'Right, you need to attach the device within a few feet of the screen.' Nathan said, clearly trying to stay calm.

This is it, she thought. *I've done my part, got us into the chamber as promised. Now it's your turn.*

Jen looked down through the tinted green floor and spotted armed guards, three in total, plus a droid, patrolling the server room below. One of the guards nodded but didn't smile. The scene reminded her of something she had watched as a child. A cartoon about a man inside the belly of a whale. She felt like that man, and if someone lit a fire, all hell would break loose. She stood at the console, which was comprised of a voice board, mind interface and three holographic feedback screens. She grabbed a chair, sat and slid herself up to the desk.

'Right, look busy,' Nathan suggested.

Jen attached a small device to the underside of the steel console. It gripped the surface and immediately went to work. For a few seconds she held her breath. If Nathan told her it wasn't working, then all this could be for nothing. All of it. Jen glanced down to see a guard watching her. *Look busy? How the hell am I supposed to do that?* She nodded, forcing herself not to smile.

When Nathan's voice returned, he was excited.

'I can see the server,' he said, almost shouting. 'Jen, I can see it all.'

'Okay, good.' She spoke deliberately, lifting her hands in a gesture that suggested to the guards below that the people back at base were giving her a hard time. 'I will sit here and *look busy.* Just be quick, okay?'

'Search algorithm is running,' Nathan whispered. 'We're going to be okay.'

Jen told him he was doing well, but her mind was elsewhere, trying to figure out how to ask him a question, one that had been burning since leaving England. She'd assured herself there was no point raising it before now. What if they hadn't made it this far? They could have had an argument for no reason.

'Nathan,' she asked quietly, wringing her hands.

'Hmmm?'

'I need you to do something else.'

'Sorry? What?'

'You need to do something else while we're here.'

'Yes, I heard that bit,' he said, briskly. 'What do you need? Pizza?'

He was jovial, trying to keep her relaxed. He's good at this, Jen thought, better than expected. He'd managed to keep his cool in situations where she'd seen lesser men crumble.

She swallowed and said clearly, 'I need you to search for someone. A man named Conrad Fowler.'

'I'm sorry, what?' Nathan shouted, incredulous. 'Who the hell is he?'

'He's on a witness protection programme. You'll need to do a wider search.'

Jen explained the deal she'd made with Lynch, knowing immediately it had been a mistake not to tell him. She tried to persuade him that it had been their only chance to get to Russia, that Conrad Fowler was a bad man, that it was a good trade, but as she talked she felt more and more empty, embarrassed by her secrecy.

'So, we find this guy, give Lynch the details and then what?' Nathan hissed. 'Fowler is tracked down and killed, along with a few others, probably.'

Jen remained silent.

'Brilliant.' Nathan's optimism seemed to have left him entirely. 'Now I'm a fucking hit-man, too. Sentencing some guy to death. Nice, Jen, thanks a lot. What happened to teamwork? Sharing? In this together?'

You're right. I'm a bitch.

There was a long pause broken by Nathan's voice, horribly monotone and stripped of feeling. 'If we have time – and I have no idea how long this is going to take – then maybe, maybe I'll do it.' He sighed loudly. 'You should have told me.'

'You're right,' Jen replied. 'No more excuses. I'm sorry.'

There, deep in the Shiryaevo Vault, buried under tonnes of limestone, Jennifer Logan felt something she hadn't for a long time: a genuine, personal connection. She wanted to tell him that she really *was* sorry – and that, perhaps more importantly, that she cared about him.

★ ★ ★

Victor Reyland's sleep was interrupted by his neural comms tugging at his consciousness, lifting him out of his selected dream. He was annoyed until he noticed the caller's name.

< *Zido Zitagi.* >

Reyland cleared his throat and answered.

'Were you asleep?' Zitagi asked.

'I was.' He tapped the light next to his bed and checked the time. 2.05am. 'This better be good.'

'It is. We've found her.'

'Logan?' he asked.

'Yes, Sir.'

'Where?'

'Samara, Russia. Picked up her image on a mind sweep, local trapper in the Zhiguli Mountain Range. She got caught in a storm, took shelter.'

Victor Reyland was fully awake now and calculating options. 'Shiryaevo? The Vault?'

'Yes, Sir. She's already there.'

'If she lets loose with the Histeridae in that Vault, we could have a serious situation on our hands. Governments and major corps pay good money for their data to be secure.'

'I know, Sir, I understand.'

'We can't afford an incident, Zitagi.'

'I understand,' she said again.

'What the hell does she think she's going to achieve? That place is impenetrable.' He paused a beat. 'Even with that *device*. There's no way she's getting anything.' It was a statement and somehow also a question.

'We have her trapped.' Zitagi said. 'We can contain her, bring her in and –'

'She's inside?' he interrupted. 'You're sure?'

'Yes. Posing as a technician.'

'Alright.' Reyland composed himself.

'Sir, what *are* the risks?' Zitagi asked. 'If she did manage to steal something and escape, what secrets do we have down there?'

Reyland frowned. He could sometimes forget there was so much she didn't know. He often thought it was a strange game they were made to play.

'Zitagi,' he said, his mind made up. 'Authorise a strike team. Even if she does find something, make sure she doesn't leave with it.' Reyland sighed. 'Are you sure this blocker of yours is going to work?'

'Absolutely. She won't stand a chance.'

'Keep me informed,' Reyland said and hung up.

Finding a way to block the Histeridae had cost the lives of three people. That in itself didn't concern Zido. What did was her inability to test the newly developed technology. She was confident it would work, but the only way to truly know was to go up against Logan.

Her sighting had been confirmed seven hours ago. Zitagi hadn't waited for approval. She immediately began preparing everything, hoping Reyland would authorise her initiative. Her strike team were assembled in readiness. It would take them fifteen minutes to reach the vault.

She looked around the busy command centre at the team of operators initiating the mission, *her* mission. A central screen displayed a team of soldiers running towards two combat helicopters. Reyland had decided Zitagi was ready for bigger things and the recovery of the Histeridae would validate his decision. She would take it back and Jennifer Logan would be dead. Failure wasn't anywhere near her mind.

You're trapped, Logan, Zitagi thought and smiled, her tongue flicking across her dry lips.

Trapped like a rat.

CHAPTER 49

Nathan was nearly done. He'd found Conrad Fowler too but wasn't going to tell Jen that. He was still seething at her *extra* request.

He pulled his eyes away from the screen and blinked, gazing around the bare hotel room. A packed case was placed in the centre, bathed in the tangerine glow of the collective heaters. He would finish here, pick her up and they would head to the safe house. There they would wait two weeks for things to die down, for security to become lax.

He rubbed his face and turned back to the screen. It was flashing. Multiple alerts.

'Shit,' he said, dropping all thoughts of planning, of success.

'What?' Jen asked.

'Shit, shit shit.' His voice was accelerating. 'No!'

'Talk to me, Nathan. What is it?'

'You need to get out of there.' He swallowed, his throat clicking loudly. 'They've initiated a silent lockdown, a manual shutdown of the main frame. All doors, exits, and systems.' He tapped ferociously. 'I've got 60 seconds max before they lock me out.'

Nathan watched his link to the server disappear. They had found what they came for. Secret files. Baden, the Government, Histeridae project files. He needed to park all of that now.

The only thing *he* had was a list of files. The actual data was on the drive in Jen's hand. He needed to get her back safely or it was all for nothing.

Jen's mind was racing, her body tingling with adrenalin.

Silent lockdown?

'Then… they know we're here,' she said slowly.

The guards below her looked up, eyes darting, clearly listening to unseen voices. It wouldn't take them long to reach her. There were no sirens, no flashing lights, nothing to worry an intruder. A silent lockdown meant they *knew* she was here but didn't want to alert *her* to the fact. Nathan had given her a chance, and if she was quick, she might be able to use it.

'How could they know?' Nathan screamed. 'I was so careful!'

'It's not your fault,' Jen replied, the face of the trapper who saved her flashing into her mind.

I should never have let him go.

Jen grabbed the device from under the table. 'Just get me out of here.'

She had counted three guards and the first was already inside, pistol raised, shuffling towards her. Another followed. She guessed the other one was hiding behind the doorway. He popped his head out confirming her suspicion.

The nearest guard closed in and Jen noticed his hands were shaking. They didn't expect anyone to break in, let alone get this far.

'You can't escape,' the guard said, sounding like he was trying to persuade himself, too.

Below, Jen saw the droid, large and heavy. It couldn't move to her level. Her relief was temporary, though, as it flashed a blue laser across a console on a nearby wall. With a loud metallic scraping sound, steel security shutters began to descend from gaps in the ceiling. The guard's expressions turned from shock to panic as the shutters descended rapidly on all sides around them. Jen raised her hands, lit red by security lights as the metal sheets completed their journey, trapping her and two guards inside.

The Histeridae's tendrils flickered and spun around the cylindrical tomb, unseen by all except her. Flashes of blue and purple danced around and then through the guards. Jen made her selection, the weaker of the two: Leo Guskov. Leo had no idea why he ordered Mikhail, his colleague, to drop his gun and kick it away. Mikhail shook his head and asked why Leo would betray him like this. They had worked together for over two years, made jokes, managed against all odds to find some fun down there in the depths. Leo had even eaten a meal at Mikhail's home. Leo raised his gun and asked again. As the gun skidded past her feet, Jen resisted the temptation to grab the weapon. As the guards continued confused talk of betrayal and broken trust, she asked Nathan for a way out.

'There isn't one. I can't control those shutters.' Nathan's voice was robotic and broken.

'Are you locked out completely?' Jen asked.

'Not yet, but it won't be long. I'm opening doors on other levels where I can. You just need to get there.'

Just, Jen thought, deciding it was time to turn things up a notch. She turned on Leo Guskov.

'How do you open the door?' she screamed into his mind.

His expression turned to abject horror. He clearly had no idea how this woman was doing these things. He blinked, a tear streaking down his cheek, followed by another. Jen crept towards him, her face bathed in the blood-red security lights. She could read Leo Guskov's mind. He was convinced he was being controlled by some kind of she-devil, the mind from the stories his father read to him as a child, stories of demons and evil spirits. Jen used it and transformed into the demon from his darkest fears. She approached him, her face red, eyes like black wet marbles.

'Tell me how to open them!' Jen boomed into the corners of his brain. 'Or I burn the flesh from your bones.'

'It's a timed door,' Leo sobbed. 'T – timed door... it's impossible.'

Mikhail, his partner, was at the door, his face pressed against the window frantically gesturing to the third guard. Jen accessed him too. Mikhail, against his knowledge, revealed that the door could only be opened using a combination of an external keypad override and a reversal of the droid's original instruction. Jen sent her mind through the door, taking control of the remaining guard, chaining them all together in a powerful neural network. It was the third guard's job to press the buttons and sort out that droid.

Minutes later the security mechanism clattered back to life. Jen stood, eerily still as the bluish light from the server room traveled up her body. The shutters rose and banged to a halt and the door clicked open. She jogged past the guards and then walked the third man into the tunnel to join his comrades. The droid had been reset and sensing fresh movement above flashed its blue laser across the nearby console. Again, the shutters began to descend, trapping the confused guards. They huddled together, shivering, their backs against each other, not speaking. They were just relieved the devil was leaving them.

'I'm out,' Jen said.

'Straight ahead, then left,' Nathan shouted, his voice clearer again.

'Lock all the doors behind me,' Jen replied.

'Already doing it.'

Jen traveled the white corridors, retracing her steps. She was sprinting now and it felt good, her boots gripping well, pounding the smooth floor.

'I've got guards massing on the level above,' Nathan informed her. 'Take the next left. That door is open.'

Ahead of her, in the distance, she could see movement. She stopped and slipped through the doorway on her left as instructed. It was a stairwell, steel steps surrounded by white block walls.

'Where now?' she asked, her breath laboured.

'Okay. Got it!' he shouted. 'We need to get to… yes, the original excavation tunnel. Up three flights. I'll work on getting the doors open.'

'Original tunnel? What about the heat vent?' Jen didn't wait, launching herself at the flight of stairs, jumping two steps at a time.

'We lost that. I can't get you there. Nearly all exits are locked. I'm going to try and get you out via the visitor centre. There's an access tunnel… I think we can get to it.'

'Are you sure it's still there?' Jen asked.

'This is where the older version of the maps might actually be a good thing.' Jen heard the distant clatter and crashing of people and doors. 'They're closing in on me,' she panted, bounding up the steps.

'Listen to this,' Nathan said and patched her into the base's communication chatter. She heard multiple voices.

'What is this, some kind of drill? Stand down? Is that correct? Confirm order.'

Another voice. *'Can someone tell me what's going on? Is this safe?'*

Nathan explained. 'I'm sending out random secure messages via their comms centre. Some think it's a drill, others a chemical leak. All of them, confused.'

It was clever. In fact, it was genius. Jen resisted the urge to tell him. She wasn't out yet. One more flight of stairs.

Nathan shouted encouragement, but as the words left his mouth, he felt his heart sink. He closed his eyes, sat back in his chair and swore loudly.

'What is it?' Jen shouted, the sound of her boots hitting the steel stair treads banging in his ears.

He stared blankly at the message filling his screen. It was winking. Mocking him.

//System offline //

'They've locked me out,' he admitted with a heavy sigh. 'I'm sorry.'

CHAPTER 50

Jen sprinted ahead, her mind spinning, adrenalin through the roof. She could hear shouting and footfalls but couldn't tell where the sounds originated. At least she was warm now, the air on her face the only reminder of the actual temperature. Nathan might be locked out of the system, but thankfully they could still talk. She didn't want to be alone down here.

'Did we get the files?' she panted. 'Are they any use?'

The drive was stuffed inside her rucksack.

'I've checked the inventory.' Nathan replied, 'We got enough.'

The white limestone corridors were behind her now, replaced by dull grey concrete walls with rusted light fittings. There were bulbs out and the air seemed stale, suggesting it wasn't used very often.

'You should be in the older section of the vault,' Nathan said, as if reading her thoughts. 'I managed to get most of the doors ahead open. These are the original service tunnels – tricky route, but you can still get out.'

Through the gloom she saw movement. The end of the long corridor joined a circular access tunnel, and in the centre was a large blast door, hinged and open. Jen guessed the door was around twenty feet in width. A row of ten steel rods protruded from its open edge. They matched ten cylindrical holes in the wall next to it. It was a nuclear-grade blast door, and it was closing.

'Right. Follow the corridor until you come to a door, probably old-looking,' Nathan calmly instructed. 'Looks like an old bunker – '

'Too late – I'm here and it's closing!' she screamed. 'What do I do?' She had already made the mental calculation; she might make it, but it would be tight.

'Run!' Nathan shouted. 'If that closes…'

She put her head down and heard the man's voice before she saw him. He was shouting at her to stop. Jen accessed the Histeridae and pushed him awkwardly aside. He lurched to the right and fell back, hitting his head on the jagged limestone wall. Jen ran and launched herself into the narrow gap between the huge door and the studded circular frame that would seal shut in a matter of seconds. The thought of the door crushing her like a melon entered her mind just as she felt her rucksack snag on one of door's stubby locking pins. The bags strap looped, tugged and then slipped from the steel, spinning her a little in the air. She just managed to stay on her feet as the huge door banged shut behind her. It shook the mountain and resonated up through her boots, sending a vibration down the cavernous chamber and away.

'Jen?' Nathan cried out.

'Too close,' she bellowed, sliding to a stop, resting her hands on her knees. 'Too fucking close. More notice next time.'

Jen accessed the guard on the other side of the door. He was out cold.

Nathan apologised and she heard him whispering multiple calculations under his breath. Eventually he said, 'Up ahead, follow the tunnel to your left.'

'The files,' Jen said, running again, shaking off the vision of being crushed alive. 'You're sure they're useful to us?'

'I don't know yet. All I have are file names. The secure data is on the drive. It will take time to trawl through them, but first we need to get you and that drive out of there.'

She didn't reply. She knew if she was captured they would get the Histeridae and the drive. It was all down to her.

What's new.

The tunnel, which had become circular and smooth, came to an abrupt end. The walls seemed to just stop and open out into a dark void, like an exhaust into space. The only indication that the world ended here on purpose were two painted yellow lines on the floor ahead. She crept towards the edge, eyes adapting to the absence of light. In the darkness, and all around, she saw the jagged texture of rock. As her eyes adjusted fully she saw another bigger tunnel running parallel to the smaller one she was leaving. She peered over the edge to see a small drop onto a tarmac road. To her right, complete darkness, to her left a faint glow in the distance.

'Left?' she suggested hopefully, her words echoing away.

'Yes. About half a mile. The visitor centre. We can get you out there.'

She dropped down onto the road. Every hundred yards or so a dim green security light set her bearings. The distant glow was becoming brighter with each step. She jogged, wondering about the contents of the drive. For years she had thought about her father, imagined his work, his research. Since finding the hidden memory, her need to understand him had become more heightened. After everything – Mac's betrayal, Hibernation, Baden – it seemed even more crucial to understand and remember him correctly. As an adult. She wanted to know the *real* him, what he believed, to understand why he'd taken the Histeridae.

Ahead, a building emerged from the muddy grey darkness: a prefabricated steel structure built into the rock that stretched far into the distance. There was a single window, long and without panels – a viewing room perhaps – and a door. She ran to it and pulled the handle down. The door creaked open loudly.

Nathan's voice. 'Okay, you should be in sublevel one. Make your way through and up the stairwell to your left. We can get you out on the ground floor.'

Jen stepped inside, squinting. The corridor ahead seemed to be lit from all sides, its white brilliance burning her eyes. Framed pictures of the vault during various stages of construction hung on the walls, and above a sign reminded her that this area was for AUTHORISED PERSONNEL ONLY. She crept forward, passing a corkboard decorated with team member names and rota-duties. It was quiet. Deserted.

'Where is everyone?' Jen asked.

'It's 7pm,' Nathan replied. 'It closed over an hour ago. There might be stragglers, so be careful. I opened the main doors, before I got kicked out of the system; hopefully they stayed open.'

Jen took a deep breath. 'You did well, Nathan. It wasn't your fault.'

She felt controlled air again, warm and not unpleasant, but she craved the real thing, wanted out of this hole, this underground coffin. She wanted to feel real warmth and safety and most of all to see Nathan again.

She passed through a set of double doors and out into a hallway. There she saw the stairs, exactly as Nathan had described. She stuck to the edges, staying low, her boots squeaking against the recently cleaned steps. As her eye-line reached the ground floor, she paused, scanning the lobby. In the centre was a huge spiral drill bit like an arrowhead reaching almost the full height of the large open space. Placed evenly throughout the lobby were glass cabinets and exhibits. She crept forward, hugging the edges, darting between the cabinets. In the corner a holographic film displayed a dimensional model of the facility. There were cameras everywhere.

'Won't they spot me?' she whispered.

'Maybe. But they are focused on the vault right now. They won't be expecting you here – we might get away with it. Let me check their radio transmissions, get a better idea where they're heading. Hang on.'

Jen entered the foyer and gift shop. Still no one. The place was empty. She peered carefully out through the main glass doors to see snow flickering yellow against the glow of raised floodlights, and below that, car parks and roads. It looked familiar, but she was struggling to get her bearings. In the distance she heard a sound, a repetitive droning, whistling noise interspersed with a kind of whipping sound.

Shlack, shlack, shlack.

She hunched down behind a display of toy metal diggers. The sound was getting louder, becoming more and more familiar. She cocked her head, trying to form a mental image. The answer came quickly and triumphantly, like a person's name that had been close to mind but painfully elusive. Her relief turned to fear as she watched the snow curling up from the ground like milk being poured into an invisible wine glass and felt the whip of air pass beneath the doors and rush over her.

'Jen,' Nathan shouted suddenly. 'I'm picking up transmissions, they've got two choppers...'

'They're here,' she said, her voice cracking. 'I can see them.'

Only combat choppers made that specific sound. They hovered perfectly still as two teams of six repelled onto the tarmac below. Jen noted their attire. White snow fatigues, balaclavas and assault rifles.

Special Forces.

CHAPTER 51

Jen watched, helpless, as the strike team crossed the car park. They were in tight formation, organised, their rifles scanning left and right, moving gracefully.

'I can see a team of twelve heading towards the Vault's entrance.' She crept along the shop display and poked her head out, craning her neck to see the men before they disappeared from view.

With an unseen signal, they stopped. One of them – Jen presumed he was the point man – gestured towards her position. Two broke away from the group and jogged towards the visitors centre, towards her. She could see their eyes glowing green – night vision – and they would have heat sensors too.

'I'm screwed,' Jen whispered, backing into the shop, clambering, searching for cover and ideas, running through her options. The Histeridae was central to most of them, but she knew that if she used it, it wouldn't be long before the rest of their team showed up. These guys were serious. They would have a backup plan. Whatever it took until she was captured or dead. There was no quiet exit now. She would need to control multiple guards in order to escape, but twelve? *Really?*

The two men crossed the road, about two hundred yards from her, and a plan formed in her mind.

Control the approaching men, turn them against their own and in the confusion, make a run for it.

Nathan was frantic, blind to all of this. All he could hear was the empty hiss of unused radio channels. The arrival of the helicopters had brought radio silence. These men were here to do a job and get out with minimal fuss and disruption. He felt utterly helpless. He glanced out the window, knowing that just over that range of hills Jen was trapped, and there was nothing he could do. His chest felt tight and he swallowed hard against the sticky lump that had formed in his throat. He couldn't help feeling he had failed her, that this was his fault.

Working against everything her body was telling her, Jen calmed herself and accessed the Histeridae. The thought tendrils rushed greedily outward, searching for prey, attaching easily to the vibrant, alert minds of the approaching men. She had a good connection and could see through their eyes immediately: the visitor centre just ahead. She was about to stop them, to turn them around and begin firing back at their own squad, when she felt the most extraordinary sensation. It felt as if the world were suddenly quiet and peaceful. As if time had stopped. It was calm.

But something was wrong.

It reminded her of that awful moment of silence before a crash, those sickening seconds that seem to drag out the inevitable. There was a sudden push, and although it was purely psychic, it felt as if she had been punched hard in the stomach and slapped across the face simultaneously. She cried out in pain, stumbling back into stands and shop displays, sending them crashing noisily to the floor around her.

'Jen, are you okay? Jen?' Nathan's desperate voice sounded distant and hollow. She was flat on the floor, her mind resetting somehow after the mental beating it had just endured.

'What happened?' Nathan's voice, still thin and distant.

She felt dizzy and found herself staggering, pushing herself up. Her body felt like a lump of metal that had been banged with a sledge-hammer, the vibrations still pulsing though her. She could see the two soldiers now, running straight towards her.

Nathan's warning came at exactly the same time as her understanding of the situation. 'They've just broken radio silence,' he shouted. 'They know your location.'

Whoever these people were, they were expecting the Histeridae, and they were somehow immune. Her mind was racing faster than ever and she could feel her pulse banging against her temples.

'The Histeridae,' she said. 'It doesn't work on them... it doesn't work...'

Zitagi.

She felt creeping fear working itself over her. They were going to capture her, torture her, take everything she had discovered and then bury it with her. A whimper escaped her mouth and she felt the tears of frustration pushing at her eyeballs. Without the Histeridae, she was lost.

Nathan's voice pulled her back. 'It worked before. Search again, find anyone *except* these guys, anyone else you can use. You need to create a diversion.' His voice was firm and direct. 'Jen. Do it now.'

She shook her head, her mouth stretched into a grimace, and without thinking she searched with the Histeridae again, this time avoiding the approaching men and reaching out into the corners of the base.

There, crouched behind a cluster of cars she found what she was looking for. One of the Shiryaevo guards. He had decided to wait out whatever *situation* was occurring. Jen had other ideas. She took control of him, seeing what he could see, and raised his gun towards two of the Special Forces soldiers running towards the visitors centre.

Taking aim wasn't easy. She had to close her own eyes and see through his, but the clarity came. It was a standard-issue assault rifle. Decent scope. She closed one of his eyes and pressed the butt into her shoulder, resting her cheek on the cold stock. Gently she squeezed the trigger, just a little pressure, and heard the rifle click.

Nothing.

Jen looked down at the gun and the man's rough hands. She removed the safety, aimed again and fired, hitting one of the soldiers square in the back. His companion turned and crouched next to the fallen body, looking around frantically. Nathan included her in the feed as the soldier broke radio silence.

'This is Silver Team, we have a man down. East car park, please advise.'

The main strike team were now in the vaults lobby, exactly where Jen had been a few hours earlier. They stopped, regrouped and started running back towards Jen's location.

She made the shooter run across the car park and up the side of a building. The ladder rungs burnt at the guards hands. Jen didn't care; she needed him on the roof. She needed a bigger diversion. He clambered up and lay flat. Jen watched as the strike team closed in.

She switched the gun to semiautomatic and opened fire, aiming to kill. It was too late for compromise or attempts at stealth. Through the scope of the guard's rifle, Jen watched as the strike team members individually seemed to appear and then evaporated again, each time somehow making progress. There was no way to make a shot. They were too good.

'I need to draw them away,' she whispered to Nathan, her body slumped against a pillar in the gift shop. 'I can't hold them like this. They will be here soon no matter what I do.' She fired off a couple more rounds from the roof.

'There's a back-up generator,' Nathan said. 'Look to the left outside the visitor centre, between two buildings. Two massive fuel towers.'

Jen searched for another mind and found a guard, who moments ago had been assisting the new arrivals. Now he was hers. She took control, running him towards the towers.

'I'm listening to their communications. They're short and controlled, but I'm finally getting the gist. They know where you are and they know about the Histeridae,' Nathan advised. 'And they've been instructed to shoot any guards who get in their way.'

There was a thudding sound and Jen was suddenly thrust back into her own body. She saw a green flashing object attach to the glass doors and managed to shield her eyes in time as splintering glass exploded over her, the explosive charge blowing the windows out in a piercing rush of air. She crawled back, crunching glass underfoot as a bullet whipped past her. Too close. She'd lost control of the two guards, her mind forced into singularity. She was up and running, back into the foyer as searchlights flashed across the shop front. She passed the exhibits and skidded along the floor, hiding behind the huge drill bit that dominated the centre of the room.

Stay calm, Jen. Stay calm.

She focused. Guard one was still on the roof. She made him hers again and fired random shots, slowing the approaching strike team as best she could. Guard two was outside watching the team work their way into the building. Jen felt as though she were playing a game of tennis, except she was both players as well as the umpire, watching, controlling, thinking. Her mind was split and it was stretching. She turned the second guard towards the back-up generator and ran. Ahead were two black towers, ridged and tall enough to cut black shapes against the bluish night sky. They were covered in signs.

She didn't need to read them, they all meant danger. Jen opened fire, muzzle flashing, bullets ripping through the tall drums. The last thing she saw, through the eyes of her unfortunate surrogate, was a tiny flicker of flame in the darkness, and then a pure and brilliant white.

CHAPTER 52

Jen smelt fuel, smoke and burning plastic. The air had been pushed out of the room and she couldn't breathe. She stood, wincing against the heat pouring from either side of the statue that shielded her. She crawled away, instinctively sticking to the ground until she could walk again. Through shattered glass she stepped out of what remained of the foyer.

The entire side of the visitors centre was gone, replaced by glass and debris, huge pieces of stone and jagged steel erupting out like broken fingers. Fires burned all around her and she could see bodies, flames flickering over them. A river of burning fuel was spreading and flowing across the car park, bathing the surrounding area in primitive light.

She made her way from the building. As she staggered through the rubble a single word banged through her consciousness over and over.

Murderer.

'Jen?' Nathan's voice cut the confusion. 'Are you there?'

'What have I done?' She stumbled through the torturous scene, towards the perimeter fence, bodies everywhere, some in pieces, raw meat smouldering on melting tarmac.

'I heard the explosion from here,' Nathan said. 'Are you okay? Are you hurt?'

She shook her head. 'I'm okay.' She looked up at the rooftop. The sniper was gone, released from her murderous grip during the explosion. The other guard would have been obliterated. Her ears were hissing loudly, damaged by the sudden and deafening explosion, but she could hear distant shouting. She passed a man who was laying face-down. He twitched and began to crawl, groaning, his white combat jacket burned open revealing shiny red flesh, seared and fused black around the edges. He saw her and stretched out his hand. Jen knelt next to him and plucked a radio from his belt.

She looked out across the car park and through the fence. There was the mountain range she had descended earlier. Her pack was up there, hidden next to the air vent, her original exit plan before she'd blown half the building away.

It seemed a long time ago. In fact her whole life, her previous self, felt absent. Her head was spinning, dogs were barking and she could hear more shouting.

A gust of wind fanned the lake of burning fuel surrounding the wreckage, lighting her battered frame a rich golden red. She walked but felt her ankle buckle, tight in her boot, painful and stretched. She couldn't remember hurting it. The adrenalin, covering for her, enabling her to live a little longer.

'Where are you?' Nathan asked.

'Heading towards the main gate, towards the hills.' She hobbled behind a car and took a moment to catch her breath. Around her more voices, screaming and shouting. She looked back at the visitor centre, a broken construction, collapsed in on itself.

She could see at least three distinctive white shapes, people, milling around. Silver Team weren't all taken out by the blast. They spread out and began searching again.

She picked herself up, working her way along the parked cars, her ankle sending sickening waves of pain through her hip and back.

Nathan heard her cry out. 'Are you hurt?'

'I can make it,' she whispered defiantly.

A rush of air whipped past her and she heard the ding of metal. They were firing at her. She broke into a run, her ankle sending flashes of white pain through her vision. The combination of days on the run, the blizzard, using the Histeridae and huge adrenalin dumps had finally taken its toll. She couldn't believe how drained she felt, as if the energy was literally being sucked from her. It occurred to her that whatever had blocked the Histeridae might also have caused this fatigue. She'd never been so tired in all her life.

She decided to focus on something important.

The obvious thoughts came, exposing the truth and the lies, but those ideas felt somehow distant now. They were concepts that brought no warmth, no vitality. She needed something more immediate. She focused instead on the one person she still trusted, the man who hadn't let her down. She imagined his hands reaching towards her, pulling her on, willing her to be safe. Suddenly he seemed essential, like she *had* to return to him. They were a team now. Their meeting suddenly felt like fate.

Another bullet fizzed above her and into the darkness. The shouting had stopped. They were organised and closing in.

His voice came then, as if on cue. 'Jen, I'm out and heading to the meeting point.'

'Okay.' She was struggling to maintain her composure. 'Nathan.'

'Yeah?'

A pause. Words stuck in her throat. 'Be careful,' she managed.

His voice *had* spurred her on. Time had somehow passed and she was running between trees with snow underfoot. The forest had thickened, encasing and hiding her and the ground, and begun to steepen. It meant she was climbing.

A tight stitch banged in her left side but the energy in her legs had returned and her ankle had stopped complaining.

Five minutes later, as she reached a plateau, she allowed herself a single look back down the hillside. She could see lights, equally spaced. Men with night vision working their way in formation up the hillside. They were moving away from her, though. She was going to make it.

She turned and fell, her heart suddenly pounding in her ears. Her stitch was worse now and it felt as if her body was expanding. She pulled her hand away from her side. It was warm and sticky. She blinked in the gloom, not wanting to see but not being able to help herself. Her hand was stained dark, covered in her blood.

She'd been shot.

CHAPTER 53

Jen was on her knees, gasping for breath. The sight of her own blood had told her body that it was time to go into shock, that it was okay to stop pretending. She could feel death closing in on her again, but this time it meant to finish the job. Exhaustion returned with a wave of pain that threatened to knock her unconscious. The radio she had plucked from the wretched, crawling guard sparked to life.

'Logan?' She recognised the voice. Zitagi sounded calm, controlled. 'Listen to me very carefully.'

Jen snarled at the radio, grabbing it, fully expecting to throw it away but cradling it instead, eyes closed, panting.

'Logan. If you run, you're going to die. There's nowhere to go.'

Jen howled, lifted herself up and continued walking, the radio dangling at her side. She thought about that bitch, miles away, somewhere safe, controlling this whole situation.

Zitagi's voice drifted up. 'You don't understand what's *really* going on. This is bigger that you realise, bigger than you and I.' There was the slightest hint of something genuine in those words; it was a quality Jen didn't associate with this woman.

Jen coughed, wiping her lips, ignoring the dark smears glistening on the back of her hand. 'I've got evidence.' Jen hissed, 'I'm going to blow this whole thing open and take you down with it.'

'Some secrets are better left buried,' Zitagi responded. 'You don't know what you're doing.' There it was again. Jen could hear something different in Zitagi's voice. It wasn't fear. It was something else. 'Your father was a good man, Jen, he didn't do anything wrong.'

Jen had been dragging herself along and making a decent pace, the lights of men behind her still drifting away from her position. She stopped now and shook her head, sighing into the icy air. Zitagi was playing her, trying to get a radio lock. Jen was at her weakest, desperately reading into her words, wanting them to mean something, for all this mess to make sense.

Fuck this.

Jen threw the radio to the ground and lifted her leg, but before her boot landed, smashing it into pieces, Zitagi spoke again. Five simple words that echoed in Jen's mind in the silence that followed.

'We can't save them all,' Zitagi had pleaded, almost shouted it.

We can't save them all.

CHAPTER 54

The dam was also a bridge crossing the Volga, huge arcs of water pluming from its row of locks below. Nathan, hidden in its shadow, saw Jen stumble out from a line of trees and out onto the riverbank. He ran to her and she collapsed in his arms.

'Are you hurt?' he asked, cradling her. 'What's wrong?'

She looked up at him and smiled. Nathan saw her hands covered in blood and her clothes soaked in it. He held her tightly. She was cold, freezing to death.

How long had she been losing blood? Her skin was horribly pale, eyes dry and lifeless. He carried her back into the shadow of the trees.

'I'm sorry,' she said.

'You don't need to be sorry.' He wiped the hair from her face and frowned. 'I'm getting you out of here.'

Jen shook her head and pushed her bag into his hands. It wasn't the first time she had done this. The memory returned to them both.

'You need to take this.' Her voice rattled. 'Figure out what's going on.'

She's dying, Nathan thought in horror, the calming distant thrum of the dam giving the moment an ethereal, otherworldly quality.

'Just promise me,' Jen whispered, 'you'll finish this.'

Nathan shook his head, breathing rapidly. 'No. Don't talk that way. We can still escape.'

That's when the sound came, gentle and strange – creaking and whistling. They listened, the air cracking around them before tinkling away in a mystical chorus.

'What *is* that?' Nathan asked, confused as the sound came again, surrounding them.

Jen smiled, her face still. 'It's our breath freezing and then hitting the ground. The Russians call it the whisper of stars.'

Nathan stroked her face. 'It's beautiful.'

Jen nodded, pushing the Histeridae into his hands. 'Yes, it is.'

He cupped her hands, the device gripped inside them, and wrapped them in his own. As the Histeridae bonded them together there was no indication, no visual signs, no tendrils or glowing. There was just an overwhelming inner peace.

They both felt it, as if a warm breeze had suddenly surrounded them. The wind died down and in that moment, they both felt love. An undeniable, uncomplicated, unconditional love.

Jen had spent her life searching for that feeling. She had craved it, and yet for reasons unknown, it had eluded her. And now, here, as she lay dying, she felt it. He loved her, with all his heart.

She tried to speak but the words wouldn't leave her mouth. Instead, she felt as if the stars themselves were communicating for her. It was a connection, a truth that would change them both forever. They didn't need to *say* anything. They could feel the universe; they *were* the universe and joined completely to all things.

His lips joined hers and they kissed. It was the only thing left to do. His mouth warmed her, filling her mind, leaving no room for fear, or panic.

She died then, wrapped up in him, his body protecting her.

Nathan wasn't sure how long they had stayed like that. Was it minutes? Hours? His trance was broken by the distant sound of shouting. He stared down at her body, her frozen beauty. He cried for a while, his tears like daggers, but stopped abruptly. He had to move. He dragged her towards the dam knowing that the real pain would come later. For now he was numb, and that wasn't a bad thing. He didn't want them to have her, to use her body in any way. Her last words drove him on.

Promise me you'll finish this.

He pulled her nearer to the rushing water. He was operating on autopilot, knowing he needed to escape, but it was impossible to imagine her gone. How could she be gone? She was an amazing woman. Surely the world wouldn't work without her in it. And she had loved him, he'd felt it.

The experience of joining with her was fading. Maybe that wasn't such a bad thing. There was no way to function in such an intense state. He thought he heard voices again but it was impossible to tell over the roar of the dam. He looked up at the towering waterfalls crashing into the white river below, swirling patters of white foam dancing on the glassy surface below. He crouched and held her one last time, her limp body ice cold. Kissing her forehead, he glanced down and saw her necklace – a small silver ring tied on a bootlace. It was obviously personal, something sentimental. He pulled it from her and stuffed it into his jacket pocket.

There was nothing left to do.

A guttural shout left him as he pushed her off the ledge and watched, through distorted tears, as her body flopped into the icy river, rolled once and was gone. He screamed at the world, clenching his fists in pain, inhalation impossible.

He was alone, again.

In that single moment, Nathan changed forever. He had spent the last few years trying to become somebody new, somebody he thought he needed to be. That night he became something he could never have imagined. It was as if he'd been truly reborn and his purpose reset. He walked away, whispering dark affirmations to himself, the Histeridae glowing silently in the bag beside him.

He would expose the truth, and then – when the world knew everything – he would hunt down those responsible and kill them.

All of them.

EPILOGUE

Seven months later.

Nathan counted six passengers, including himself. Yesterday the bus had been full. It banged its way over what was left of the road, the thin plastic seats offering almost no protection from the constant barrage. Nathan didn't care, it was better than being outside. The rain had started a few days ago and not stopped, not even for a moment. Nathan was sure he had never experienced rain like it, such a constant and consistent deluge of water. It seemed impossible to him that the whole of India wasn't underwater by now.

He was trying to remember his history and became increasingly sure it was Pakistan that had first been declared a failed state, and that India followed quickly behind. One thing he knew for sure: by 2055, the entire region had been classified uninhabitable.

Large beads of water traveled along the window panes, racing the gushing rapids in the roadside below. He gazed out at the shacks and abandoned cars, groups of people walking, carrying heavy loads above their heads, tall palm trees swaying alarmingly in the high winds above them. Humans still lived here, they just weren't *official*. Yet, they managed somehow. People always managed. Tens of millions of refugees had attempted to leave the country. That was just the beginning.

What followed had been much worse.

The bus hit another pothole and punched him up out of his seat. His expression didn't change. Since losing Jen he had killed two men. His expression hadn't changed then either. The first, as he was leaving Afghanistan, was a straightforward mugging. He'd stabbed the assailant in the neck with his own knife, pushing him to the ground, sending his accomplice running. The man bled out, his sticky hands wrestling against Nathan's firm grip. The second was more complicated. After paying a decent sum to cross the Pakistani border, his contact then sent an assassin to retrieve the rest of Nathan's stash – a common scam, he suspected. He had been ready, waiting in the darkness, his dead eyes watching the door. He strangled the assassin with a bootlace, cutting into his skin. The man's face had bulged purple, legs thrashing. Nathan had felt nothing. He had stared at the ceiling. No emotion. Nothing. He was breathing, the man was dead. No big deal.

The bus's engine groaned, popped and backfired. Nathan opened his eyes suddenly, realising he must have fallen asleep.

Sweet dreams, he thought bitterly, rubbing his shoulders.

The driver was shouting and waving his arms and the passengers were shouting back. Nathan got the gist. The journey was over. He walked to the front of the bus. Flash flooding had caused a landslide and half the road was gone. A couple of days back the driver had asked everyone to stand on one side of the bus as he negotiated a similar, half-eaten road. This was different, though; they were higher up now and the bus had been sliding sideways for a while, losing traction. This was *literally* the end of the road. Nathan slung his rucksack over his shoulder, walked past the arguing passengers and jumped off the bus. He studied the jagged triangular holes cut into the mountain where the road should have been.

Parts missing, gone for good.

Pulling his hood forward he began to walk, thick orange mud cloying his boots. Two days later he arrived at a crossing, exactly as described. A roughly built wooden bridge stretched over an angry-looking river. In the distance, against an ash-white sky, he spotted a thin line of smoke leaving the hillside.

It was dusk by the time he arrived at the hut, which was surrounded by thick trees, its stone walls packed and sealed with mud, windows covered. Thin shafts of light emanated from cracks in the walls. He knocked. There was no reply. He twisted the cold metal handle and opened the door. Pushing it slowly, he raised a hand defensively and stepped inside. The house was small and tidy with oil lamps lighting the edges. In the centre a large wooden staircase and beyond that, in the far corner he saw a figure, a man sitting with his back to him.

'Mr Mohanty?' Nathan asked. There was no reply.

Nathan shook his coat, closed the door behind him and approached. The man appeared to be writing. To his right there was a fire, warm and welcoming with an old-fashioned black cauldron hanging above it. It was like stepping back in time. It had taken Nathan months to find this place, to find this man, and a part of him just wanted to sit by that fire, dry his clothes and not speak. He stood in awkward silence staring at the figure hunched over the desk.

'Professor George Mohanty?' Nathan asked, clearer this time. Still the man didn't move. 'My Name is Nathan O'Brien. I'm here about Jacob Logan.'

The man bowed his head, turned and faced him. He was Indian and elderly, with thin white hair that hung messily over his collar. Nathan noticed he was holding a gun in his right hand.

Mohanty met Nathan's gaze. 'I heard about the Vault. I figured it was only a matter of time before you started looking for me.'

'Jacob's daughter,' Nathan said, the words pinching his heart. 'She's dead.'

Mohanty frowned and nodded. 'I know. I was very sorry to hear it.'

Nathan hadn't expected this but didn't show any surprise. He gestured towards the gun. 'Please. There's no need for that.'

Mohanty's eyes narrowed. 'I protect myself, Mr O'Brien. That's how I have survived all these years. I've known about you for a while now, known you were coming. And when I heard about the vault, it made me wonder.' He paused and studied Nathan, his voice becoming a hopeful whisper. 'Did she find it?'

Nathan slipped the bag from his shoulder and reached inside.

'Slowly,' Mohanty warned, raising the gun.

Nathan carefully lifted a small box from his satchel, opened its lid and showed him the Histeridae.

'That explains everything.' Mohanty let out a long sigh and gestured towards a seat by the fire. 'Please sit.'

'I'm not here to hurt you,' Nathan assured him.

'I know that.' George replied, placing the gun on the table. 'Let's start again,' he said, offering Nathan his hand. 'Professor George Mohanty. Tell me everything.'

As Nathan talked, Mohanty listened intently. Nathan told him about his wife, about his journey. He explained how he had met Jennifer Logan and how together they had discovered the link between Baden and Hibernation. They had retrieved files from the Vault, classified documents, proof that hibernators were being searched and manipulated. He had also found original 'Histeridae Project' files and Mohanty's name had been all over them. Nathan wanted answers.

George had listened politely but interrupted constantly, and as the hours passed Nathan became increasingly frustrated. He had managed to track down a man many considered to be dead, yet one who seemed interested in only one thing.

Mohanty sank back into his chair, 'Tell me again about his daughter,'

'I told you. She was tough. Determined.'

George nodded, 'Like her father.' He poured himself another slug of green liquid, filling a small ornate glass to the brim. He checked again if Nathan would like to join him. Nathan refused. He shrugged, knocked back the drink – his fourth in the last hour – and gazed at Nathan, eyes wet and swimming. 'And she could use the Histeridae well?'

'Can't everyone?'

George ignored him and prodded the fire absently. 'Do you know why it's called the Histeridae?'

Nathan sighed heavily and shook his head, unable to hide his frustration.

'We named it.' Mohanty was attempting a smile but his eyes were sad, his lips trembling slightly. 'Well, Jacob did, really. Named it after the beetle, said it reminded him of one. Means "actor" in Latin, I think, which is quite fitting really.'

There was a long pause.

'Tell me,' Mohanty asked, staring at the fire. 'How did she die?'

Nathan felt the blood rising up in his throat. He had traveled for weeks to find this man, and for what? To be dragged through the pain of her death again, by a drunkard?

'How is this relevant? I've already –'

'Please, Mr O'Brien,' George interrupted, raising his hand and placing it on Nathan's shoulder. 'Trust me… it's important. Tell me how she died. Exactly.'

Nathan sighed. He was tired and aching and wasn't in the mood for a fight.

'Near the vault, after retrieving the files.' Nathan swallowed, the pain in his chest tightening like cooling metal. He instinctively reached for the ring around his neck, his only connection to her. 'She died in my arms. She asked me to figure this out, expose the truth. That's why I came to –'

'The truth,' George whispered, interrupting him again, staring intently at the fire. 'The Histeridae is an incredible object. They didn't have a *clue* of its potential. Jacob and I were only beginning to understand its power.'

'Well, now I have it,' Nathan said simply, staring back at him, wondering where all this was going. 'And I haven't got a clue what to do.'

'You have the Histeridae and a pile of evidence,' George cackled to himself, 'and a world that has forgotten how to listen.'

They sat in silence for a while, and when Nathan looked over he saw that Mohanty's eyes were rolling, the small glass about to fall from his fingers.

Fragile and ready to smash, Nathan thought.

He could feel despair ripping at him. Mohanty was a strange old man, whom Nathan suspected had spent too long alone. He saved the glass and reached for a blanket.

George's eyes opened, like a snake waiting. He said, 'Tell me. Was she touching the Histeridae as she died?'

Nathan recoiled slightly. 'Yes. Why?'

'And you were holding her?' Mohanty asked, pulling him closer.

Nathan nodded quickly and George smiled. He was staring at the fire, its reflection dancing in his watery gaze. Nathan turned and watched the shape of the wood collapse, grey ash crumbling to reveal the glowing rocks beneath. A fresh log now lay over the embers and the fire flared up excitedly.

'Because, Mr O'Brien.' His voice was a whisper, his face glowing in the warm light. 'When it comes to the Histeridae, death is a very *relative* term.'

Author's note

Thank you for reading 'The Whisper of Stars'.

As an unpublished author (in the old fashioned sense anyway), reaching new readers is one of the hardest things to do.

By far, the best way to get noticed is via reviews on Amazon. Positive reviews can literally lift a book from obscurity to bestseller, and your help in that journey would be very much appreciated. So, if you enjoyed the book why not add a review?

Search for 'The Whisper of Stars Nick Jones'. Then click on 'Write a customer review'.

Thanks again. It is a real thrill for me to know people are reading my novel. The sequel is well underway. Keep an eye on my website for news, preview chapters and updates.

www.iamnickjones.com

Printed in Great Britain
by Amazon